Stolen Treasures

by Laurie Ryan

www.laurieryanauthor.com

eBook ISBN: 978-0-9861198-5-9

Print ISBN: 978-1-967127-09-2

Cover design by C. Friesen at DefianceBooks.com

Unearth more about Laurie Ryan and her books at laurieryanauthor.com. For up-to-date information about releases, please consider joining Laurie's mailing list. Sign up here.

No Generative AI Training Use.

Author's Note: No artificial intelligence (A.I) or predictive language software was used in any part of the creation of this book, nor will it ever be use for any of my works.

tions of this text, other than for review purposes, contact laurie@laurieryanauthor.com

Acknowledgements

Special Notes: Contains stormy waters, intrigue, and danger, and steamy intimate scenes.

Stolen Treasures holds a very special place in my heart as my first story published. This re-released version has been updated for current times.

I spent a lot of time wandering amongst the gallant ships at a local Tall Ships Festival. That's where the first seeds for this story, and the two that follow it, came from. There's something totally romantic about being at sea and I envisioned my darkly handsome Dion Gaetani at the helm, completely in his element.

Of course, like any good author, I then threw a few wrenches into his machinery, mostly in the form of the heroine, Claire Saunders, who had her own hang-ups to get past.

I have had the opportunity to sail on a tall ship for several nights, and it was an amazing experience. Thank you to the Tall Ships Festivals and Zodiac (and her crew) for helping to inspire this story. To my brother-in-law, Michael, for his enthusiastic willingness to teach me to sail. And to the best critique partner an author could ask for, Lavada Dee.

Lastly, to my readers. I hope you've enjoyed this story and I both thank you and appreciate you for your support.

Laurie Ryan

DEDICATION

To my husband, Mark, who gave me wings.
To Lavada, both mentor and friend, for her invaluable support.
And a special thanks to Michael, now sailing heavenly seas, whose enthusiasm for sailboats sent my imagination soaring.

CHAPTER ONE

San Diego, present day

Claire Saunders closed her eyes and let her hands guide the way. She skimmed the surface, caressed the beveled edges, and moved on to the legs, searching each curve for imperfections. A small sigh of satisfaction escaped. Smooth as glass and not a single rough edge. She smiled and opened her eyes. There were no discernible flaws in the antique table. And if she couldn't find any, no one else would, either.

She'd been right about the rosewood grain, too.

Claire stroked the surface once more, following the striations in the wood. Light and dark in perfect harmony. Under three layers of paint! It had taken a lot of patience, but the stripping and sanding had been worth it. The table was lovely.

As she pulled her facemask down and inhaled the pungent, woodsy scent, Claire braced herself for the memories, paying silent homage to the man who had taught her how to make the wood come alive. A master craftsman who happened to also be her father. This was his legacy, and the only connection to him she had left. At least, the only one she wanted to acknowledge.

"You'd have liked this one, Dad," she whispered.

Except no one was there to hear. Not anymore. She'd give anything to have him back. Claire threw the sanding block to the floor as the inevitable resentment followed. If he were here, he could clean up his own mess. It would take her years to do it for him.

She wiped a hand across her brow, moving damp, honey-colored hair out of her way. A week into September and the unseasonably warm San Diego temperatures still topped eighty degrees by midday. Her workshop, a converted garage below her apartment, had no windows, and only a small, valiant fan near the big door worked to push the heat back outside. It wasn't doing too good of a job at it, either.

A month of painstakingly slow work had cost her, but the promised elegance would be delivered on time. She hoped. As long as she could get the first clear finish coat on today.

Stretching to ease muscles cramped from too many hours hunched over, Claire reached for a broom as her stomach growled. She'd grab some breakfast while the dust settled, then apply the first coat. A quick glance at the clock on the wall confirmed that timing would be tight. She needed to be down at the waterfront by mid-afternoon.

Claire frowned. Her day job as an administrative assistant at the Harbor Island Yacht Club was a necessity, though not one she particularly liked. She should have never agreed to organize the four-day Festival of Ships. Even worse, she'd practically begged for the opportunity. It had turned out to be a nightmare of egos and regulations, and she'd come close to giving up more times than she could count.

Her apartment felt like a cooler in comparison to the workshop. With no air conditioning, though, the feeling wouldn't last long. *Still*, Claire thought as she rubbed the goose bumps on her arms, *I'll enjoy it while I can.*

The incessant chime of her cell phone called her. Breakfast would have to wait a couple more minutes. Tracking the phone down in her bedroom, she tapped voicemail. There were three messages, all from her boss. Each one said the same thing.

Call me immediately.

Great. What did he think was wrong now? Claire punched her boss's number.

"Good morning, Mr. Seton."

"Claire?" his voice boomed. "Where are you?"

"I'm home at the moment, sir."

"At home? Why are you still at home? All hell is breaking loose down here! How many times have you told me you could handle this? Now here we have this mess and you're not here?"

Her goose bumps returned, and her legs threatened to buckle, so Claire sat down on the nearest piece of furniture, her bed, or the mattress on the floor that passed as her bed. It wasn't much, but it supported her now.

"What's wrong? Everything was ready when I left last night."

"It's not about the preparations, it's about the boats. They've arrived early! They aren't supposed to be here until tomorrow, and there are already ships out here waiting for berths. What are you going to do?"

Claire's shoulders slumped in relief. "It's fine, Mr. Seton. Some of them won't be in the parade of ships. They were scheduled to arrive early."

"Why didn't I know this? Why wasn't I told?"

Claire raised her eyes to the ceiling in a silent prayer, remembering the exact conversation she'd had with him only one week ago to overview the plan.

"We have too many ships for the line," she explained again. "Plus, some of the ships need to be docked before ones in the parade can come in."

Quite sure at that moment that she heard a "harrumph" on the other end of the line, Claire stifled a laugh at the vision of her boss standing on the dock with one arm wildly waving as he spoke, his face red and slightly puffed. A tall man with a commanding presence and a full head of white hair, he would be noticeable.

"Well, I don't remember this at all. Besides, just how are they going to berth without you here to direct them? They have no idea where to go. This is your fault, Claire Saunders. You wanted this responsibility. You are supposed to be here."

The fleeting smile disappeared. "I'll be there shortly, Mr. Seton," she said stiffly. "Anthony is there to direct the ships, and I've already spoken with him this morning."

"Anthony? Who, pray tell, is Anthony?"

"He's the harbor patrol liaison who volunteered to help out with the festival this year. You met him last week."

"Oh. Um, yes, I believe I do remember him after all. Now, what did he look like again?"

"Dark hair, older, not too tall. He should be out there, radio in hand, giving orders, and directing movement on the water."

"Yes. Yes, I see him now."

"Mr. Seton, it's important that you stay out of his way," Claire begged. "He needs total concentration to get these yachts into the right slips. Do you understand me?"

"Of *course,* I do. I think I'll just go see if he's got everything under control."

"No, Mr. Seton! Please—"

Her plea came too late. Her boss had already hung up. Claire knew from experience that he would bungle everything.

Damn. Why couldn't he trust her this once? She had every-thing under control.

She hoped.

A second "damn" came out as she rushed to change into clean clothes grabbed from the neatly folded piles around the room. She needed a dresser, but didn't have the money for one yet. She needed a bed and something to replace the cardboard box beside it, too.

Her living area was perfection defined. She had meticulously restored cast off furniture from others to create an illusion of comfort and wealth. That had led to outside orders, like the table currently waiting in her shop. Along with her meager salary from the yacht club though, it still fell short. As yet, she hadn't the money to pay off the mountain of debts and close in on her dreams. Her bedroom was certainly visible proof of that. This festival had to be a success! The new job she'd been promised meant her goals would be in sight.

Claire splashed some water on her face and glanced at her watch. Damn. She grabbed her makeup bag and keys and raced out. Stopping to lock her workshop, she took one last, regretful look at the table sitting there.

She would miss her deadline on the table. She needed to be down at the waterfront now instead of in three hours—thanks to the irritating ineptitude of one Mr. George Seton, of the Mayflower Setons, of course.

It had turned into the day from hell. Everything that could go wrong, did, from her boss guiding boats into slips willy-nilly, then this schooner berthing where she shouldn't be. Claire just wanted to get off the waterfront with her sanity intact. Was that too much to ask?

"Ahoy, the *Treasure*," she called out.

Claire took a moment to appreciate the old-world character of the schooner, with its wood construction and graceful lines. She knew the specs on each ship participating. Small by festival standards, only sixty-one feet on deck, sixty-nine overall, this one easily evoked memories of sailing times long past. The schooner's previous owner had been a major contributor up until his death the prior year. His grandson owned the boat now, and everyone involved with the festival had been enormously grateful that he'd continued his grandfather's contribution. She'd heard somewhere that he lived overseas. Still, flagship of the festival had seemed a fitting show of gratitude to the old gentleman. Keeping the donors happy was a major part of her job.

Getting no answer to her hail, Claire tried again, tapping her feet.

"Ahoy, anyone aboard the *Treasure*?"

Still no answer. Finally, after a third hail, a head appeared above her, slowly followed by a body hard to ignore. Tanned, muscular legs gave way to khaki cut-offs, complete with frayed ends. The t-shirt was modern but dirt-smudged and tight enough to show off an impressive chest and arms. Further up, longish, brown hair, scruffy stubble, and unreadable dark eyes completed the illusion. The man looked like a pirate. Claire glanced up at the mast, half expecting to see the infamous Jolly Roger flying there.

He didn't say a word, and her cheeks flared with heat as he observed her. Using her clipboard as a fan, Claire let her brain delude her into believing the warmth seeping slowly through her body was weather related.

That's when he raised a leg to place a sandaled foot on the boat's railing, flexing well-defined muscles. The tempo of her fanning increased.

Yes, this man could easily pass for a pirate. One of those old-time swashbucklers who stole their women away to ravage them in the privacy of the captain's quarters. Tall, dark and...scowling? Wait a minute. That wasn't the way the fairytale went, was it?

Struggling to regain some composure, she adjusted her sunglasses and dug deep to remember why she stood here.

"I'm afraid you're not supposed to be here."

He just stared at her. That's all. No response, no raised eyebrow. Nothing, damn it.

"Did you hear me?"

"Yes."

She quickly suppressed the small shiver that trailed down her back. "Well, then?"

"Where is it you think I'm not supposed to be?"

"Here!" she said, pointing at the dock for effect.

He simply stared at her again. Claire stiffened. She had a long to-do list today and, muscled or not, this sailor stood directly in her path.

"You need to move this boat."

"No. I don't," he replied casually.

"What?" She tried very hard not to shriek.

"I said, 'No, I don't.'" He turned away and disappeared as if the conversation was over.

Claire's mouth dropped open. Instinct overrode thought as she hurried to the gangplank. She struggled to quickly navigate the steep angle and halfway up, tripped.

That figures. Limping now, she chose to ignore the standard "permission to come aboard" courtesy and kept going until she caught up to him.

As she took a moment to consider him, something began to thread its way around her anger. He was taller than her, but not too tall. Danger oozed from him in waves of intimidation.

His eyes weren't just dark. They were like deep night, black, distant, and dispassionate. His mouth was the opposite of unemotional, however. Nothing more than thin lines showed, and Claire faltered.

He really did resemble a pirate, even more so up close. She glanced back and realized how far she'd have to run if escape became necessary.

"Permission to come aboard granted," he said with slow, smooth precision.

Claire swallowed. "Look," she started, pleased to hear no quaver in her voice.

His eyes narrowed.

Claire took a step back and tried a different tack. "I'm sorry," she said, holding out a hand which shook only slightly. "We've gotten off on the wrong foot. I'm Claire Saunders, from the Harbor Island Yacht Club. I'm the festival liaison."

He didn't take the hand, instead watching her until she dropped it to her side.

"And you are?" she tried again.

"Busy."

"Well, I can understand that. You've just docked. However, you have to understand. The Festival needs you to move. This slip is assigned to a different boat."

"Not anymore, it isn't."

Her jaw fell again, her eyes widened, and a very unladylike, "Huh?" was all that her brain could format for speech.

"I said, 'Not anymore, it isn't.'"

"I *heard* what you said. But—" Claire stopped and tapped her clipboard against her leg. There had to be some way to resolve this. She stared at him for a moment, then switched gears again. "I'd like to speak to the captain."

He glanced around. "I guess that's me at the moment."

"Well, then, did you receive the paperwork indicating where you *should* be docked?"

He reached behind him then, and she backed up a step. Only she didn't have another step. The raised cabin roof stopped her short and, off balance, she fell backward. Her clipboard clattered to the deck as strong, calloused hands broke her fall and righted her by pulling her close to a hard body.

He smelled of musky earth, sweat, and sea salt. Somehow, it worked for him. And for her. Instinct took control, and Claire leaned forward.

She almost missed the hint of emotion in those dark, unreadable eyes. They flared, just for the tiniest moment. Then he set her away from him, holding her with one hand until she found her balance.

His other hand held a letter.

Straightening, she reached for it.

"Uh-uh," he said, wagging his finger. "Look, don't touch."

Her glare returned as she bent slightly to read the note, which bore the yacht club logo at the top. Confused, she read:

To Whom It May Concern:

This letter serves as notice that the Treasure *and her crew have been awarded carte-blanche to berth where they want, when they want. All members of the yacht club, security forces and any other official persons tied to the Festival of Ships will give the schooner their full cooperation.*

It was signed by none other than her boss, George Seton! She didn't know a thing about it, either. Claire felt like the word "idiot" had been branded on her forehead. He'd gone behind her back again. Was he trying to undermine everything she'd accomplished? She straightened as she realized how true that could actually be. After all, his own daughter had suggested an interest in the same job that Claire was up for...if the festival ended up a success.

"Why did they give you this authority?" she asked.

"Being the flagship for the festival has some perks, I guess."

"I don't understand."

He reached down, picked up the clipboard, and handed it to her.

"If you would be so kind as to disembark, Miss Saunders, I'd like to return to my duties." With that dismissal, he resumed his work.

His arrogance was as much a slap across the face as the letter. Fuming, Claire knew any options had disappeared with that note, so she clutched the clipboard to her chest and disembarked, leaving him to his damn sheets and halyards.

Dion Gaetani coiled the rope and tossed it toward a hook, but it missed and fell directly to the deck. The schooner seemed as out of sorts as he was. He stared at the rope for a moment, made a decision, and left it there. The rope could rot away on the deck for all he cared right now. Lifting one foot to the railing, he massaged his bad knee as he surveyed the waterfront. She was still there, at the edge of the pier. He watched her long hair sway from side to side as she nodded toward the *Treasure*, consulted her clipboard, then stared at the docks again. She'd been doing that for close to an hour.

Claire Saunders. She looked no different than any other of the self-proclaimed elite. She even had the standard uniform on—khaki pants, polo and the ever-present sweater across her shoulders. Dion had left the lifestyle of the rich and famous behind long ago. She appeared to be entrenched in it. Still, he could have sworn he'd caught a whiff of sawdust when he'd steadied her. She didn't look like she'd ever done, or ever had to do, any sort of manual labor. He frowned.

She wore makeup she didn't need. Wondering what beauty hid beneath it, he imagined himself gently washing it away, caressing her skin first with cloth, then with his fingers, slowly tracing the soft lines of her cheek, followed by gentle kisses, finding that dimple at the corner of her mouth, and finally rewarded as he reached those lips. They would be soft, inviting...

Abruptly, he pulled out of the trance and felt the hard ache his thoughts had brought on. Hell, did he need a woman that bad? Straightening, he scuffed his sandals against a spot on the deck and reminded himself that she was everything he'd turned his back on. She was trouble.

Claire walked slowly along the Embarcadero as dusk settled over the docks. The hot day had melted into night without her notice. A million small details were what made a festival like this a success, and she had spent the day dealing with the worst of them. Her boss took top spot on that list. What's-his-face on that schooner, since he never had given her his name, placed a very close second.

Another huge snag of the day came from a meeting she hadn't planned on. Security was already in place for the festival, but some new guys with the International Marine Bureau had wanted her to provide additional precautions for the smaller yachts, at festival expense, and at the last minute, too. She had heard about the recent hijackings and personally knew two of the families involved as they were from the club. It was impossible to increase the force on such short notice, and the two agents from the International Marine Bureau hadn't taken too kindly to that news.

At that moment, the darkness deepened. Claire looked up at the shadowed form of the aircraft carrier, *Midway*, now permanently moored here. Normally reassuring, tonight it seemed more a portent of doom, and Claire hurried past. This festival had to go well. That was her mantra these days, and all her hopes were pinned to it. The position of director was the carrot her boss dangled in front of her, and exactly what she needed to finally leave the past behind. But everything she did would have to be flawless in order to beat the boss's daughter.

Shaking herself free of her apprehension, she reached her car and left the waterfront behind. After a quick stop at the grocery store to pick up enough vegetables for a salad, she'd be done.

She picked up the wine being advertised as great with salads but replaced it, knowing it was over her budget. There were still too many days to payday.

CHAPTER TWO

The rope landed with a thud on the cabin roof as Dion bent over to pick up yet another food wrapper tossed to the deck by one of the visiting hoards.

"How in hell did Grandfather tolerate this?" he grumbled, still irritated by the sheer number of people who had boarded the *Treasure* over the past few days. He'd even had to pry gum off the wood in a couple of spots. Thankfully, tours had ended for the day an hour ago.

He was grateful to his partner, Roger Borland, for stepping into the role as captain. He'd have tossed some unruly visitor overboard before the first day's end. And Roger loved playing the charismatic English Captain. It was right up his alley.

They'd been partners for close to ten years, and Dion had called him friend for almost as long. Towering over most people, Roger was British in both tone and demeanor. But who had ever seen a proper, pipe-smoking Brit with a ponytail?

Dion looked around. He hadn't observed any suspicious activity yet. Of course, he hadn't seen much of anything except all the bodies clambering aboard, leaving fingerprints everywhere, and their post-tornado mess for him to clean up. He and Roger had been busy scrubbing footprints off the deck for over an hour now. The other crew used the need to scout as an excuse to hightail it off the boat about the time cleanup had started.

"I'm going for grub. Can I get you something?" Roger called, fresh from a shower and already headed toward the dock.

"No. I'll finish here, then go collapse."

Dion picked up the rope and tossed it toward a hook, but it missed. Again. Scowling at the offending cord, he picked it up and forcefully placed it on the hook, then turned to the dock, surveying the crowds that still wandered the waterfront. Most of the vendors were still open, as well as the more permanent restaurants and tourist shops. The *Treasure* was perfectly situated for observing the masses, but lousy for footprints and bubblegum.

He saw her then, talking to one of the vendors. Claire. The enigma. An apparent princess by caste, yet he'd seen her on the waterfront off and on throughout the festival. She seemed to actually be working. The sweater wasn't around her shoulders any longer. She had it on now. Her wrinkled pants spoke volumes about how active she had been. Why was she still here when all her people had been gone for hours?

Shaking his head, he started below. A wail somewhere on the dock stopped him. Before he could isolate the noise, he spied Claire already on the move to the side of a little boy, around three years old, who stood alone, in the center of the sidewalk, crying.

Dion jumped to the dock and winced as he landed on his injured leg. He'd pay for that later. By the time he reached them, Claire was seated in the middle of the cement sidewalk with the little boy on her lap. The dirt of a thousand footprints already clung to her light pants.

Here was another puzzle. People in her circle would never sit on cement, certainly not for some little urchin.

As she tried to calm the boy, Dion found himself drawn by the low, quiet quality of her voice. It circled around him, saying "trust me" in deep, silky undertones. It worked its magic on the child, too. He was noticeably calmer.

"Do you need some help?" he asked.

"I don't know."

He almost, but not quite, missed the slight narrowing of her eyes as she recognized him.

"I think he's lost," she finally said.

He looked around, silently agreed with her and noticed they had become something of a spectacle.

"Maybe we should move," he said.

Claire nodded her head and tried to stand, a nearly impossible feat with the boy on her lap.

"Here, let me." Dion carefully picked up the boy, at which point the child's sniffles returned to a full-fledged howl.

Claire jumped up. "It's okay, honey. It's okay." She kept her hand on the boy's arm, following Dion to the bench where he quickly placed him back on her lap.

"It's okay, sweetie. We won't let anything happen to you. Can you tell us your name?"

"B-b-b-illy," he said in between sniffles. "Mommy!" He began to wail again.

"I know, Billy." She kept talking to him, soothing him. "We're going to try to find her."

She looked at Dion over the boy's head and shrugged, obviously indecisive as to their next move. The boy was clean and his blond hair was combed, but his shirt seemed a little too small, stained, and faded from too much use. The shorts were thin in spots, and his sandals were about two sizes too big for his feet.

"You've got a police contingent on the waterfront for the festival, right?" Dion asked.

"Yes. Good idea. I'll call them right now."

At that moment, a young woman caught Dion's eye. "Hold on a moment. I'll be right back."

He returned moments later with the bedraggled and worried woman. Billy's face lit up with recognition.

"Mommy!"

"Billy!" The woman reached out to take him from Claire.

"I was so worried about you! Where did you go?"

"I saw doggy!" He pointed, but the dog was gone, and his face fell. The sniffling started in earnest again.

"It doesn't matter, sweetheart," the mother said and hugged him tighter. "I've found you, and you're okay. That's all that matters."

She spoke to Claire and Dion, tears threatening to spill.

"Thank you so much. I don't know what I would have done—" her voice cracked as it trailed off.

"You're very welcome. He's a sweet boy." Claire ruffled the boy's hair, then searched the mother's face.

"When's the last time you ate?" she asked quietly.

"We had a good breakfast this morning."

"And dinner?"

"Well, we'll get something later, I'm sure," the woman said, worry lines deeply etched in her face.

"Do you eat at the mission?"

The color in the mother's face deepened. "Sometimes."

Reaching into her purse, Claire pulled out an envelope. Dion could see the word "groceries" written on it, but she didn't hesitate, handing the envelope over.

"The mission is already closed for the night. Use this to get some dinner, okay? I think you both need food in your stomach and a good night's sleep." She smiled then and tapped Billy on the nose.

"It was nice to meet you, Billy. You stick real close to your mom now, okay?"

"'Kay," he said, bobbing his head up and down.

As they walked away, the boy turned in his mother's arms and lit up the night with one last toothy grin and a ragged wave over her shoulder. When Dion turned back to Claire, she was beaming.

He was spellbound. He'd been right. She didn't need makeup. A rare natural beauty shone through when she smiled. Tiny little freckles that she tried to hide dotted her face. The highlights in her hair made it the color of dark honey. Her eyes, deep cocoa pools, sparkled with her obvious contentment. He could fall for those eyes and be distracted by that smile.

Hell. He needed to get away from her and fast.

Claire chose that moment to turn his way, her smile replaced with a tight line. She stared at him for a bit, then ground out the words as if surrendering to the enemy. "Thank you for your help."

Claire Saunders walked off then, and this time, it was Dion's mouth left hanging open.

Oh, yeah. She was definitely trouble. He watched her leave and reminded himself that, for many reasons, he'd better stay far, far away from her. He didn't need the complication or the responsibility. Frowning, he went back on board, tossed down a pain pill, then decided it was time to vacate the schooner for a while and went off in search of Roger.

Later that evening, Claire walked along the Embarcadero, looking with pride at what remained of the festival. It *had* been a success. Most of that was due to the hard work and long hours she and a host of volunteers had put in. The members of her yacht club had done little except be a presence, or, more appropriately, a nuisance.

"Look what I did," she said quietly to the air around her. "Ah, Dad." The bitterness was evident in her voice. "I wish you could see."

Now, only a few vendors remained, tearing down their pavilions. Clean-up would start very early in the morning. For now, quiet had almost returned to the waterfront.

Walking past the *Treasure*, Claire stopped and, unable to help herself, glanced up. No one seemed to be on board. Maybe they were off for one last dinner on land before heading out to their next port of call.

She'd managed to avoid the pirate, as she'd come to think of him, for the rest of the festival, but a nagging awareness of him had driven her nuts. Hell, she didn't even know his name. He was handsome, if you liked the dark and brooding type, which she certainly did not. As arrogant as he appeared, he *had* helped her with that little boy. Claire smiled as she remembered little Billy.

The man knew his way around a boat, but seemed to be a hired hand, probably some type of laborer.

A vision of her father again filled her mind and brought the instant sting of tears to her eyes. He'd been a laborer, too, of sorts, working in Martha's Vineyard at some of the upscale homes when he'd wanted the work. Most of his time was spent with her, especially after her mother died. Smiling, she remembered the walks they had taken, the games they had played. He'd shown her how wood could be crafted into anything she could imagine.

He had been her world. He still was, even with what she knew now.

Crash!

The noise came from the boat, although no one seemed to be topside.

"Ahoy aboard the *Treasure*," she called out.

Only silence answered her.

Claire saw no one nearby. She walked closer.

"Hello, schooner *Treasure*. Anyone aboard?"

Again, no one answered. At the top of the boarding ramp she tried again.

"Hello? Anyone home?"

Nothing. She stepped onto the deck, walking past the cabin to the other side of the boat. Claire didn't see anything or anyone that could have caused the noise. She started to turn back, then stars exploded in her head and everything went black.

CHAPTER THREE

The first sensation that found its way into Claire's muddled mind was a slow, gentle swaying. She was being rocked, back and forth, side to side. Mmmm. That felt nice. She stretched then, and reality tossed her from her dream hammock. Movement hurt. Where was she? She opened her eyes but saw only a blur of white. Hit by a wave of nausea, she quickly closed them and gave in to the symphony orchestra playing a painful march in her head.

She tried to take stock, shifting her head to ease the pressure against her neck. Her hammock felt rock hard. Movement this time didn't make the pain better, but thankfully it didn't get worse, either. Fingers and toes wiggled. Arms and legs worked, too. Claire reached her hand up to her head slowly to check the large gash that her pain level dictated was there. While no blood appeared to be seeping out, she found a king-size lump which quickly identified itself as the cause of the clashing cymbals.

Smarter this time, she only opened one eye. Things were still blurry, but she could see that some sort of blanket covered her. She reached behind her neck and came in contact with a flat, hard surface. There was some sort of opening underneath. She touched the blanket above her with her leg. It barely budged. Was she tied down?

What had happened? Everything seemed a blank. As well, she swore the throbbing in her head increased with each attempt at thought.

Feeling a bit less woozy, she maneuvered herself into a slightly more comfortable position and opened both eyes. As her vision cleared, she could see that it wasn't a blanket covering her, but some sort of tarp. There appeared to be a loose area at the side. Shifting carefully to reach it, Claire lifted enough of it to see out. She squinted as daylight confronted her. All she could see was sky, ropes, and pulleys. Waiting for her eyes to adjust to the light, she rose higher and saw a railing of sorts. And a...a sidewalk? No. Not a sidewalk. It was wood. Beyond that, all she could see was—

"Water!" The sound of her own voice startled her, and she jumped back from the opening, once again setting off the jangle of bells in her head.

More slowly, she scrambled to the other side, praying all the while. *Please let me see the skyline of San Diego. Please!* Lifting the tarp, she was confronted with more of the same.

Ropes. Deck. And water. Lots of it, too. The motion she'd been feeling sunk in. She was on a boat. Worse, she appeared to be out to sea!

She sank down, hitting her head and increasing the crescendo of jarring music.

What had happened? How had she ended up here? She needed time to think—to figure out what to do. She probed the back of her head again.

"Ouch."

She needed aspirin, too. Or something stronger.

Safe for the moment under the tarp, Claire tried to settle into a more comfortable position.

She was at sea, on a boat, hidden in some sort of smaller vessel. A life raft? That made sense. How in the hell had she gotten here?

The last thing she could recall was the final night of the ship festival. How long ago had that been? She'd walked along the Embarcadero, checking out the docks, making sure everyone knew their time slot to weigh anchor. Scrunching her eyes, she tried hard to remember. She'd been walking past the *Treasure*. That was it!

That schooner had become her albatross. Claire tried to focus on the last thing she remembered. She'd seen nothing and only had a vague sense of some movement behind her. Then came the pain and everything went dark.

Reaching up, Claire carefully felt the knot on her head as the realization hit her. She'd been knocked out and dumped into this raft. By whom? Were they still aboard? Her eyes widened. Were they her captors? Had she become another victim of the pirates preying on these waters?

The heat had become stifling. She squirmed quietly, trying to find a more comfortable spot. Was she a prisoner? She certainly wasn't a guest. If she was a hostage, they knew where she was. If not, then who had done this to her?

She didn't feel prepared to give up the relative safety of the lifeboat. The temperature, though, now bordered on insufferable, and dying of heat prostration would do her no good. Crawling forward, she peeked out front. There was no one around as far as she could see. The vessel appeared larger than she originally thought. If they had a radio, maybe she could get to it before someone spotted her.

Moving to the one place where the tarp wasn't tight, she scanned the deck again. No one was there. Carefully, quietly, she climbed out, almost surrendering to the dizziness and nausea that overwhelmed her as she tried to stand. She lost precious minutes waiting to regain her balance. When she did, she recognized the schooner. It figured. She was indeed on board the *Treasure*.

One unsteady, measured step at a time she moved toward the opening she knew would be stairs down into the cabin. Why did she feel so dizzy and sick to her stomach? As she reached the companionway, someone started topside and they both stopped short, shock evident as they came face to face. Wavy, dark hair and unreadable eyes immediately identified the man.

"You!" she said, wincing at the effort.

"What the hell?" he followed quickly on her verbal heels.

Just then, the *Treasure* bucked on a wave, throwing Claire forward into the surprised arms of her pirate. Then, blissful darkness took over as Claire lost her hold on reality and blacked out.

Dion Gaetani watched her as she lay on the bunk. Her face was pale, giving her the appearance of a porcelain doll, most likely due to the concussion she must have. That was one hell of a knot on her head. Her long hair fanned out slightly, framing her face with the color of the teakwood he polished every day. Even with her eyes now closed, he could picture them. The cocoa color, a rich, intelligent, dark brown, was seared in his memory.

Claire Saunders. Not a name he would likely forget. She fit the stereotype of a yacht-club princess. She didn't act like it, though. During that festival, long after all the yachting royalty had departed for home or club, he'd watched as she stayed, apparently not afraid to get her hands dirty.

Her hands looked so small. He gathered one in his, and it seemed even more delicate. Turning it over, it surprised him to feel calluses. These were not hands belonging to the rich and want-to-be famous. No, this woman wouldn't be easily categorized.

She moaned then. The quiet sound echoed in his head. He laid her hand back on the bunk, but couldn't resist another touch. His thumb traced her hairline down the side of her heart-shaped face. She shifted then, leaning her cheek into his touch. Her skin felt like warm silk.

Dion yanked his hand back and straightened, searching the cabin for something, anything, to take his mind off the unconscious woman in his bunk. He refused to go soft over some wisp of a princess. A bad feeling settled in his stomach. She was going to be trouble, and lots of it.

Quietly shutting the cabin door, he grabbed a bottle of water from the galley before joining the rest of the crew topside.

"She awake?" Aidan asked, generally the most vocal of the team. His long, trendy brown hair almost covered green eyes that hinted at his Irish heritage.

"Not yet." Dion leaned over the railing to watch the water go by. "How the hell did she get here?" he said, smacking the railing as he turned to the two men.

"We'll not find that out," Roger answered, "until she wakes up."

Always one to point out the obvious, Dion thought. He watched his partner take a long draught on his pipe.

Dion's smile disappeared quickly as Aidan spoke.

"She hid in the life raft."

"And that rather large knot on her head most likely means being here isn't by choice," Roger added.

Dion remained quiet, letting Aidan and Roger run the situation for possibilities.

"Who would do this?" Roger asked.

"The pirates?"

"It's possible. Or it could be local thieves. We left the schooner unmanned for what, about an hour last night? Enough time to let the pirates have a look and decide the *Treasure's* worthiness."

Dion winced.

"Right," Aidan said. "I'm guessing that's when our lucky lady boarded."

"Yes, except we don't know if she boarded as a voluntary act or coercion," Roger said.

Dion hadn't considered that possibility. That was some lump she'd taken for a set-up, though.

He needed time to think. "We don't know."

"Yet," Roger confirmed. "The only other item to ponder right now is what to do with her."

They grew silent. Finally, Dion spoke.

"We can't decide that until we have some answers. I think, until we know more, we should all keep a very close eye on our new ship-mate."

"Agreed."

"I also think we need to maintain the same visible hierarchy as we did back in port," Dion said.

Roger groaned. "You're just saying that, mate, so you don't have to deal with her."

"Even if I were, it still makes sense until we know more."

"Damnation! I hate it when you're right."

"Yeah." He grinned, but the weight of this new responsibility turned it into more of a grimace. "I know."

"Just for that, you can take over my watch. I need some grub."

"Aidan," Dion said, looking forward to where Mike Stone, the last member of their team, stood on watch duty. "Let Mike know what's up."

"Aye-aye, cap'n." Aidan gave a lopsided salute and sauntered off.

Alone with his thoughts, Dion tried to make some sense of recent events. A week ago, he'd been in England, finishing up medical leave. The tide had turned against him when he'd stopped by the headquarters of the International Marine Bureau, Piracy Division, to drop off the paperwork.

"Gaetani!" The roar bellowed down the hall, invading it and bouncing off the dull ivory walls with nothing to muffle the sound except a few posters hyping workplace regulations.

"Exactly the man I want to see!" The floor vibrated with the man's footfalls. The source of the small earthquakes was the massive form of Chuck Ecker, director of the International Marine Bureau, seeming more like a bear in oxfords than a polished, politically oriented leader. He was a walking controversy, with a head overflowing with dark hair, mustache, and beard longer than fashionable, yet impeccably clothed in a well-cut gray suit, white dress shirt, and muted tie.

"Step into my office, Gaetani. I've got a proposition for you."

Dion groaned inwardly when the sudden sensation of being fed to the lions nudged his alert system.

"We've got a problem," his boss said, lowering his voice as he closed the door. Dion settled into a chair.

There's always trouble somewhere. He'd been fighting piracy for too many years to be fazed by another problem. "Where's the hot spot now?"

"San Diego."

Dion sat up. "San Diego?" He'd expected Malaysia or Somalia, someplace that always had problems. But the west coast of the United States? That was unusual.

"What's the situation?"

The director sighed. "Moderate to luxurious yachts have been hijacked in the waters off Mexico. Five in the last three months."

"And we're just getting wind of this?"

"Hell, no!" Ecker's voice returned to its usual boom. "Brass is screaming from the highest levels. My ass is in the ringer on this one."

"Who's on the case?"

"Stone and Walker have been out there for three weeks and have come up empty-handed. Nothing. And the last boat was stolen only six days ago almost right under their noses."

Dion waited. His boss had a plan, and Dion knew he would be part of it. San Diego had been his home away from home, and he would bet a year's wages the director knew that.

"You used to live in San Diego, didn't you, Gaetani?" The quiet voice was back.

Yep. He knew. "I spent a few summers there."

"With your grandfather, right? On that boat of his, what was it called again?"

The sensation was back. Dion's internal warning system went on full alert.

"The *Treasure*, sir."

"Ah, yes, the *Treasure*. Sturdy little schooner, as I recall. In good shape and long enough, too."

Dion's eyes narrowed. "Long enough for what?"

"Long enough to attract the attention of the right people."

He could almost hear that last nail being pounded into his coffin. There was the punch line.

"You want me to use my grandfather's schooner to bait the pirates," he said flatly.

Director Ecker rose then, moving to sit on the side of his desk near Dion. "You know I wouldn't ask if I had any other options. Your boat is already on the docket for the Festival of Ships that kicks off in a couple days. It's the perfect situation."

"I'm not even officially back to work yet. I just dropped off my paperwork a few minutes ago."

"Oh, yes, that." The Director picked up the phone and a minute later, his assistant arrived, folder in hand. Signing the documents inside, he continued, "You are now."

And that had been that. The next thing Dion knew, he was on a plane to San Diego with his partner, ready for action. A mere two months after...

Out of nowhere, his mind threw him further back in time, to the fight of his life. Another sting operation. Only this one had gone terribly wrong. He could see her lying there on the floor, crimson spreading out from beneath her as if it were trying to reach him, engulf him, take him with her. He couldn't forget. He couldn't forgive himself, either. God, he wished he could.

Roger watched Dion at the helm. Alert always, running the lines with his eyes, checking for flaws that would need repairing. Well, he was *almost* always alert. Roger knew each time Dion's flashbacks occurred. The man felt guilty about Mary's death. That was apparent. The inquiry had absolved him of culpability, but that didn't seem to be enough for Dion.

Turning to the water, Roger gave in for a moment and let the pain wash over him. Mary. His Mary. His hand slipped into the pocket of his shorts and curled around the small black box. He'd had the ring inside specially designed, then never got the chance to ask her to wear it.

Abruptly he removed his hand and shook his head. Dion wasn't the only one with ghosts to bury. Wondering what it would take to put the past to rest, he bit into his sandwich, trying to blank his mind to the inevitable misery.

CHAPTER FOUR

This is what heaven feels like, Claire thought, as she snuggled deeper into the softness beneath her. The gentle to and fro motion made her ache to drift back off to sleep. She needed to get up but could not remember why. She lifted her head off the pillow and moaned as reality crashed back in on her.

"Ooooh!"

"Easy there, my dear." A restraining hand on her shoulder nudged her back, and she sank down into the bed.

"That's quite a lump you've got."

Claire opened her eyes slowly, one at a time, relieved to find the blurred vision had disappeared. Surprise replaced relief as she recognized the blond-haired, gangly man standing beside her bed.

"Captain Borland?"

"Roger, please."

Rolling her head gingerly from side to side, she sighed. "At least it doesn't hurt as much to move my head."

"I'll bet that's pretty painful. You may have gotten a bit concussed. It's hard to tell. However, fainting the way you did is certainly a symptom."

"I fainted?" Scrunching her face, she tried to dredge it up, but the memory was lost. "What's going on? What have you done to me?" Fear crept into her voice as the realization hit her again that this man could be the enemy.

"Nothing, luv. In fact, I have a few questions about that myself, if you feel up to it." Roger Borland pulled up a chair and sat down. "Do you remember anything about how you got here?"

"No...yes, well...some." She paused. "It was after dark, maybe ten thirty? I heard a noise as I walked by your boat. No one answered my hails, so I investigated, and the next thing I knew, I woke up under a tarp in your dinghy."

"That's why we didn't spy you before we sailed, then."

Sitting up cautiously, she took a better look at her surroundings, a cozy cabin wrapped in wood. She rested in a large bunk on one side. There appeared to be a small bunk or couch on the other, with drawers underneath and cupboards above. The well-worn wood shone with protective polish. In between them, at the narrow end, were more cupboards as well as a desk and chair, currently occupied by the captain.

"How did I get here? What's going on, Cap—umm, Roger?"

"I don't know, but first things first. Let's get you fixed up." He held out a mug. "Here. Have a drink of this."

"What is it?" she asked, taking the cup and sniffing. She drew her head back quickly, setting off another chorus of discordant music in her ears.

"Whew!"

Roger chuckled.

"It's an old sailor's brew. Guaranteed to put out the fires raging in your head."

"Or start new ones. No, thank you." She held the cup out to him.

He prodded the cup back toward her. "It will help, Claire. Bottoms up, now. All at once."

Skeptical, she obediently downed the liquid and her body mutinied in the form of an immediate, wracking cough. That, in turn, tripled her misery. Claire felt as if she would explode into a thousand pieces. She held her head in her hands and several long and painful moments passed before she could draw a deep breath.

"What are you trying to do, kill me?"

"Wait it out."

"Wait for what? My meeting with the Maker?"

"Trust me. I'm on your side. How does your head feel now?"

"Like it's about to separate from my body. Oh! Wait a minute. It does seem a little better." Claire shot him an annoyed look. "If you think I'm going to thank you, think again. You could have warned me that it was a trial by fire."

"You're welcome," he chuckled.

"I think you should get some more rest now," he continued. "Let the medicine and rest help you heal."

"I can't. I've got to get to the club. Have we arrived back in San Diego yet?"

The roof of the cabin was low, so Roger Borland had to stoop when he stood. Still, he moved to the door of the cabin in an instant, like a rabbit spooked by some predator.

"We're not in San Diego, Claire."

"*What?*"

"We can't go back. Not yet."

"Excuse me? Now that you've found me on board, you have to take me back."

"I'm very sorry. We can't. At least, not right now."

"You can't keep me here against my will!" Her head started to pound again, so she lowered her voice and tried again. "Captain, you don't understand. My whole future hinges on what happens today." She stopped. "It is today, right? The festival just ended last night?"

"Yes. You've only lost a few hours."

Claire stood up slowly. "Then I insist you take me home."

He didn't speak for a long moment. "I'm sorry. I can't. Even if I could, it would take hours to reach the harbor. You'll have missed today either way. Now try to get some sleep, and we'll talk more about this later." This last filtered through an almost closed door as he took the cowardly way out and let the solid wood muffle his words.

"Ohhh!" Reaching for something, anything to vent her fury with, Claire fingers closed around the cup that had held remnants of the vile remedy. It shattered as it hit the door.

"She wants to go back."

"You knew she would."

"Is it really right for us to keep her?" Roger asked.

Dion lifted his leg to the railing and tried to rub away the ache. "We've gone over this. I don't like it any more than you do. We didn't put her here. We certainly don't *want* her here, but we can't put her ashore without jeopardizing everything. She has to stay aboard for now."

"That means taking her along on the op."

"I know what it means," Dion cut in bitterly. "I don't see any other way. Damn it! What the hell happened for her to have ended up here?"

"I don't know," Roger said. "She says she heard a noise, came on board to check it out, and got hit over the head. Next thing she knew she woke up in the zodiac with the devil's own headache."

"What civilian does that? You don't check out noises, especially if they might be illegal. You call the authorities. Is she nuts?"

Giving in to his frustration, Dion picked up a rope. Ready to toss it at the hook, he thought better of it. Lips tight, he walked over and slammed it onto the hook, staring at it, daring the schooner to toss it back at him.

Agents Mike Stone and Aidan Walker came up from below then, looking like beach bums in cut-offs, sandals and tanks.

"It's quiet in the cabin. Maybe she's asleep," Mike said. He brushed a fly off biceps that gym workouts had sculpted to a competition level. His slight accent seemed a remnant from an eastern European country.

"Not bloody likely," Roger answered.

"Yeah, she's probably carving epitaphs in that nice polished wood," Aidan joked. "We heard something break as you left the cabin."

Dion cringed. "Any suggestions?"

"What do we lose if we put her ashore?" Aidan asked.

Dion surveyed a shore he couldn't see, measuring distance, determining time. "Day and half, maybe two," he finally said.

"So, what do we lose?"

"Our satellite window."

"Good point." Mike, who had been sitting on the lazarette behind the wheel, got up, moved forward, and leaned onto the cabin roof the wheel abutted.

"Could we get her transferred to another vessel?"

"Most of the ships headed north to the next festival in Seattle, not south like us. Have you sighted any other boats since we left?"

"No." A pause, then Mike continued. "Radio?"

"Have someone pick her up?" Aidan suggested.

Dion considered the possibilities.

"We can't do that without taking the chance of alerting the pirates to what we are and why we're here. That could throw the whole operation. So far," he continued, "no one has been hurt."

As Aidan opened his mouth to speak, Dion held up his hand. "I know. That doesn't mean they *won't* hurt someone. All it would take is one botched attempt at escape and bam! Someone dies."

The blood-red flash took only a second to shoot through his mind. Except this time, the bullet riddled body wasn't his teammate. It wasn't Mary's blood that reached for him. This time, he stared into the lifeless doe-colored eyes of Claire Saunders.

Horror engulfed him like a vise, squeezing his chest and stealing his breath. For a long moment, Dion fought for some equilibrium. He filled his lungs with a long, slow breath, ran shaky hands through his hair, and looked up. His team members watched him like he was the specimen under a microscope.

"You all right, boss?" Aidan asked, placing a hand on Dion's shoulder.

"I'm fine. Just fine," Dion ground out. He forced his voice to sound normal. "Considering possibilities, that's all. In the past, these thieves have stranded people on islands."

"I wouldn't call them islands," Aidan said. "More like sparsely vegetated bumps in the middle of the ocean."

"Regardless, they've been rescued each time. I think we're going to have to place some trust in that, keep the girl with us and make damn sure we keep her safe."

As he scanned the water, Dion's shoulders drooped with the weight of that decision. He didn't want the responsibility. He certainly didn't *need* it. Closing his eyes, he thought how much he would give to not have her here. The stab of memory threatened to swamp him again. He forced it to the back of his mind and turned to the others, waiting for his decision. No, he didn't want anything to do with the safety of another woman. They might never get another chance at these thieves, though. He couldn't let this opportunity slip by. He straightened. He would have to keep her here, protect her, and hope that it will be enough.

"We take her with us," he said.

"You know," Roger said, rubbing the light stubble on his chin. "She told me she has something she absolutely had to be in San Diego for. She's not going to like this."

Dion knew Roger waited for a reprieve, but remained silent.

"Who gets to tell her?" Roger asked.

"It has to be you," Dion answered without hesitation.

That earned him a scowl.

"You're the captain," he supplied as explanation. With a glare, Roger grabbed the rope off the hook and threw it at Dion.

"You'll pay for this, Gaetani. I'll make you pay."

A small chuckle escaped as Dion tossed the rope back toward the hook. Missing completely, he watched it fly right past and into the water, quickly disappearing behind them. Both he and Roger sobered. They had worked together for a long time and thought alike.

Roger put a voice to it. "This raises the stakes. We can't afford to have anything go wrong."

"I know." Dion frowned. He knew only too well.

CHAPTER FIVE

Claire wilted, hitting the captain's chair with a thud. The ceramic fragments from the cup littered the cabin floor, and she refused to care. They could damn well clean it up themselves.

She couldn't be here. Not now, of all times. Her future hinged on making sure her boss remembered who was responsible for the festival's raging success. The newspapers had validated it that first day. George Seton would happily take the credit and forget who had done the legwork, who deserved the raise...oh, God. One hand clutched her stomach as it gurgled an unhappy tune. She absolutely had to get home to San Diego.

Her free hand worked the wood desk instinctively, feeling the imperfections, gouges, and places worn by long use.

Think, Claire. Connect the dots and find a way out of here.

The rhythm of the wood distracted her. The variations were too smooth to be accidental. She ran her fingers over the markings, reading them like Braille.

Mi Tesoro, Mi Amor.

Tesoro? Treasure? Treasure! Whoever had named this schooner must have carved this. My Treasure, My Love. Had the previous owner done this? And did the current owner, the grandson, know? If he was on board, he would help her. But who was he? The captain? No, he'd made it abundantly clear he wouldn't help her.

The first mate? Clair ran her fingers gently across the words again, doubting that anyone so arrogant could spring from such devotion. She didn't even know the man's name.

This vessel seemed larger than two people could safely sail, so there must be others on board. The owner had to be one of them. She needed to find out for sure and enlist his aid. In the meantime, all she could do was pray that it wasn't Roger.

Claire started to pace the small cabin, wobbling back and forth. The floor had a list to it, which meant they were under sail. Damn. She needed to be home, and she moved further and further away with each dip and swell. Her stomach continued to churn, and she doubted it was nerves.

She pounded the wall with both fists. "I will *not* be sick. I will *not* get sick."

A nagging thought kept tickling the back of her mind. Why wouldn't they take her home? What was so important that they couldn't delay long enough to drop her ashore? She knew most of the ships in San Diego had sailed north to the next festival. She checked the nearby vent and felt the warm air breeze in. This didn't feel like a northbound voyage, which meant they were heading west or south. Nothing she could imagine would make timing so crucial.

She stopped then. Timing. It had to be something to do with timing. Were they meeting someone? Were they...

Lunging for the bunk, she dropped onto it, afraid to trust her legs.

Could they possibly be the pirates? She visualized them both. The first mate, now, that was pretty easy to believe. Roger as a pirate, though, did not fit at all.

What had those agents told her at that security meeting? The leader was tall and blond. Roger could pass for a blond and he certainly qualified as tall. The rest were stockier, darker, and maybe Hispanic. The mate certainly qualified under that description. She tried to remember the names of the agents at that meeting. Stone and Walker, that was it. She'd seen them on board the *Treasure* more than once during the festival. Had they been checking it out? Did they know who the pirates were?

Damn. She needed answers. The only thing she knew for a fact was that she couldn't take anything for granted or trust anyone. She was on her own.

She had to get out of here. And she had to do it by herself, at least for now. Crossing to the door, she opened it slowly, hoping it didn't need to be oiled. Peering out, she saw a short hallway leading into what must be the main cabin. No one was in sight, so she stepped through the door.

"Oomph!"

She tripped over the gasket seal around the hatch and froze with her heart thumping away in her throat. Hearing no other sounds, she moved at a turtle's pace down the short corridor, and kept her eyes peeled on the stairs topside for any sign someone was headed her way. As she glanced around, she saw an alcove of electronics immediately to her left. Claire squeezed into the room and hid behind the wall while she tried to decipher the panel.

She saw something with the letters EPIRB. Claire wondered if that was some sort of emergency beacon but didn't know for sure. Then she saw it. VHF FM. She was almost positive this was the radio, and she knew that the Coast Guard monitored channel sixteen. She didn't know if it was monitored internationally or not. Turning the dial to sixteen, she searched for the mike.

"Looking for this?"

Claire jumped straight into the wall, immediately yelping as the corner of a shelf jabbed into her shoulder. Off balance, she lurched in the opposite direction, right toward the electronics panel.

Her momentum was re-directed as she was yanked away from the electronics and smack into the first mate's firm, muscled chest. Then they were both falling. She couldn't see anything. There was too much of him blocking her view. She felt the bunched muscles tighten their hold on her as he arched to the side.

They landed with a thud on the floor of the main cabin.

"Oooph!"

"Aghhh!"

"Everything all right down there?" Roger stuck his head through the companionway hatch. "What the hell!"

Jumping down the stairs, he was quickly followed by two other men Claire couldn't see. Roger bodily lifted her off Dion and placed her none too gently on a nearby bench with a firm "stay" thrown in her direction.

He kept his voice low as he helped his first mate up.

"Are you buggers letting her out of y—the cabin?"

The man coughed, obviously still trying to catch his breath. Claire smiled. *Serves him right.*

"I didn't let her out," he said, one word at a time through gritted teeth.

"Well if you didn't, who did?"

"There's no lock on the door, remember?"

"Uh, oh. Yes. A bit of a quandary, that."

"So it's a good thing I grabbed the mike before I went topside, isn't it?" he ground out, dangling the cord in front of him. "I found her trying to use the radio. Channel sixteen."

Claire knew then she'd been on the right path. She saw his scowl deepen as he watched her smile. Her smirk fled when she got her first good look at the other men. Agents Stone and Walker? The men from the International Marine Bureau she'd met in San Diego. She felt all the blood drain from her face. What were they doing here? Were they part of this? And what, exactly, was *this*? Could they possibly be undercover, infiltrating the pirate ring? Or worse, could they be part of it?

Aidan Walker leaned back against the counter with a wide grin on his face. With his reddish hair and relaxed disposition, he didn't seem very pirate-like. The other one, though, frowned as if everything in life inconvenienced him. Claire rubbed her bruised shoulder. If attitude were any indication, Agent Stone could be the first mate's brother.

She couldn't breathe. Hell, she couldn't even think. She had to get out of here. Claire stood, digging deep for a bravado she didn't feel.

"Excuse me," she said, hoping for haughty, but getting something more like a squeak. "I've been bruised and thrown about. I'm not feeling at all well and I'm going back to my cabin."

Roger escorted her back before he issued his ultimatum.

"You can have the run of the ship, Claire. But, as you can see, you won't be able to use the radio."

"Why won't you take me home, Captain Borland?"

"Roger. And trust me. You don't want to know."

Her eyes widened.

"Get some sleep." Gently, he shut the door behind him.

Claire's queasiness finally cut loose, and she barely reached the bowl on the table. Then she curled up into a tight ball on the mattress. Seasick and unable to sort out anything, she drifted into an uneasy sleep, dreaming of pirates with deep, dark eyes.

Hours later, Dion knocked on her door and entered without waiting for a response. Claire sat on the side of the bunk, rubbing sleep-filled eyes.

"Dinner," he said, indicating the tray in his hands.

He watched her reach up, touch the bump on her head gingerly, then wince.

"Still hurt?"

"Yes." She glared at him, then switched her gaze to the tray.

"Headache?"

"Not too much anymore."

"I could have the captain whip up another cup of the cure if you like."

Claire frowned. "No, thank you."

He set the tray down on the lone table in the room.

"Eat. It will help. There's aspirin there, too."

As he made to leave, he felt more than heard the movement and turned back as Claire crossed the short distance between them. Placing her hand on the arm that held the door, she spoke, using that low, sultry voice that had haunted him since he'd first heard it. Even the feel of her hand on his bare arm sent shivers through his body.

"I'm sorry."

Fully awake now, she looked right at him as she spoke. Hell, she looked through him. He saw again that her eyes were a deep chocolate. Their closeness now showed him the little imperfections in the color, like swirled fudge.

"For what?"

"For being rude to you, back at the festival."

"Forget it," He knew he was staring. Even with tousled hair and tear-streaked face, she was both beautiful and vulnerable.

"I can't forget it."

Dion reminded himself that she was trouble with a capital "T." He shifted his focus to the hand resting on his arm, which seemed almost as bad. Slender wrists, long fingers, and manicured nails had him imagining what it would be like to have them blazing a trail across his body. The shivers increased, and he would start visibly shaking if he didn't get out of there. Either that or he was going to do something he'd most certainly regret.

What was she talking about? He'd let the conversation drift away from him.

"You can't what?"

"Stop worrying about having insulted you," she said.

"It's history." He could feel his reaction to her nearness. Hell. He needed to get out of here. Fast.

"Well, thank you, then."

"For what," he asked, even more confused.

"For saving me from being hurt. You know, earlier."

It was too intoxicating, being this close. She smelled of spring. He wanted to inhale deeply and let more of her scent surround him. He returned his gaze to her face then, knowing he had to end the conversation.

"I wasn't saving you. I was protecting the electronics."

He didn't wait for her to respond, pulling the door closed behind him. He heard it open back up, warning him she wasn't done. How much more could he endure?

"Wait. Please."

The plea worked. Dion stopped. He didn't want to talk to her, get to know her, or be responsible for her. He couldn't ignore her, either. The *Treasure* wasn't that big, and they had several days of sailing ahead of them.

"I don't even know your name."

No. I won't give you that power. "Dion."

"Dion." She smiled. "It has a nice sound to it."

His name rolled off her lips like liquid sunshine. He liked how she said it much more than he should.

"Dion, can you help me to find a way to get home? Or at least put me ashore somewhere?"

"No."

"Please. I've got to get back."

"I'm sorry. We can't."

He looked then, but shouldn't have. He watched her shoulders droop and tears well in her eyes. It added a layer of fragility to her he didn't want to see. She retreated to the cabin, and he followed. Only to reassure her, and nothing else.

"Please understand, Claire. What the captain told you is true. We have something to do that's time sensitive. You won't be hurt in any way. I promise you that."

Wincing, he realized what he'd just done. He was right back where he'd been, working hard to keep someone he cared about safe. Only the last time it hadn't worked out so well.

This time when she met his eyes, fire flashed in hers.

"Oh, and that makes me feel *so* much better when my life in San Diego is falling apart while he keeps me captive here. Get out of here!" she cried, picking furiously at the tray of food.

"Claire—"

"Get out!" On the heels of those words came the tray of food, flying directly at him. He barely got an arm up before it caught him full in the face and chest, then clattered to the floor.

Dion looked down at the mess slowly oozing down his t-shirt, then up at her, but she had turned her back to him. He knew if he spoke, he'd regret it, and for totally different reasons this time. So he left, closing the door quietly behind him.

Reaching for a towel as he passed the galley, he went topside, where all three men grinned at the spectacle he made. He glared at them as he ripped the dripping shirt off over his head.

"Ah, lover's spat, then," stated Roger, his grin widening.

"Shut up."

Mike Stone took a more serious tone, although the struggle to maintain a stern face was minimal at best. "Didn't your girlfriend like the food?"

"Leave. It. Be. Damn it."

"Are you the only one doused in food?" Aidan asked, hooting in a poorly disguised attempt to smother his smile. "I mean, I'd be happy to go help Claire if she's as covered as you are."

The food-soaked rag and shirt landed square in Aidan's lap as Dion gave up. He limped back down into the galley, serenaded by laughter. His leg ached, and he could feel one bastard of a headache coming on. The only aspirin he had now sat in the captain's cabin with Claire. Damn.

"I'm heading for a shower and bed," he said, but no one was there to hear.

Claire woke the next morning with full knowledge of her surroundings and, thankfully, with much less of a headache. Still, she was no closer to figuring out how to escape. Roger said she could move around the boat, so she decided the best thing to do was to be where she could keep an eye out for opportunities. Maybe she could find out where Dion hid the radio mike, or if the owner was on board.

For now, though, her stomach reminded her that she had tossed supper instead of eating it last night, so she ventured out from the cabin. She found the galley beyond the electronics room and started rummaging for something to eat. She found mugs hanging from hooks in the ceiling and grabbed one, pouring herself a cup of coffee. A bagel from the cupboard and some cream cheese in the fridge would do for breakfast. She was halfway finished when she heard the noise. She wasn't alone.

Dion sat in the navigation room, watching her, a scowl firmly entrenched. He looked...formidable, and it did little to quell her nerves. Was it the scowl that frightened her or the way his eyes seemed to pin her to the wall?

Claire stood up straight and stared right back. She refused to give him the satisfaction of intimidating her. And she sure as hell didn't plan to apologize for throwing the food at him. He deserved it. They all did, keeping her here against her will.

Defiantly, she continued to eat. Swallowing was difficult, though, with her throat so constricted. It took an enormous effort to stand up to his gaze. To help, she decided to use the age old speaker's trick and envision him naked, all dark and muscled and...

The bagel hit the floor. Okay, that was a bad idea. She picked her breakfast up and tried a different tack, deciphering what she could see instead of what she could imagine.

His dark hair and broodiness made him seem dangerous. For all she knew, he was. His eyes were always the toughest to get past. The color of strong coffee, they seemed infinite and unyielding. The tight line of his mouth added to the feeling that a very well-built wall surrounded him. His face was sun-weathered, with tiny, white crow's feet at the corner of each eye, as if the sun had somehow missed them when tanning the rest of his face. Had he earned them by actually smiling a time or two in his life? Claire doubted it.

Still, the smoky circles under his eyes almost overshadowed any sense of danger he radiated. Something haunted him. The urge to ease his burden flared in her, and she hastily suppressed it.

She'd be damned if she'd feel sorry for him. He was no better than that captain, keeping her here against her will. She met his stare without wavering.

Dion broke first, throwing the chart he held to the counter as he stomped topside.

Good. He deserved to be uncomfortable. A ghost of a smile touched Claire's face and, for the first time, it felt good.

She set her mug on the counter and tried to understand the layout of the ship. It was more spacious below deck than she expected. The cabin she occupied was at the stern, right behind the ladder. The galley abutted the main cabin. She could see five or six places to bunk, some with curtained privacy, some out in the open.

Opening one door, Claire was elated to find a shower. This was exactly what she needed. She ran quickly back to her cabin, yanked drawers open in a search for any type of clothing she could wear, and settled for a pair of men's shorts and an over-sized t-shirt. She also found a belt. That should help. A small cupboard yielded a towel and shampoo.

It took only moments for her to begin indulging in a luke-warm shower, not even bothered that it wasn't hot. It was the first good thing that had happened since she'd been hit over the head. Claire closed her eyes in pleasure as she rinsed her now clean hair. A whoosh of air alerted her in time to see Dion pull the curtain aside.

"Wha—"

Without a word, he shut off the water.

"How dare you," she sputtered, hastily grabbing a towel for coverage. "Get out of here."

"You're done," he said as he spun on his heel and left.

Oh, no I'm not! Claire followed him out to the main cabin.

"How dare you?" she repeated. "What gives you the right to intrude on me like that?"

His pivot was so fast, Claire took a step back, afraid his momentum would carry him smack into her. His face, set with more steel than the polished edge of a sword, added to her distress. He stared at her as she had done to him earlier, taking time to scrutinize the towel behind which she now desperately tried to hide.

"The desire to survive gives me the right. You were showering with our drinking water."

She hadn't realized that. Even still, he didn't have the right to march in like he did. Another thought crossed Claire's mind, though, and she jumped on it.

"Does that mean the captain will have to put ashore to re-supply?"

"No such luck, lady. Trust me when I tell you that the captain will put us all on rations before he would screw this up just to get you off the ship. And believe me, he'd like nothing better than to do exactly that. Go get dressed, Claire," he continued.

"You're displaying much more than you think. Oh, and while you're at it, remember to take care of your dirty dishes. Anything left sitting out can go flying with one rogue wave."

She watched him take a long, leisurely tour around the edges of the towel, surveying her like she was a yacht for sale. A brief flash of fire filled his eyes, and she felt her body responding at a deep, guttural level. She wanted to drop the towel and give him what he was looking for. Her arms actually started to dip before she realized what she was doing.

"Argh!" Turning on her heels, she stomped back into the shower, slamming the door behind her. She caught her reflection in the mirror, all flushed and...and...naked! Claire slid to the floor, covering a face that flamed with heat, as she recognized that she had just given Dion a clear view of her undressed backside. The towel only covered her in front.

She pounded the floor with her hand. It didn't help. So she once again gave vent to the only thing that might. "Argh!"

CHAPTER SIX

Dion stood still and silent for a long while after Claire slammed the door to the bathroom behind her, trying to regain some composure. She was nothing but a spoiled debutant. His mind knew that. His body, however, forced him to retract that thought. That body did not belong to a little girl. Not by any definition. He shook his head. How had he managed to keep his jaw from hitting the floor? The towel she'd held over her breasts had only enhanced their perfect roundness, and he'd broken into an instant sweat when they had almost spilled over the top. He had even seen one rose- colored nipple trying to burst free. Even angry, his body had reacted powerfully. He'd gone from pissed off to rock hard in about two seconds. It had taken every bit of willpower to not approach her, rip the towel away and show her what she did to him.

Damn. Do I need a woman that bad?

He scowled, reminding himself that she was a princess. He'd better stay as far away from her as he could while on board. Otherwise, he'd be constantly torn between throwing her overboard and throwing her into his bunk. Her bunk, he corrected. The bunk she'd slept in since she'd come on board.

Dion headed up the stairs. He found Roger, Mike, and Aidan all standing around the wheel, smiling, not even trying to disguise having heard the conversation from below. The boat wasn't that big.

"Don't you all have things to do?"

"Nope. Not a thing," Aidan answered, his smile never wavering.

"Then find something," Dion responded, deepening his scowl.

Laughing, both Mike and Aidan went forward to begin the daily chore of washing down the deck. Dion slumped down onto the bench of the storage bin behind the wheel.

"Wipe that damn grin off your face," he told Roger.

"Sorry, partner. This is just too much fun."

"This is serious. She's impossible! We'll never get her to cooperate."

Roger sobered at that comment. "I know. It won't work the way things are right now. We have to tell her."

"No."

"Why not."

"We don't know her. We can't take the chance."

"Do you really think she'll find someone to tell out here?"

To bring the point home, Roger waved both arms, indicating the ocean all around them. "There's no land in sight. Besides, have you considered the possibility that she thinks *we* may be the pirates?"

Dion stared out at the water, trying to find a solution they could all live with. "We can't take the chance," he said again.

"What are you going to do, Dion? Lock her in the shower and hope they don't find her when they take over the ship?"

"I don't know." He smacked the bench. "Hell. We don't need this complication."

"I know, partner. But we've got it. And we're running out of time to decide what to do about it."

"True."

At that moment, Claire appeared on deck, wearing Dion's shorts and t-shirt, held up by his belt. And no bra. She held it, dripping with water, in her hand. He'd have known anyhow, the way his t-shirt, even oversized, molded to her breasts.

"Man, what I would have given to be down below for that, umm, discussion you and she had." Roger's smile returned. "What a sight that must have been."

Dion's glare deepened. He wasn't about to validate that with a comment. He hated to admit it, but Roger was right. They needed Claire on board with what would be going down, since she was also literally on board. "Fine, he said to Roger. "Tell her."

Tossing one last glare in her direction, he headed below. Access to his cabin had been severely limited since she'd been found, and there were some things he needed.

Holding clothes damp from a quick washing, Claire found Dion sitting with Roger when she came topside and promptly headed in the other direction. Movement was hard with the deck somewhat angled since they were under sail. She held on tight to ropes and railings to navigate. She watched Dion head below like walking on a canted, rolling deck was child's play.

Agent Walker stood polishing some metal fittings at the bow of the schooner, so she crossed over to him.

"Agent Walker," she whispered.

"Aidan," he answered warily.

"Do you know how I can dry my clothes?" She held up the garments for effect.

"Well, we can rig a line, although they'd dry just as quick if you laid them out on the cabin roof.

"A line would be fine, Aidan." She smiled at him. "Can you string one for me?"

"Yes, ma'am." He ran to grab a line from below and deftly secured it. Her clothes were soon fluttering in the gentle breeze.

"I expected there to be more breeze since the boat is under sail," she commented.

"That's a common misconception. We're running with the wind right now, which reduces the apparent wind, meaning the wind you feel."

"I guess that makes sense. Agent Walker?"

"Aidan."

"Aidan, then."

"Yes."

"Um, you know, you can tell me if this is some sort of operation," she said, her voice back to a whisper.

"An operation?" he repeated.

"Yes. Have you and Agent Stone infiltrated a smuggling ring?" she asked.

"A smuggling ring?"

"Yes! Are you and Agent Stone undercover?"

He stared at her like she was speaking a foreign language, so she tried again.

"Are you and Agent Stone, um, what do they call it? Deep undercover? Are you trying to get evidence on the captain and first mate?"

Finally, a light dawned in Aidan's eyes. He understood, and laughed heartily. Not exactly the reaction she expected.

In between gulps of air he managed a few words. "You think we're trying to capture Dion and Roger?" Aidan wiped at the tears streaming down his face.

Claire watched him struggle to sober up long enough to answer her. "Believe me, that's about as far from the truth as you can get. But thanks for the laugh," he finished, heading below.

Chagrinned, Claire had no idea what to make of the conversation. What did he mean? Had she made a mistake in confiding in him? Was he one of the pirates, masquerading as an agent?

Roger gestured for her to join him. She made her way slowly back to the stern took a seat on the lazarette and waited. He didn't make her wait long. "We need to talk."

"Funny. You weren't too interested in doing that last night."

Wincing, he continued. "You've a right to know why we can't take you back to San Diego."

"Yes, I do," she answered, with arched eyebrows and a quick nod.

"What do you know about piracy?"

She didn't answer, but remained still, poised for the punch line.

"Most people know about the olden-day swashbucklers, like Blackbeard, Francis Drake, even women like Anne Bonney.

It's easy to believe that overtaking ships became a venture of the past as the modern age was ushered in."

While he spoke, Roger reached for a pouch and loaded his pipe with tobacco.

"It didn't. Piracy is alive and thriving on the high seas. Ninety-five percent of world commerce is transported by sea. Did you know that?"

She shook her head.

"Last year," he continued, "there were well over three hundred assaults at sea. And those are only the reported ones. A lot more go unreported."

"Why?"

"Well, for one, small yachts, boarded by thieves for the valuables on board, don't want to be held over in ports for long investigations."

He took a long draw on his pipe. The wind drew the oaky aroma in Claire's direction, and she moved, feeling her queasiness resurfacing. She grabbed at the rigging to maintain her balance.

"Be careful what you hold onto, Claire. Never put your hand near any of the blocks."

"Blocks?"

"The pulleys that the sheets, or ropes, move through. You can get bloody pretty quick getting in the way of those."

Making sure her hands were nowhere near the blocks, she moved upwind and waited for Roger to continue.

"At any rate, most piracy attempts are against large vessels, even the large crude oil tankers. You may have heard about the failed attempt last year on a cruise ship. They're not after the vessel. It's the valuables. Money, computers, televisions—items they can sell quickly on the black market. They don't use muskets and skiffs anymore, though. It's powerboats and automatic rifles."

Taking a moment to step to port and check the waters ahead, he took another long pull on his pipe.

"Most piracy occurs in and around Asia, Africa and South America. Places like the Malacca Straights and Somalia. This is the first time a U.S. port has been routinely preyed upon. Five yachts have been stolen, Claire. Five. All over a relatively short period. And all from San Diego. We believe there is a rogue band working these waters."

"We?"

"We. Agents Stone and Walker are not pirates, as you may have been fretting over. *We* are from a division of the International Marine Bureau. We fight piracy."

"All of you?"

"Yes."

She remained silent, waiting for him to finish.

"You landed in the middle of a covert operation, an attempt to capture these thieves." Gesturing around, he continued. "The *Treasure* is the bait."

"Expensive piece of bait."

"Yes. There is a lot at stake here."

"And the owner agreed to this?"

"Not exactly."

Claire's eyes widened. "Is the owner on board? Or did you steal this boat?"

"We didn't steal the boat, Claire. We have the owner's permission."

"Forgive me if I find this just a little hard to believe."

Roger leaned forward. "Believe it, luv. You know there have been hijackings. We need to stop them before things escalate and someone gets hurt."

"If I understand correctly the trend is that they haven't hurt anyone yet?"

"Correct."

"So you're risking my safety on a hunch that they won't change their methods?"

This time, Roger's wince was much more pronounced. "Frankly, yes. That, and our own ability to protect you. I'm sorry. I do wish we could take you home, but it's just not possible."

"Why not?"

"Because these pirates have a certain window of opportunity they seem to prefer. Putting you ashore places us outside that window. We believe we won't get another chance at this."

"What do your superiors think about you having an untrained civilian in on this…operation of yours?"

"They don't know. This op is covert, Claire. There's no radio contact until it's over."

"What do you expect from me, Captain?"

"We hope for your cooperation."

"How can you ask that from me? I'm here against my will. I have a life back home, and not being there right now could be disastrous for me."

"I truly am sorry. You need to understand that if you don't go along, if you work against us, you will be increasing the danger, both to yourself and to the agents on board who now must protect you."

Claire tried to digest it all, but each word added to the weight on her shoulders until it seemed overwhelming.

"I can't think."

She got up and searched for someplace she could be alone. There weren't many options. The cabin felt too much like jail, so she headed for the only other place she could see would afford her some quiet. Moving toward the bow, she walked past the life raft where this whole mess started, thumping it as she passed. Reaching the forward-most point of the schooner, she tried to settle into a comfortable position.

Everybody wanted her cooperation, and no one gave a hoot what her needs were. This was familiar territory. Her boss, and even the other members of the yacht club made it very clear what her role should be. Before that, it had been the so-called friends she'd had at St. Mary's High School. Friends. That's a word that brought only contempt to mind.

Damn it. It wasn't fair! She was so close to turning her life around and then this. It was ridiculous how often these setbacks happened to her.

No. Claire hit the deck beside her. It didn't keep happening to her. She kept letting it happen. Well, she was tired of being everybody's fool, and done with being played.

Roger came up from below and joined Dion at the wheel. He'd taken over watch about the time Roger's conversation with Claire had finished.

"How long has she been there now?"

"Three hours."

"Do you think I ought to go talk to her again?" Roger asked.

"No. You did your part. We can only hope that time will help it all sink in. It has to." But Dion wasn't so sure. He turned to Roger.

"What did she say again about her life in San Diego?"

"That not being there right now would be disastrous."

Dion watched her for a few more minutes and then made up his mind.

"Take the wheel," he said without waiting for a reply. He went below and came up with a bottle of water and a long-sleeved white shirt.

As he moved forward, he felt a little like a pirate being nudged out onto a plank. Nevertheless, it needed to be done. He settled beside her. "Water and shade," he said, holding out the offerings.

She looked up as if gauging the strength of the sun, then shrugged into the shirt he brought. Dion saw the lingering trails of salt on her face.

She grabbed the water out of his hand and nailed him to the railing with cocoa-colored eyes full of defiance. Tear-stained cheeks muted the effect, and felt so much more dangerous than her anger. He ached to reach over and wipe them clean, to tell her everything would be all right. To tell her he would take her home.

Dion watched the horizon for a while, unsure of how to break the silence.

Claire took a long draught from the bottle. "What do you want?" she asked.

"You okay?"

"No. I'm not. Don't expect me to let your captain off the hook, either. I've been knocked out and put to sea against my will. He won't take me home or even put me ashore somewhere. And to top it all off, he wants me to join in some dangerous operation to capture the bad guys. Hell, for all I know, you *are* the bad guys, and he's just handing me some line. No, Agent, if that's what you are. I'm not okay at all. I want to go home," she said, bitterness apparent in her tone.

He prayed time would change her opinion. There wasn't much he could do to sway her in that respect, so he picked a different aspect to discuss.

"What's so crucial back in San Diego?"

She looked at him now. "You wouldn't understand."

"Try me."

For a moment, he thought she wouldn't answer.

"I need to finish the festival," she said.

"Someone else will do it."

"That's what I'm afraid of," she continued so softly he almost didn't hear.

"Why?"

She turned a withering glance his way and hesitated, as if she didn't want to answer. "I'm up for a promotion if the festival does well. I need to be there to follow up on that."

"The festival was a success. You've got to know that."

"The promotion was to be decided immediately following the festival."

"You'll know when you get back then."

"Again, you wouldn't understand."

"Again," he repeated. "Try me."

Claire gazed out at the water once again. The silence dragged on.

"I'm afraid," she finally said, "my absence will be the momentum that will allow them to give someone else the job."

"Isn't that a bit ridiculous?"

"Is it really?" she said, facing him. "You've never been around this type of people, have you? Do you know how centered on their own comfort and reputation they all are? They'll do what is best for them every time. If I'm not there to remind them it will all fall apart."

"Then why is it so important for you to be part of what they offer?"

"Once again—"

"I wouldn't understand. I know. You said that."

She stood up then, grabbing for anything to keep her balance. Dion found it hard to keep from staring at her legs, clothed in his shorts. Except that, on her, the shadows offered him enticing glimpses of things he'd like to investigate further. He forced his eyes upward, where the shimmer of tears had resurfaced on her face.

She ignored the tears, looking directly at him. "It doesn't matter why. It's important to me, the result of a lot of hard work and destined to go down the toilet if I'm not there. And right now, thanks to this little adventure of yours, I can't do anything about it."

Claire crouched down in front of him until their faces were only inches apart. His breath stopped, and Dion realized he was sweating. The closer she got, the more beautiful she became. Chocolate eyes fanned by long, dark lashes threatened to swallow him alive. He'd been in some tough situations. Right now, though, none of them seemed as dangerous as this.

"So," she said quietly. "If I'm having a hard time accepting your boss's ultimatum, well, you'll all just have to deal with it." She stood again and walked aft, disappearing from sight down the companionway.

He gulped a deep breath as he watched her go, torn between following her and his own remorse over not taking her back. Was he doing the right thing? For the greater good, yes. But for Claire? Most definitely not. And he couldn't figure out for the life of him how to make it up to her. Once again, he'd need to wait and see what happened. His intuition was screaming. The last time he'd had this feeling...

Suddenly, he was back in Somalia, acting as cook on a large crude oil carrier, Mary at his side, playing assistant. The boarding was sudden. They were overrun before they could react. Herded into one main area, he'd seen Mary signal that she had her gun.

"No. No!"

"Dion. Come around. Come around, man."

Roger crouched down in front of him. Dion shook his head to right his world. Still, it took him several moments to recognize he was on the *Treasure*.

"I blanked out, didn't I?" He sighed.

"Not exactly. You were shouting this time." Roger nodded toward Mike, Aidan and Claire.

"Damn."

"I thought the nightmares were gone."

"So did I." Glancing back, he saw they hadn't moved. "Damn it to hell. That's all I need is for them to think I'm some kind of nut case."

"You're not loony, you know that. Something must have triggered this. Any idea what?"

Dion looked at Claire. Yeah, something had triggered it, all right.

"No." He saw Roger follow his gaze but refused to acknowledge it.

After a long moment, Roger glanced once again at Dion.

"Well, you'd best figure it out soon, partner. You'll need all your wits around you for what's to come. We all do."

"I know," he said, watching as Claire descended below deck. "I know."

It was working out perfectly. Dion was distracted, just as he'd guessed would happen. The man would never even see it coming.

Watching them now, talking quietly, he knew that his plans were about to come full circle.

CHAPTER SEVEN

Hours later, Claire left her cabin at the same time Dion came below. Once again, she tripped over the doorway. Wondering if she would ever find her sea legs, she lurched as she rounded the final corner to the main cabin, and fell right into Dion's arms.

He reached out to steady her just as momentum sent her into his embrace. His hand felt warm against her back, even through the t-shirt she wore. Claire hated that she reacted, could feel her nipples hardening to well-defined points against his chest. Hot embers branded her in every place their bodies touched.

She needed to push him away, to douse the flames. Instead, she rested her head on his chest, just for a moment. His head bent toward her, just for a moment. Had he sniffed her hair?

She would rest her head for just a moment, she told herself. Just long enough to hide her reaction to him. To stop the raging tremors coursing through her and calm her breathing. Just for a minute. Oh, God, he smelled good, all oil and sunshine and wood polish.

His hand moved in a gentle caress along her back. It was enough to bring reality back in focus. Claire flinched. This wasn't right. She pulled away, quite certain her face was a deep shade of red. Mortified at her reaction, not daring to look at Dion, she moved quickly to the sink for a cup of water, where mortification took on a whole new meaning as she realized they weren't alone.

"Oh, good," Aidan said, a wide grin on his face as he dried his hands on a towel tucked into his waistband. "More hands to help." Apparently good at ignoring scowls, Aidan shoved a bag of lettuce and a bowl at Dion, shooing him off to the table with his hands. "Make salad."

"Claire, why don't you get plates and utensils out?"

"And where would those be?" she asked, her voice overlaid with a touch of venom.

Aidan continued on as if he hadn't heard the I've-got-the-perfect-place-for-those-dishes tone to her voice. "Cupboard above the table, drawer to the left of the sink."

She'd lost control of both her circumstance and her emotions over the past couple days. She wasn't much in the mood to add to that by getting close to Dion again, so indecision held her hostage until Aidan forced the issue.

"Dishes, missy. Dishes. Everybody does their part around here."

Claire's eyes narrowed. "Even the ones who are here against their will, right?"

"Right. Sorry, no excuses allowed," he finished with his signature slapstick smile.

Unable to come up with a response, she opted for the lesser of two evils, heading for the silverware drawer. That only delayed the inevitable. Resolutely, she crossed the small galley area and opened the cupboard over Dion's head, pulling out a pile of plates.

"You're not going to drop those on my head, are you?"

"Not accidentally, if that's what your worried about," she shot back, moving away. Her arm brushed his hair, and she started, almost losing her balance again. Dion moved to help, so she righted herself and settled the plates on the table with a bit more clang than intended. The quick shake of Dion's head as he sat back down didn't make matters any better.

His dark hair had a coarse and unruly look to it. She hadn't expected it to feel so soft. Claire rubbed her arms, feeling the goose bumps that had turned her normally smooth skin into tree bark. Goose bumps! In this tropical heat? She closed her eyes, disgusted with herself and trying to will her body and mind into submission.

She couldn't get interested in Dion. She wouldn't. For one thing, she ticked off mental fingers as she went down the list, he didn't care one whit about what she wanted. Also, it was apparent the job topped his priority list. If he was undercover a lot, he played a lot of different parts. She would probably never know the real Dion. Third, he was not someone who would fit well with her own plans.

Claire wondered again about things back in San Diego. Had they notified the police of her disappearance? Sent out search parties? They'd probably be combing the waterfront, since she'd left her car there. She sighed. They wouldn't think to check into the boats leaving the harbor. She was most likely on her own out here.

She opened her eyes and watched Dion make salad, trying to look at him with the dispassion of a plastic surgeon. He had a strong face, angular, but not hollow. His nose had been broken at some point, and his skin was bronzed, maybe by heritage, maybe by the sun. She couldn't tell. His eyes, though, still drew her. Unreadable, yet always the shadows were there. Sorrow seemed ever-present. She refused to think about the story behind them. A story she sensed he needed to tell, but it would not be to her.

Dion was someone she'd be better off staying far away from. Only, how do you do that on a boat? Rotating her neck, trying to release the tension in her muscles, she tried to expel thoughts of Dion. She had enough on her plate. Movement. She needed movement and backed away to sit on the berth across from the table.

Dinner, consisting of salad, spaghetti out of a jar and loaf bread with margarine, was wholesome if not totally appetizing. Afterwards, Claire headed topside to find some coolness in the evening breeze. Roger was on watch, so Claire grabbed a deck chair and set it as far away from him as possible, settling in to watch the water pass by. Maybe he'd leave her alone. Maybe they all would. Dion, claiming it was his turn, stayed below to do dishes. Relieved of duty, Mike and Aidan soon joined Roger at the wheel, grabbing seats on top of the lazarette storage locker.

Claire heard the quiet banter, forcing it to the back of her mind as her thoughts deepened with the dusk. She would never admit it, but it was peaceful here. This ship felt...comfortable, almost as if it was trying to lull her into a sense of contentment. It invited her to relax.

Relaxing wasn't in Claire's nature, however, and her thoughts returned to home. Had someone closed down the festival for her? Had they let Trish Seton finish things up? She'd never do it right, and Claire would be blamed. Trish was incompetent and the President's daughter, a deadly combination for Claire. The girl could do no wrong, and someone else was always at fault.

Mr. Seton wouldn't finalize things and make sure everything got cleaned up. He would remember less than half of what needed to be done. The temporary piers needed to be scheduled for return. The electricians had probably already picked up all their connections. Who saw to the water hookups, the phones, the garbage cans? Damn it. Claire needed to be there.

She had started organizing the festival with an end result in mind. A promotion. Somewhere in the process, it had become more. She'd taken a very proprietary pride in how well things had come together, and she couldn't stand that she wasn't there to finish things.

Wrapped in her own thoughts, she started at the voice beside her. "Pardon?"

"I said," Roger began again, squatting beside her chair. "Have you made a decision, Claire?"

Everything grew quiet at that moment. Even the dishes stopped jangling down below.

A sigh escaped as the finality of answering hit Claire. At times this boat was too small.

"Yes. Take me home."

"We can't do that."

"Then put me ashore with some money and I'll find my own way home."

"Claire, even if we had the time," he stood and leaned against the railing, "you don't have your passport with you. The nearest land is well within Mexico's jurisdiction. You'd be delayed days trying to get through the paperwork to cross the border."

"Then take me home," she repeated more forcefully. "If you really are agents, you know it's against the law for you to hold me against my will."

"Not when you're interfering with a covert operation, it isn't."

"Interfering!" The water, the boat, even Roger faded away as red filled Claire's vision. "I'm here against my will! If I'm such interference, take me back to San Diego."

"I'm sorry, Claire. That's not going to happen."

"Then you can all go to hell," she finished, toppling the chair as she got up. Heading forward, she tried to stare at the stars, to return to some semblance of peace. Instead she felt three sets of eyes boring holes in her back.

She couldn't do it. She wouldn't. Acceptance meant they won. And it meant letting go of a dream. Her dream.

Frustrated, she grabbed her laundry off the line and climbed down the forward ladder and through the galley. Dion stood there, dishtowel in hand, eyeing her like she'd disappointed them all. Claire glared at him, then rounded the companion-way and entered her cabin, slamming the door behind her.

It was no better for her inside. The room was small and stuffy and she could find no way to vent her fury. Picking up a lamp, she pulled back from throwing it as she remembered the mess her meal dishes had made when they'd hit the floor last night. Someone had cleaned it up.

Claire set the lamp down and slumped onto the bunk. These agents and their mission were going to make her give up on the most important things in her life. Solvency and the respect of her peers, neither of which would be there when she got home. She knew that for certain.

Curling up on the bunk she wiped at her eyes and gave in to the misery she felt.

Claire woke the next morning to a different world, a stifling one. She was hot and sweaty. Even breathing seemed a challenge, as if the blankets were piled high on top of her, weighing her down, warming her almost beyond endurance. She threw the heavy covers back, surprised to find only a sheet. The scorched air pressed in on her. The mugginess had increased, too, amplifying the effect.

She reached for a glass of ice water and took a long drink, turning the glass in her hand. When had it appeared in her cabin? Someone had entered while she slept. She'd heard nothing.

She took a closer look and found no lock that she could bar entry with. So she grabbed the chair and placed it under the doorknob. It seemed to sit pretty securely. It would have to do for now.

Replacing the chair, she threw on the shorts she'd worn yesterday along with a scrounged tank top that was too large. It would have to do, however. With her bra underneath, at least she was covered.

Topside, no one acknowledged her presence. The stillness seemed almost as oppressive as the heat. With little movement on the water, the schooner appeared poised on a sheet of dark, undulating glass. The sails sat lashed to the mast and an awning had been stretched across the boat to provide shade.

Aidan, Mike and Roger lay at various points under the canopy, faces flushed and outfitted in water-soaked hats and t-shirts, as if they'd just come from the sauna.

There was no wind, not even a puff. Even the schooner seemed wilted.

Only Dion moved about, and Claire froze when she saw him. He had taken his shirt off as he tied down a sail. His arms reach over the boom, then under, tendons dancing with each change, ripples crossing his back each time he shifted the weight of the sail. He was sun-bronzed. Very...her thoughts stopped suddenly and zeroed in on what she saw.

A pock marked scar on his right side, just above his waistline, marred the muscled back.

He shifted enough that she could see no scar on his abdomen. Had he been shot? In the back? Then she saw the ragged wound around his knee, healed now, but jagged and angry looking like the reason for his limp.

Was this the meaning of the shadows beneath his eyes?

She felt cold all of a sudden, even as the sun beat down. How had he been injured? How close to danger were they asking her to get? Not asking, she reminded herself. Forcing. Just how much risk would be involved in this operation of theirs?

At that moment, Dion noticed her. Adopting his usual scowl, he reached down for his shirt and pulled it over his head.

Claire turned away.

"What's for breakfast?" she asked Mike.

He pulled the hat off his face to peer up at her. "We haven't felt much like anything in this heat," he answered. "And we don't want to run the generator any more than we have to in order to conserve fuel. As well, when things are this quiet, it's generally noisy enough to drive a person nuts."

She went below, rummaged around, and found enough to make a cold fruit salad and a tall glass of iced tea. Just as she reached for a fork, noise topside reminded her she wasn't alone. As if she could forget that. She stabbed the fork into the fruit. Well, they can damn well go hungry.

She chomped down angrily on the fork then calmed as the taste of the fruit held the heat at bay just a small bit. She took another slow, languorous bite, and the temperature took another imaginary dip.

Whap!

Claire jumped as something hit the roof of the cabin.

"Come on, wind, damn it! Give us something! Anything!"

That had to be Aidan. He was the only one who seemed willing to show some emotion. Dion's face came to mind. Well, the only one if you didn't count Mr. Eternal Scowl.

Mike said they hadn't the energy to eat that morning. Claire's eyes kept darting to the stairs as she gulped bits of the fruit. Somehow, it just didn't seem right to be sitting here eating...

Hell. The fruit tasted almost sour now. Tossing the dish on the counter, she began opening cupboards until she found the salad bowl. She'd make salad for them all and maybe some iced tea. But that was all she'd do. They could damn well clean up the mess themselves.

Several minutes later, Claire loaded up trays with fruit salad, bowls, silverware, napkins, cups and a pitcher of tea.

Heading up with the first tray, she almost collided with Dion on the ladder.

He reached to steady them both, his hands covering hers as she held the tray. She froze as his fingers passed like a whisper over hers. His scowl was gone, replaced by something more intense and indefinable. It felt like he was claiming her, and she couldn't move. She didn't want to. Then, abruptly, he released her, took the tray and turned with ease on his good leg, calling for Roger to take it. Claire leaned against the stair wall, taking slow, deep breaths. One touch, one look and she felt turned inside out. She wanted more. She wanted...

"Claire?"

It was Dion who quietly brought her to her senses. He had a slight smile on his face, as if he knew what he did to her. Claire's ardor turned quickly to irritation as she felt the rush of what must be a deep, blushing red flood her face. He knew, damn it.

She turned away, reached down for the second tray and handed it up. Soon everything for breakfast was topside, and they were all seated under the canopy out of the sun. Claire settled in as far away as she could from the others while still being in the shade. She felt Dion's eyes on her, but refused to meet his stare.

"Ah, this is excellent," Roger said, tipping his bowl in Claire's direction. "It seemed too hot to even think about eating. You've hit the nail on the head here."

"Here, here," Mike and Aidan added.

Dion just nodded in acknowledgement of Roger's comment, not trusting himself to speak. He'd gone hard as a rock from one simple, innocent touch. How the hell could one touch make him want a woman that way? His pulse still raced, and he felt the ache of desire spiral almost out of control. He wanted to reach for her. He could almost touch her from here. It would be easy to pick her up, to take her to his cabin, to lay her in the bunk she'd slept in. He wanted to slowly run his hands along the gaping edges of the tank top she wore, feel the lace of her bra that peeked out, brush across a nipple that would instantly harden. He knew she would respond. She wasn't immune to him. Her body would reach out for his, and he would answer both their needs. Find fulfillment…

"Why has it gotten so hot, so still all of a sudden?"

Claire's silky voice drew him back to the present.

Aidan answered her. "It has to do with dry air and high pressure. Basically, we're passing through an area of little or no air movement called the doldrums. We'll pick up the trade winds soon. Until then, though, we struggle for gasps."

"So we just sit here?"

"Bottom line is yes. We wait it out," Roger supplied, moving to sit down next to her. "We don't really want to be under power if we don't have to. So we'll give it a few hours and see if it passes."

"What if it doesn't?"

"It will. Weather changes. It's just a matter of how long it will take."

"So what do you do while you wait?"

"Not much in this heat." Roger gave a short laugh. "There are a few maintenance items we can take care of if we have the energy. Other than that, we pass the time however we can."

Claire knew then it would be a long day. Since inactivity wasn't her style, she started to pick up the breakfast dishes, but Aidan stopped her.

"Cook doesn't clean up."

"I need something to do."

"Sorry, that's the rule," he quipped. He stepped over a bucket and ducked under the boom as if they weren't there. All the while, he balanced a tray laden with dirty dishes.

Claire stared at the bucket, and a revelation struck her. "I'm not sick," she murmured.

The others stared at her, uncomprehending.

"I'm not sick," she said again. "Why am I not sick?"

Only Dion understood. "Because you weren't seasick. You were nervous."

It made sense. Especially in light of how good she felt this morning. More at ease than she had since her reluctant boarding, she relaxed back against the railing and watched Dion and the others in silence. He made it look easy, moving about the boat. For that matter, they all did. She might not be queasy anymore, but she did still wobble and reached out for walls and railings to help her navigate the schooner. Not these guys. They stepped in, around, and under things instinctively, as if they knew when the schooner would rise and fall on the water's whim. She envied them the ability, doubting she'd ever be that comfortable on board.

"Claire," Roger said. "Would you like to become more familiar with the *Treasure*?"

She stayed quiet for a moment. Had he read her thoughts? Seeing Dion squirming out of the corner of her eye, she wondered why he'd gone all antsy. He got up and walked forward, placing a hand on the foremast as he checked the water.

"Maybe," Claire answered Roger, not willing to commit.

"It might make you more comfortable."

"It won't change my mind."

"Fair enough," he said with a smile meant to charm the Queen Mum.

Dion returned aft as Roger continued.

"How about we let Dion show you the ropes?"

She saw the grimace on Dion's face and added her own glower to the mix.

"Maybe Aidan or Mike would be better?"

"No. They aren't sailors."

"Hey!" Aidan arrived topside, and both he and Mike's faces took on the appearance of caricatures as they worked up their protests.

"They know how to sail," Roger pacified, holding up a hand. "But they don't know the *Treasure* as well as Dion and I do. You're better off with Dion."

I doubt that. However, Claire couldn't see another alternative. She didn't want Roger instructing her. She didn't like him much. He was too...unyielding.

Claire tipped her head in silent consent. She watched Dion as he responded in kind, still leveling a prickly stare at his boss.

"Great. These guys will catch the dishes and cover watch for a while. I've got some logs to complete. Thank you for breakfast, Claire," he finished as he ducked below.

Dion sighed, picked up his tea and raised his glass in a toast toward Claire. "It's good. Thank you." His eyes didn't mirror his gratitude. In fact, they looked more like he'd just been tossed in the lion's den. He drained his tea and stood with exaggerated difficulty.

Did he dread this as much as she did? A shadow touched her heart like an icy needle. Did he?

"Remember to watch out for the boom," Dion reminded her.

Claire mimicked his sigh, then placed her hand on the spar that the sail was lashed to. "That's this pole, right?"

"Yes. With the sails furled, the boom is settled into a bracket, so it's lower than you're used to."

"Okay. Thanks for the warning."

He lost no time and dove right in to what she needed to know. Did he want to get this over with? She did. The shadow returned. Maybe.

"We're standing at the wheel, where navigation is controlled. You've seen us maneuver with this," he began, placing a hand on two of the spiked points of the wheel. "It's attached to a rudder underneath. That's what steers the *Treasure*."

His hand ran over the wooden wheel as he spoke. She could find no other way to describe it except lovingly. Claire found his voice, his words, fading, replaced by a vision of those strong hands wandering over her, moving along her curves with the same apparent adoration.

She shook her head and dug for a question that sounded at least minimally intelligent. "I thought the wind determined the direction we went."

"Everything out here is in relation to the wind. Unless you're running with it directly behind you, though, you have some leeway, or sideways push. The keel, or centerboard helps to resist that sideways force, giving us a little directional control. So there's a certain interrelationship between rudder and wind." He moved his hands in concert through the air.

"It's like a dance," he continued. "You have to move in a certain rhythm and sequence in order to get where you want to go."

He looked up then, his face turned as if in answer to the wind, except there was none. The man appeared every bit the master, at ease on the sea. Despite his injury, he stood confidently. Claire wondered how much time he'd spent at sea. He'd have to be a seasoned sailor for the agency to put him aboard a ship like this. Of course, Roger was captain. He's the one who would be responsible if anything happened to the schooner, she guessed.

"How long have you been sailing?"

"All my life," he answered absently, moving a hand along the foremast.

Claire gave herself up to the particulars of sailing a schooner this size and actually found it held her interest. Even in this stifling heat, she could almost feel the wind as he talked about jibing and tacking and direction. The way he spoke brought the *Treasure* to life. It started to feel almost like a sentient being.

This was the most animated—and talkative—she'd seen him. He didn't just make the schooner seem alive. He joined with it, appearing to almost know it intimately.

He touched the well-polished teak wood on the cabin roof and she found herself again wondering what it would be like if he touched her that way.

He caressed the sheets, moving his hands gently up and down them as he explained their purpose. What would it be like if he did that to her spine? A shiver coursed through her at the thought.

Claire asked a question here and there, but mostly found his explanations easy to understand. The quintessential seaman, he seemed to be always checking for problems as he spoke.

"The running rigging is what we use to raise and furl the sails. You can see here." He laid one hand under the boom and reached up to point out the spar on top of the sail. "There is a pole, called a spar pole, at the top of the mainsail. The slides attached to the spar wrap around the mainmast and sheets, or ropes, are used to raise and lower the sail."

After a couple of hours, she had a basic feel for what she needed to know in an emergency. She knew that port meant left and starboard right. He'd explained that a sheet was a rope, not a sail. Of course, a halyard was also a rope. In fact, none of the ropes seemed to actually be called that. She now knew how to lower the sails in an emergency, help with tacking, and some basic steering guidelines.

She learned that when the captain said "prepare to come about" they would be tacking, which turned the boat through the wind and onto a new course. If she didn't have a job during this process, she should steer clear of the sails and the men working.

"Always be aware of what the wind and the sails are doing when you head topside, Claire. We have preventers to make sure the booms don't swing too far in either direction, but you don't want to be caught unawares. If you are, well, that headache you started this trip with would return with a vengeance."

"Been there. Did that," she said.

"Yeah," he agreed. As he spoke, his eyes traveled up the main mast. He seemed to be checking it visually, and when he reached the top, she saw him stare for a long moment, a frown reappearing.

"What's the matter?" she asked.

Dion muttered something about slides and moved away.

He could tell that Claire was wilting. She'd shown a knack for sailing, once again surprising him. Now she had trouble putting coherent thoughts together into sentences.

Dion shielded his eyes as he looked skyward, the sun appearing larger than life as it blazed almost directly above them. It baked them with its heat, made suffocating by the absence of wind and enough humidity to give the air the feel of a sauna.

Concerned, he glanced again at the main mast. The slide didn't seem to be moving freely and he needed to check that out later. Not with Claire on deck, though. He didn't want her to see him climb the mast. Dion massaged his knee, feeling the ache from being on it too long. He caught Claire watching him and abruptly turned away.

He went below for iced tea and returned to find her seated on the shaded side of the deck, her long legs stretched out in front of her. She wasn't that tall, maybe five seven. Right now, she seemed to be all long, shapely legs, partially sheathed in his shorts. Too much leg for his peace of mind. He sat next to her facing the opposite direction so he wouldn't be distracted by them. It put him in too close a proximity to her, but he considered it the lesser of two evils.

For a while, they simply sat in silence. Even in the shade, it felt like they were baking. Certainly, the sheen of sweat covering both of them reflected the scorching heat. He watched the water, searching for any sign that might signal a return of the wind. Nothing. The swells, even this far out, moved slowly against, under, and beyond the schooner, lapping gently at the hull as they passed. The water looked like an endless sheet of glass. It felt more like a magnifying glass, and they were the ants. He could see no discernible sign of changes to the water in any direction. It would be a while before the wind returned.

"Do you know any of the history of this schooner, Dion?"

He hedged. "Some."

She raised her eyebrows. "And…?"

"What do you want to know?"

"Well, for starters, how old is she?"

"She, and that is the correct term, was built in England in 1924 for a man named Horace Manchester. Her design was ahead of its time, intended to increase speed and durability at the same time. Manchester was the first to order the new hull."

"What was he like?" she prompted.

Dion gave a short laugh. "Most of his wealth came from smuggling booze during the prohibition, first in Russia, then in the United States. He had a reputation for ruthlessness. Some also say, he had a weakness. He was in love."

Claire glanced at Dion and then turned back to the water. "You think love is a weakness?" she asked.

"No," Dion replied after a moment's silence. "But it turned out to be for him. The original name of the schooner was 'Mi Corazon', meaning 'My Heart'. He couldn't give it his lover's name. He had many enemies who would use her against him if they could. So he hid her."

"How sad."

"It gets worse. Apparently, he arranged for her to meet him in South America where he'd gone to take ownership of the schooner, and they began the long trip north to Florida, his home. Shortly after leaving a little quay called Vitoria just north of Rio de Janeiro, they were overtaken by pirates and both killed."

A single tear escaped and slid down Claire's cheek. He wanted to wipe it away, to make her smile. He forced himself to sit there like stone, his gut tight with emotion he couldn't show.

Claire wiped irritably at the tear. "I'm not usually so emotional. Just so you know."

"Sure."

"I'm not. It's this...this whole situation. I've lost all control. And I can't stand it."

"You like to be in control?"

She turned from the water to him. "I like being home."

"I'm sorry, Claire."

After a bit of silence, he continued.

"You know, Grandfather...meaning the owner's grandfather, bought this schooner at auction."

Claire appeared interested, so he kept going.

"He was a man of strong principles. He was also deeply in love with his wife, Emily. They say he always called her his treasure. So once again, the schooner is named for a life-long love."

"Just like my parents," Claire whispered.

"Your folks?"

She shook her head. "Never mind. So, did they sail together, these grandparents?" she asked.

"At every opportunity. They lived aboard the *Treasure*, sailing the waterways of the world, for twenty years."

Looking over the deck, he wondered if she could imagine his grandparents working in tandem, hauling sail, weathering storms, always together.

"And they lived happily ever after," she sighed.

"Well, they had twenty good years, at any rate," he said, crushing her vision.

"Emily died of pneumonia when she was fifty-three years old. The old man never got over it."

"He didn't stop sailing, did he?"

"Not entirely. He sailed local waters, belonged to the yacht club, and even helped with the tall ship festivals, as you know.

He never again went on another voyage, though. He said his heart wasn't in it anymore."

"I can understand that. He lost the love of his life."

"But he had twenty memorable years with her."

"And how many lonely ones after that? I don't think I could bear it."

Dion was quiet then, and she followed suit for a while. Eventually, she broke the silence. "You know, it's kind of poetic justice that a prohibition smuggling vessel is being used to capture a band of pirates, don't you think?"

"This boat smuggled a lot of liquor into the country. There's even a hidden cache, below the captain's cabin, for stashing contraband. I heard a rumor that the current owner found it, along with a case of very old whiskey."

"That must have brought a huge price at auction."

"I don't know. The story goes that nothing ever hit the market. Maybe he kept it for his own private collection."

"Maybe," she said. "How long has it been since you were injured, Dion?"

He froze, holding his breath as the bloody image once again filled his vision. Cold fear hit him like a sledgehammer, and he balled his fists to keep from pounding something. Long moments passed before it faded and he could answer her. "Three months." he said.

"How—"

"Don't."

Silence.

The she tried again.

"How long have the four of you worked together?"

Dion's breathing returned to normal at the change in subject. "Roger and I have been partners for ten years now. Mike and Aidan have only been with the IMB for a couple of years."

"Roger. Hmmm. I don't think I like him much."

Dion squinted at Claire. "Why not?"

"He's too narrow minded, unwilling to consider options."

Dion almost spit out the drink of iced tea he'd just taken. He gulped and asked what he already knew. "Because he won't take you home or put you ashore?"

"Yes."

Looking away from her so she wouldn't see the guilt, he tried to decide how to answer. He wasn't looking forward to her finding out it had been his orders, not Roger's, that had kept her captive onboard. He'd seen her anger. Been the brunt of it, too. No, that would not be fun.

"Roger is just doing his job."

"I know, but I'm not sure I care."

"Did he tell you much about this particular band of pirates?"

"Not really."

"Well," he said, putting his hands behind him to prop himself up. "The last hijacking, two weeks ago, was their fifth."

"Over how much time?"

"The first one was about three months ago, give or take."

"What makes you think they'll strike again so soon?"

"It's too perfect for them not to. They've only been preying on yachts out of San Diego. The festival brought all sorts of boats in and there were just too many good choices. We felt they would at least take a look."

"Why take the *Treasure*, then? Why not some other sailboat?"

"For a couple of reasons. First, she would be easy to transform for sale." He stifled a wince as he said that.

"Also, they've only hijacked sailboats that are owned outright, like this one. Lastly, she was the first boat to leave the harbor after the festival. We made sure all the rest waited until the next day."

"I don't remember passing that information around."

"You didn't. Mike and Aidan went around quietly behind you and passed the word." That earned him narrowed eyes and pursed lips, but she only asked another question.

"Why would that keep them from going after another boat the next day?"

"Because somehow they manage to overtake these yachts during a time when the satellites aren't covering the area so we can't get any footage of the incident. That happens again the day after tomorrow, which is why this is so time sensitive. If we take you back, we lose our window. We have to be in a certain region at a certain time. Do you understand?"

It was as near an entreaty as he could get. He could only hope that, when she found out the truth, she'd remember this.

She stared out at the water. Leaning forward again, he reached over her lap and braced his arm on the other side of her legs. She turned back to him, her brown eyes larger than life.

He shouldn't be here. He knew that. Except he couldn't seem to help himself.

He asked again. "Do you understand now?"

"Yes." The word was a whisper.

"Will you help, or at least not hinder, the op?"

"It seems I don't have much choice, do I?"

His eyes were drawn to her lips. Slightly parted, they invited him. The upper one was thinner, giving way to the fullness of her lower lip. An irresistible urge to taste it gripped him. Reaching up with his free hand, he ran his fingers lightly over her lower lip. The edges quirked slightly upward, sending shards of white-hot desire straight through him. Her lips were so soft. He gave up any lingering resistance, his only thought to keep it light and quick. Get it over with and out of his system.

The first contact created a tremor that racked his body, turning aside reason and will, leaving only a sensual urge for more. He knew she felt it, too. She shuddered, as if cold, and didn't resist. In fact, she leaned into it, tried to deepen the kiss. He welcomed it, reached up into her hair, and pillowed the back of her head with his free hand, entangling his fingers without notice. Nothing mattered except the powerful erotic sensations screaming through his body, shattering his sense of reason.

Then her hand brushed his injured knee, and it had the effect of ice-cold water. Breaking contact, he jumped up quickly, breathing deeply to gain some control, elusive though it was.

"I'm sorry," he said finally.

"What?"

"I'm sorry. That should never have happened."

"Wait. We need to talk about this," Claire said.

He didn't stick around to hear what she said. He couldn't. He had to get away from there. He walked away as quickly as he could. Right now, this boat seemed smaller than it ever had. As he turned to climb down the ladder, he saw her still sitting there, eyes focused on only one thing. Him. Dion paused for a moment more and then went below.

Where was that damn tracking device? He searched yet another cupboard, opened another drawer. Dion had hidden it well, damn him. It had to be here somewhere. This was the only room he hadn't been able to search so far. He'd covered the rest of the boat. Finally, lifting up the mattress, he found it. Tucked back in the corner, LED light flashing its activity to some unseen vessel.

"Finally," he muttered, picking it up and putting it in the bag at his side. Then he smiled. This was the last thing he had to do. His contract was now complete, and he could just watch as it all came down. Soon, he'd be long gone from here. And some would finally suffer in a way he'd been waiting patiently to dish out.

CHAPTER EIGHT

It was a long time before Claire moved. She felt weak, like she hadn't eaten in days. She wasn't a virgin, for crying out loud. She'd certainly been kissed before, but never...never quite like that. She felt shredded, like he'd blasted through every defense she had, reaching right into her core.

She held her hand out and stared at how it shook. Arms wrapped around knees, she felt chilled, even in this sweltering heat. Dion was right. It shouldn't have happened. It had, though, and now she didn't know what to do about it.

Lightheaded, it took all her energy just to stand. What had that kiss done to her? Sluggishly, she climbed down the nearest ladder.

Below deck, she found everyone except Dion sitting in the main cabin, wet towels wrapped around necks, trying anything to beat the heat. This area had the most vents and the best possibility of any breeze creeping in. Wetting a towel in the sink, she wound it around her neck and reached for more iced tea. Suddenly, the room started to swirl around her.

"Whoa there, missy."

Aidan. That was Aidan talking. Her mind knew it. She just couldn't answer him.

"Come on over here and have a seat."

He settled her at the table while Mike re-wet and replaced the cloth around her neck, then got her some ice-cold water.

"Thankfully, this old lady has a few modern conveniences so we have ice. You've gotten a little too much heat," Aidan said.

"I thin' I jus' did too mush," she slurred, placing the cold glass against her flaming cheek. It felt so good. Like that first burst of water on a burned finger. She moved the glass to her forehead. Someone took the towel off her neck.

"Don'. Give it back."

"I will, Claire. We're just cooling it down," Aidan said.

The towel returned and Claire pulled it up over her lips, sucking the moisture out. Ahhhhh.

"Claire?"

"Hmmmm?"

"Claire?" Roger tried again. "If you go topside again, make sure you stay in shade, okay? For now, though, I think you had best lie down for a bit."

"Really, I'm 'kay. It was jus' a stupid kiss." She stood, her legs wobbling like pudding. "Maybe I'll sit." And she flopped back down on the chair.

Mike and Aidan helped her over to one of the galley bunks.

"My cabin's tha' way," she said, trying unsuccessfully to point behind her.

"I think that will be a bit too stuffy. You'd better stay out here where there's at least a puff of air now and then."

Just then she caught a whiff from the nearby vent. Snuggling closer to the opening, she threw the wet towel over her head and promptly fell asleep.

Waking up, once again disoriented, Claire tried to sit up, but her pounding head and a gentle hand on her shoulder forced her to lie back down again.

"Oh, God." She grabbed her head with both hands. "Who hit me over the head this time?"

"The sun."

"What is it about you that makes my head hurt all the time?"

"My winning personality," Dion supplied in answer, placing a cooling cloth on her forehead. "It was the sun, Claire. You got too much of it today. The heat amplified the effect."

She opened her eyes then, turning to him and was amazed. Gentle eyes and a conciliatory smile had replaced Dion's normally brooding Marlon Brando fierceness. He was actually smiling. She could feel the transformation clawing at her inner barricades as effectively as…that kiss. Closing her eyes, she felt the tingle again. All the way to her toes.

He was gorgeous. And dangerous. Very dangerous. So was this line of thought. Claire clamped a tight lid on her mind and opened her eyes once again, seeing that the mirage had not disappeared. He still stood there, and still smiled.

"Oh, is that it. The sun. I feel like someone's building railroad tracks in my head."

"I don't doubt it."

Claire tried to sit up.

"Get your wits about you before you sit up," Dion said. He sat down facing her on the bunk. "What did you mean earlier, about your father and mother? That the prior owners were just like them."

She smiled. "Dad loved my mother beyond anything else."

"And she him?"

"I believe so. I only know her through him."

Dion waited.

"She died giving birth to me."

"And your father?"

"Never got over her. He also never held it against me. I've heard of that happening."

"Never *held*?"

Claire looked at the wall. "He passed away. Two years ago, now."

Dion's gentle smile returned. "I'm sorry. I think I would have liked your father."

Here," he continued, reaching underneath her shoulders. "Let me help you sit up, and then you can take some aspirin."

Not a good idea, being this close to him. Still, the steady, strong arm surrounding her did feel rather nice.

"Take these." He handed her two pills and reached for some nearby water, keeping his hand behind her to keep her steady.

Did he know what he did to her? Swaying slightly, she focused on the aspirin, managing to get them down with some water.

"How long did I sleep?"

"About four hours. You really had too much sun today. I apologize. I know better."

"It wasn't your fault. I should have figured that out for myself."

"You haven't spent as much time in these waters as I have."

"It doesn't matter, Dion." His proximity was getting to her. She needed some space. She got up too suddenly, almost falling to the floor because of it.

"Hang on," he said. "You shouldn't get up so fast." He held her while she found some equilibrium, and it seemed natural to lean into his strength. He was so solid, so comforting. She looked up, wanting to see that smile again. But Brando had returned.

A moment later, the support disappeared. He placed her hand on the chair and moved to the other side of the galley.

"What's wrong?"

"Nothing." Dion's scowl remained firmly in place.

He didn't want anything to do with her. Claire's hand shook as she sat down. He made that pretty darn apparent. Why, then had he kissed her?

"Fine, then. Thank you for the aspirin. I'm sure I'll be okay now. I'll just sit here for a bit."

Without a word, simply giving her a curt nod of acknowledgement, he headed topside.

Dion headed for the port side of the Treasure, pulling his shirt over his head as he went.

"Seen anything in the water?" he asked over his shoulder to Roger, who manned the helm.

"Nope," he answered with a smile.

"Good." Without a pause, he stepped up onto the railing and dove in, cleanly slicing through a swell into the glassy sea. He swam around the schooner once, twice, a third time. It wasn't enough. He could see Mike and Roger keeping an eye on him, both grinning broadly, and increased the ferocity of his strokes. This wasn't the best idea, swimming at sea. But he needed action. He needed to do something so he wouldn't be thinking about Claire. What was happening to him? Somehow, she had gotten under his skin. And somehow, he had to get her out from beneath it.

Feeling his knee aching and his leg starting to cramp from too much activity, he closed the distance to the boat. Roger and Mike put the ladder down and he climbed aboard, muttering a stilted "thanks" as he threw on his discarded shirt and sat heavily in one of the deck chairs. Chuckling, Mike headed below, leaving Dion to his thoughts.

"Did it help?"

"What?"

"The swim," Roger said, throwing a thumb toward the water. "Did it help?"

"Help what?"

"With whatever demons you're trying to rid yourself of," Roger explained.

Dion debated even answering. "No," he said finally.

"What's going on, partner? I've never seen you this jumpy before. Are you worried about the takeover? We've done everything we can to prepare. We're ready."

"I know we are. Except there are always variables."

"This is something else though, isn't it?"

Dion was silent, picking up a nearby rope and beginning to coil it. He knew what the problem was. He just didn't want to talk about it. Still, his partner had a right to know. Anything that might affect the operation should be commonly discussed. It was rule number one. Any good operative knew that.

"Claire." He saw his partner's grin broaden, and he tossed the rope, almost managing once again to clear the railing and land it in the water.

"Let me guess. You're lusting after her."

"Something like that."

Roger blew a puff of pipe smoke out, and they both watched it disappear slowly behind them. "Do you think it's a problem?" he finally asked.

"No. We're ready. There's nothing more we can do. I just...don't need the distraction. I don't want it."

Roger placed a hand on Dion's shoulder in apparent sympathy. "Then you've got a problem."

"Yes. I do."

"Better figure it out quick. You're running out of time."

"Yeah. I know."

"And Dion?"

"What?"

"If I were you," Roger managed a completely straight face as he delivered the punch line, "I wouldn't go kissing her anymore."

Dion put his head in his hands. "Don't I know it," he mumbled. "Don't I know."

Dinner didn't consist of much that evening, just sandwiches. No one had the energy for much discussion, either. Going below was not an option. The cabin heat had climbed as the day progressed. Even with the setting sun, it was still stifling.

Dion knew that, more than likely, they would all be sleeping topside tonight. Even Claire. Glancing her way, he watched her finish the last bites on her plate. She was very precise when she ate, as if trained. He frowned. It seemed more than that, almost as if she were afraid to make a mistake.

Was she really a part of the yacht club society? Or was she trying to mimic it? She had seemed a spoiled brat at first, but he'd seen a resolve in her that was foreign to those people. She had calluses on her hands. She wasn't some acrylic showpiece like those yacht club babes, either. Claire had substance. She cared. If she hadn't, she'd have thwarted their attempts to keep her on board by now. The mike had been returned to the radio room shortly after her first attempt, and she either hadn't noticed or she'd chosen not to use it. Of course, someone always kept an ear out, just in case.

Roger broke the silence. "Claire?"

A pause, then she answered. "What?"

"Will you help or hinder us?"

"It seems I don't have a choice," she gave in dully. Her head came up just then, met Dion's eyes for a moment before she averted them.

"Thank you, Claire," Roger acknowledged.

Dion turned his gaze to the fading horizon, thinking about the huge concession Claire had made. Deep in his own thoughts, he almost missed the slight caress against his cheek, like the intimate touch of a lover. Standing, he waited patiently, knowing it would return. Rewarded, the barest hint of a breeze stroked him again. He sensed more than saw a subtle change in the water as the wind began to freshen. To starboard, there was the slightest bit of chop, looking like little white cat's paws dancing across a dark piece of glass.

He heard the slight luffing of the sail, an almost silent sputter, as if calling weakly to the wind. Finally, the wind was going to answer.

"Time to go to work, men," he said with quiet excitement. Since it was dusk, they set the sails for running at night, with only the fore and mainsail rigged. Before long, they were once again moving across the water.

Focused as he was, he still saw Claire go below with the dishes. She didn't reappear, and he found himself irrationally disappointed at that.

When Claire awoke the next morning, the first thing she noticed was that she felt much better. Also, that the oppressive, stifling temperature was gone, replaced by a much more comfortable, temperate heat. A breeze even drifted in through the vent. It felt wonderful! She indulged in a leisurely stretch before turning her thoughts to the day. Not looking forward to another day under Dion's tutelage, she decided that warranted a lazy morning in bed.

Eventually, a scent reached her that drew her out from underneath the sheet. Bacon? Did she smell bacon? Hurriedly dressing, she left her cabin and found Aidan in the galley cooking up what appeared to be a feast.

Affecting a poor rendition of an Irish accent, he welcomed her. "And a good mornin' to you, lass. D'ya' sleep bonny well?"

"Um. Gloriously. It's nice to have a breeze again."

"That 'tis. That 'tis," he answered.

She leaned over his shoulder, she couldn't help but ask. "What's for breakfast? I could swear I smelled bacon."

"That you did, lass. No one felt much like eatin' yesterday so we'll be feastin' this mornin' tide."

"What can I do to help?" she laughed for the first time in days.

"Throwin' together that delicious fruit salad like you did yestermorn would be a great start."

Working companionably, he cooked hotcakes and bacon, and she began whipping up a salad, pausing mid-cut on a nectarine.

"Aidan?"

"Yes, love?"

"How did Dion get injured?"

His back went stiff, then he set the spatula down and turned to her, all pretense of a brogue gone.

"You'll have to ask Dion that."

"I did. He wouldn't answer me."

"It's his story to tell, not mine. Sorry, love."

Claire sighed and returned to her work, her lips set in a thin line. This was a brotherhood she'd been forced to join, but there were boundaries she wouldn't be allowed to cross. Giving way to the anger she felt, she stabbed at a grape when Aidan reached in and took the knife from her. She watched as he sat across from her, looking like he was fighting an internal struggle of his own.

"It's not an easy story to tell. And Dion was very strongly affected by it. I really am sorry."

"I don't belong here," she almost cried as she said it. "This isn't my world. You've all asked me to become part of yours yet you shut me out. You want me to go along with this dangerous scheme of yours, except I'm not allowed to know anything about you."

"I know this can't be easy for you."

She arched her eyebrows to indicate the enormity of the understatement, but Aidan continued before she could interject a sarcastic comment.

"I know it's hard. But it's important. And you've been forced, as you say, to team up with the best there is. Dion and Roger have been partners for a very long time. I've only known them for a couple years, but trust me when I say they are the best in the business. If they are secretive, it's the nature of their job. We work undercover, Claire. We can't let anyone in."

The tears of frustration brimmed over, and she fought for some control. Finally, she squared her shoulders and went to pick up the knife Aidan had laid down.

"I don't like it. Not at all. I suppose I can understand it, though, at least a little," she conceded.

Aidan covered her free hand with his before she could return to work. With a return to his bad attempt at a brogue, he tried to reassure her. "We'll be protecting you with our lives, darlin'. Not to worry."

At that moment, Dion came down the ladder. Claire flushed. She'd been prying behind his back and felt the guilt of it. She quickly pulled her hand from beneath Aidan's, managing to nick herself with the knife as she did.

"Ouch," she said, sucking on the finger.

Aidan reached to grab a towel, but before he could turn back, the first aid kit landed with a thud on the table between them.

"Wash it," Dion said curtly. "Wash it, dry it, put antibiotics and a band aid on it. Cuts at sea can become serious fast."

Aidan, with exaggerated slowness, extracted the injured finger from Claire's mouth, taking great pains to wrap and hold the compress on to stop the bleeding.

"We'll be gettin' her all fixed up now, won't we dear?" he said, his eyes conveying his amusement.

Dion just stared at them for a moment, then turned and headed topside without a word.

CHAPTER NINE

Dion took watch during breakfast, so Claire went topside with a plate of food.

"Thanks," he mumbled. Setting the plate on the wheel housing, he ate in silence.

Claire stayed. It was peaceful here at the helm. They were making steady headway but not racing to their final port.

"Where are we sailing to?"

He moved to the rail to get a better look ahead, not answering Claire's question. So she tried again.

"Where are we going? What's our destination?"

"Huatulco, Mexico. To pick up a charter. We don't expect to get there."

"So it's basically just a story," she finished, hugging her arms. Finally, she asked the question. "What's going to happen?"

"In prior attempts, the pirates boarded almost without being seen during the hottest part of the day."

"How can they not be seen," she questioned, seeing nothing except ocean all around them.

"All the victims describe a sudden commotion and the yacht heeling over with the added weight of people boarding."

Claire shuddered. "So we won't know they're coming?"

"Not necessarily. We think we will. You know some of the people whose yachts have been stolen."

"Yes."

"Then you know that they're in their own little world. We think they see the boat in the distance and ignore it."

Taking a break for another bite of breakfast, he continued. "We'll be keeping a closer eye out."

"When—"

"Later tonight, maybe. Satellite blackout is optimal tonight, but they've never boarded at night. There's another window tomorrow afternoon. We think that's when it will happen."

"And then what?"

"Typically they've isolated the passengers together in one cabin for two to three days while they sail to one of the Revillagigedo Islands. Then, they set them adrift within reach of land."

"So we'll be stranded?"

"For a time."

This made no sense to Claire. "How does this help you capture the pirates?"

"There's a tracking device hidden on board the *Treasure*," Dion set his plate aside. "You need to understand. There is sound reasoning behind our belief that you won't be hurt. These guys just want the boat. So far, they haven't hurt anyone.

"That *belief* is what you're basing my safety on?"

"That and our own ability to protect you. To date, the pirates have only scared their hostages into submission. We think they'll do the same thing when they board the *Treasure*."

"And you can guarantee that? And my safety?"

Claire watched him move his breakfast dishes further away from them. When that was done, he looked at her like he was about to drop a bomb.

"There are things we can do to up the odds. Roger and I feel that the best way to minimize the risk is to keep you close to one of us."

Her eyes narrowed. "How are you going to do that?"

He didn't answer.

Suddenly, the bomb fell and she knew. "You're going to make them think we're involved?" Her lips felt parched.

"Yes."

"You and I?" *Good.* Her voice barely wobbled as she asked.

"Yes."

She watched him for a bit, saw the thin lines of his mouth, the complete seriousness that clouded his eyes.

"You drew the short straw, didn't you?" she concluded.

"That's not how it was."

Angry now, she reached for his dishes and got up. "Yeah, right. So you lost. You get to baby-sit," she said, her resentment soaking through her words.

She got up quickly, intent on leaving. Dion's quick grasp of her arm stopped her, though. He snatched the dishes from her and tossed them onto the wheel housing.

"Let me go!"

"Not until you listen. This isn't some random roll of the dice. We're trying to protect you."

"Yes, like I'm some sort of precious cargo, instead of a real human being who's had to throw her own life in the toilet while you cowboys go traipsing after some modern-day pirates."

"What do you want from us?" Dion asked.

"I want to go home!"

"You—"

"Don't even say it, okay? I know I can't go. I can't just sit here and do nothing, though. I'll go crazy!"

"Is that what this is about? You want a more active role?" He ran his hands through his hair. "No."

"Why not? I need something to do, Dion. You've taught me sailing basics. Let me at least help with the day-to-day stuff."

"Absolutely not."

"Yes. That's what I thought you'd say." Wrenching her arm free from his grasp, she crossed them indignantly in front of her as she watched Dion rake his hands once again through his hair. He looked about to explode. Good. It was about time he was the one sweating it out.

"Okay. In the first place, we've got the sailing covered. In the second place, you're a civilian. We're trained agents. We do this for a living. You *don't*."

"Then what have you been teaching me for?"

"I've been teaching you emergency techniques, not to be active in a sting operation. Basic survival. That's all."

"Well, it's not enough," she all but shouted.

"There isn't time for more," he said, raising his voice to match hers.

Claire spun around, then stopped before reaching the companionway. Turning back, she lowered her voice and gave him a dose of honesty.

"I don't like being out of control, Dion. Every time that happens, I lose."

He closed the gap between them, reached out, and stopped. Calmer, he gently brushed his hands along her arms in comfort.

"I can understand that," he responded, his voice back to quiet. "I promise. I'll try to be mindful of how you feel. However, I won't leave your safety up to you. Can you understand that?"

Caught up in the inviting huskiness of his voice, she closed her eyes.

"No, I don't understand." But the words were lost. She could feel his hands still caressing the skin of her arms. A tingling sensation spread out from there, enveloping her whole body. She swayed slightly. Would he kiss her again?

His lips brushed hers. At first, it was the slightest touch, as if a feather had lightly crossed her lips. She leaned into it, wanted more, and the kiss deepened. He reached to cup her face in his hands. She was on fire. Every part of her body ached for more.

Then she felt his gun, stuck into the belt of his khakis. And the reality of the situation hit her once again. He was an agent doing a job. He didn't see her for who she was, only for what cooperation he could get from her.

Pulling back, she slapped him hard.

"You're just like they were. I'm an object to you. And I will not be used in this way again. If you already know you don't like me, you don't get to taste the goods."

With that, she disappeared to her cabin.

Right behind Claire's departure came Roger's entrance. He took a long moment to examine the remnants of her slap. "What did you do to make her mad now, partner?"

"I guess I told her we were babysitting."

"Ouch. No wonder she's steamed."

"Then I kissed her."

Roger whistled through his teeth as he sat next to Dion.

"Yeah," Dion replied.

"You told her your idea?"

"Yep."

"And that's when she decided we were babysitting?"

"Yep."

"In a way, she's right. Following up with another kiss, though? Bad idea, partner," he continued, chuckling. "Diplomacy never has been your strong point, Dion. You may have gone a little overboard this time."

You've got that right. He touched the sting that had not quite faded away. *Why* had he done that? Claire Saunders did some strange things to him, not the least of which was making him break his own hard and fast rule about not getting involved, especially when undercover.

Kissing her seemed so natural. Those lips were hard to pass up. Gentle and demanding at the same time. Soft, too. He stood, turning to Roger.

"You got watch for a bit? I'm going below."

"Sure, partner. No problem."

Once in the main cabin, Dion turned, staring at the closed door to his cabin, knowing Claire was on the other side. He was tempted to go to her, have this out. Certain that his cheek still sported a red hand print, he decided it wasn't the time and instead headed for a shower. A cold one.

Claire fumed behind the door of her cabin, pacing the irritatingly short distance between the bunk and opposite wall. It didn't help. Old memories had once again forced their way to the surface.

It was high school all over again. A stage set with innuendo and complex mixed messages. A flash of blond hair and Hollywood attitude invaded her conscious mind. At least Jay had pretended to like her. Dion, however, made it abundantly clear he didn't, then he came up with that flimsy excuse to get into her pants? She hadn't understood Jay then and didn't get Dion now. What was it, a guy thing? Love 'em, then leave 'em?

The tough part was, she was starting to like this one. A lot. And this wasn't high school anymore. She was older and smarter. Yeah, right. So smart she went all gushy over a little kiss.

The pacing stopped as she thought about that kiss. She had gone weak at the knees. If he hadn't steadied her, she might have actually fallen. Even now, her legs felt like Jello. Claire slumped heavily onto the chair.

"It's happening again." She was falling for the wrong guy.

Her hands drifted over the carved letters in the table. The old man truly had treasured his wife. It must have been a long time ago. Life seemed different now. There was no such thing as love. Only muddy images of it, just enough to whet the appetite. Never enough to quench her need.

Her hands continued to wander over the table. It really could use refinishing. Claire looked up at cupboards that could stand some work, too. She knocked on the wood. Solid and basically in sound shape. She could easily fix the dings and rounded edges if she had the tools.

Claire smiled. Finally, something I can do. She didn't believe in fate. It had dealt her one too many blows. She was responsible for her own happiness. Neither fate, nor Dion, nor any other person would ever have that power over her again. She knew what she was capable of and she would show him and everyone else.

She headed out on a scavenger hunt and found most of what she needed. Sandpaper, hammer, screwdriver. Stain remover and marine refinishing stain, even some good woody putty. And rags. She would need a lot of rags.

You're gonna love this, Dad. She smiled then got to work.

It wasn't long before Claire had the table sitting in the middle of the floor stripped of all its varnish. It needed to dry before she could begin sanding and repairing it. Since she needed a break from the fumes, she searched for something else to pass the time with.

Aidan found her a little later tucked into one of the main cabin bunks, immersed in a book on sailing. She was definitely a cute little thing when she wasn't pissed off at someone. If it weren't for the sparks flying between her and the boss...Aidan smiled. *Hell, I probably couldn't keep up with her.* Uncaged, she was a little fireball of energy.

He sniffed the air.

"What stinks?" he asked.

"Varnish remover," she said without looking up.

Uh oh. He took a quick peek in the captain's cabin and turned back to Claire.

"What's up in there, anyhow?"

Claire's eyes blazed with challenge. "Just finding a way to be useful. Any problem with that?"

He held up his hands. "None at all, milady," he answered, backing toward the stairs.

"None at all." He spoke slowly to keep the smile on his face from spreading. He took the steps two at a time to reach the deck. This operation had been anything but boring thanks to

Claire Saunders. And it was about to get a whole lot more interesting. He saw Dion and headed forward.

On deck, Aidan banked the grin on his face and joined Dion and Roger.

"What's she been doing down there?" Roger asked. "I swear I can smell fingernail polish."

Aidan shrugged. No way in hell would he deprive them of seeing this for themselves.

"Go check it out, Roger," Dion said.

"Not on your life, partner. I'm not the one who kissed her. Twice. *You* go see what she's doing."

That did it. Aidan's grin would no longer be held back and he let it go. "You kissed her twice?"

Scowling, Dion settled deeper into his chair and spent several minutes staring at the water. But curiosity got to him, as Aidan knew it would.

Dion stood and grabbed the rails on the forward hatch ladder to slide down, Aidan right on his heels. One glance in the master cabin and Dion bellowed as he turned back around.

"Woman, what the hell have you done?" Each word was matched with an ominous step in her direction.

Aidan settled into a chair, smiling. Oh, yeah. This would definitely be fun. He watched as Claire plastered a smile on her face.

"Just a little fixing up, that's all," she answered.

Probably not the best attitude to use with Dion, Aidan thought.

Sure enough, Dion still roared.

"You've destroyed that table!"

Oops. There went the smile on Claire's face. Careful, Dion.

"No. I haven't."

Beside the bunk now, Dion clenched hands into tight fists, his voice only a bit calmer. "The hell you haven't! It's all splotchy, like a...a dog after a bad haircut."

"It won't be when I get done."

"You can bet your sweet ass it won't, because you won't be touching it again!"

Watching Claire, Aidan saw her face harden, like molten steel forming up in about five seconds time.

She swung her legs off the bunk, hitting Dion in the process. He backed up one step, just enough to give her room to sit, She didn't stop there standing and glaring at him as if daring him to stay put.

He held his place.

And she didn't budge.

"You don't want me to sail. You don't want me to fix something on this derelict old boat."

The schooner bucked on a wave then, and Claire had to grab a hold of the bunk to keep from stumbling. Dion remained stone faced and still.

"You don't want me to do anything at all. Except feign an interest in you. So, do I get to walk two steps behind and one to the right, also?"

"For your protection, remember? Trust me, if I could do this any other way, I would. However, you can't destroy this boat just because you're pissed off at me."

He saw Claire straighten. "For your information, I happen to work pretty well with wood. I *can* and *will* finish restoring that table. It's gone too far now, anyhow. The marine air will destroy the wood if I don't get some varnish on it soon."

Here it comes, Aidan thought, his smile widening.

"Besides," Claire continued. "What do you care? It's not your boat."

Unable to hold it in any longer, Aidan let the laughter roll out in waves. He saw both Claire and Dion scowling at him, but he was helpless to stop, even after they each stomped off, Claire to the cabin and Dion topside.

Roger and Mike entered as Aidan tried to wipe the tears from his eyes.

"That didn't sound quite so jolly from up there." Roger pointed to the deck above.

Aidan wiped his eyes again. "Ahhhhhhh! It was hilarious from down here. You should have seen it."

"We heard it. That was enough."

"No. I mean the look on Dion's face when she played her punch line." He chuckled again. "Funny thing is, she didn't even *know* it was a punch line!"

He howled again, then started to cough, tears streaming down his face. Mike hit him on the back a few times to settle him down.

"Ahhh, man. I haven't had that much fun in ages."

He peeked around the corner at Claire and watched her pick up a piece of sandpaper and attack the table. Still chuckling, Aidan headed forward.

Claire emerged from her cabin hours later physically tired but mentally satisfied. The shower was empty, but one look at it and a warmth she didn't want to feel infused her body. Images of Dion flashed through her mind. Dion pulling the shower curtain back, and pausing for that almost imperceptible moment before he turned the water off. Dion inspecting the outline of her towel with a fierceness that belied his dislike of her. He'd been affected. She'd been sure of that. So how could he remain so in control when she felt so frayed at the edges? Pulling the shower curtain closed, Claire opted for a sponge bath.

Dressed again in her own clothes, she got a bite to eat and finally felt refreshed and ready. She had a plan. All she needed now was someone to help her put it into action. Mike was at the table, studiously pouring over some charts.

She headed up to see who had watch, hopeful it would be Aidan. It was.

"Ah, survived the dragon's teeth, I see."

"Funny." She joined him, watching as he kept his hand on the wheel and his eye on the water, with an occasional glance at the compass.

"So, being on watch isn't really all that difficult, is it?" she asked, toying with a rough edge on the wood.

"I wouldn't say it's that easy," Aidan answered. "There's a lot to keep an eye on. And you have to know what to do in an emergency."

"Yes. I've been studying that." She leaned into the wheel-house to check the compass herself.

"Studying?"

"There's not much else for me to do here," she said, leaning back against the port wall of the wheel housing and eyeing the water ahead.

"True." With a quick glance at the sails, he returned his gaze to the water.

"And you never know when I might be called upon to help out in an emergency, right?"

"I doubt that will happen, but yes, it's good to be prepared."

"Good. I'm glad you agree. I have a few questions."

Aidan scrutinized her then, as if trying to decide what she was up to. "Like what?"

"Like what you do when you're on watch."

"I don't think we should be discussing this."

"Come on, Aidan. I'm going nuts here. At least let me learn to cover watch. It's not like I'd be alone doing it. There are always two people awake at night, right?"

"Almost always, but the captain will never let you take watch."

"No, he won't. Would you?"

"I highly doubt it."

"All I'm asking is for you to show me what to do while on watch. Give me a chance to prove my capabilities."

For a moment, she thought he would refuse her. Instead, he sighed, and with a quick nod, he proceeded to show her what all was involved. Claire fine-tuned her knowledge of proper and improper sail formations and how to see objects on the water, even at night.

"You know about the large container ships, right?" he asked.

"Yes."

"What you probably don't know is how often containers fall off these vessels and just float around in the oceans until someone tows them to shore for salvage rights or they hit land on their own."

"Seriously?"

"Seriously. So you have to be looking for small *and* large objects. If you're on night watch and think you see something, you call for a second set of eyes."

She honed her new skills on checking depth and direction, too.

"We're on a southeasterly course now, right?"

"Right. We started out more southerly and now have turned back toward the Mexican shoreline. We'll stay this course until we either get boarded or reach Huatulco."

Their heads were together, reviewing instrumentation in the wheelhouse when Claire sensed movement. Dion, a cup of coffee in his hands and sleep still masking reality, joined them on deck. He watched them for a long moment, his trademark scowl firmly in place.

Claire ignored him and returned to the navigation equipment.

"Aidan?" she started.

"I think we'd better shelve this for now," he replied, turning his gaze back to the water.

Dion's entrance had obviously clamped the lid on further study. That was pretty apparent. He sure seemed to have these men under his thumb. The only one who didn't jump at his orders was Roger. The man really should put Dion in his place.

She felt confident with what she had learned, though, ready and able to handle the watch. She just needed an opportunity to show the rest of them. Smug in her new knowledge, she left Aidan to his own devices and headed below to help Mike with dinner preparations.

That night, Dion rolled over in the small bunk and wished for about the hundredth time that he was in his own bed. The bed where Claire peacefully slept, wearing his t-shirt molded to her curves. He imagined her small, perfect breasts as they rose with each intake of breath.

Damn. Dion threw himself back to his other side, punching his pillow. He needed a distraction.

What the hell was with her and Aidan today? Their heads had been bent together as if sharing some sort of secret. He hadn't liked it. Not at all. He'd worked hard to squelch his awareness of her, but here, in the semi-darkness of the forward cabin, it stared him in the face and wouldn't let go.

He was falling for Claire. It was a complication he didn't need. He tried to steer clear of her, but the *Treasure* was a small boat. He wanted to touch her, hold her, kiss her until she had no will left to deny him. And each time she came near, the urge grew stronger. He wanted to claim her as his.

This wasn't helping. Dion sat up suddenly and hit his head on the cabinet above his bunk. Damn. He rubbed his head, wishing once again that he had his own cabin back.

Since his demons wouldn't let him sleep, he grabbed a cup of coffee in the main cabin, surprised to see Aidan lying on the bench, fast asleep, an open book about to fall off his chest. Who had watch? He picked up the book and set it on the table, taking the steps as fast as the steep angle would let him. He stopped short at the top, his mug slopping hot coffee over the side and onto his bare legs.

"Hell!" Dion danced as he brushed the coffee off his leg, sloshing more coffee out of his cup in the process. "What the hell are you doing at the wheel?" He put a bit more force than he'd wanted into the question. "And where the hell is everyone else?"

Claire's back went from relaxed to ramrod straight before he'd even finished.

"I'm taking watch." She paused before continuing. "And you need a rag. The captain wouldn't like you mucking up his boat."

"I know that," he ground out. "Where's Mike?"

"He's sleeping."

"Mike and Aidan are supposed to be on watch. Why aren't they?"

"Because tomorrow will be a very busy day, and you all need to be on you're A-game. Since you and Roger wouldn't assign me something, I found my own way to help."

She smiled then, and Dion was reminded of Tweety Bird after once again having foiled Sylvester's attempts at capture.

"Aidan is an idiot! You don't know the first thing about watch. Plus, there should be two people on watch. You can't catch everything from behind the wheel. He's put the *Treasure* in jeopardy through his laziness."

He turned, intent on giving Aidan a very rude awakening. Claire's next words stopped him.

"He didn't want to," she said quietly. "I had to convince him. In fact, he knew you would react this way."

Her shoulders slumped. "So did I, unfortunately. Look, Dion," she said. "I'm here. You can't get rid of me. God knows, I wish you could. The way things are now, I serve no useful purpose. Worse, all I can do is sit and stew. I have to have some control or I'll go crazy."

He leaned against the wheel housing. "You don't know what you're doing."

"Yes, I do. Maybe not as well as you, although I know enough to be safe. You taught me the basics. I've been reading the books I found below, and Aidan covered all the watch duties with me today. I've checked depth and direction regularly and kept an eye on the water for any objects on a collision course, large or small. The wind has been a steady south-southwest flow and I haven't needed to make any course corrections yet. Had there been any change, I'd have called for Aidan."

"Except he's asleep in the main cabin."

She smiled at that. "That just proves my point. You all are stretched too thin and need a good night's sleep. I can help with that."

She was right. They could all use the sleep. A small smile escaped, and Dion turned his head to hide it. Claire was pretty damn resourceful, he had to admit. She reminded him of Mary.

Except that Mary wasn't here anymore. His smile disappeared. Mary had taken matters into her own hands, too, and had ended up with a bullet in the gut.

Suddenly his vision shifted, and there she was.

He saw Mary reaching for the gun tucked into her boot, saw her giving him the signal, ignoring his frantic motion to belay the action. He saw her roll as she fired, but not fast enough. The pirate's bullet caught her dead on. He tried to reach her, to protect her, and took a bullet of his own as he launched. Two bullets, as it turned out. Doubled over on the ground, he could only watch as the blood wound a slowly widening river toward

him and the life force left an agent he'd specifically request-
ed for the operation.

"Dion?"

He shook his head. He was once again on board the
Treasure, standing at the wheel with Claire.

"What?"

"Are you all right?"

"Yes."

"Are you sure? You looked a million miles away for a
minute there, and didn't even seem to hear me."

"I'm fine. Just leave it at that."

She paused, then murmured okay and turned back to the
sea.

Dion didn't much care for the alliance, but he allowed
Claire to continue watch duties. They were running at
reduced speed due to darkness. Still, he'd be damned if he'd
leave her in charge of his boat.

They were in the tropics, so the breeze felt balmy. He
took a slow, deep breath, allowing the slightly acidic salt air
to fill his lungs. He smiled. Out here, with no land in sight,
the nights were dark and solitary and idyllic. He glanced at
Claire. Well, mostly idyllic.

The peace calmed him. Even the creaks and groans of the
old girl comforted him. He knew them well.

The foresail luffed. Dion moved to tighten the sheets. He turned to compensate at the wheel and saw Claire check the compass, then use a feather touch to adjust their heading.

He realized they had just worked in tandem without a word. He'd never considered the possibility that she might have an untapped talent for sailing. Damn. He was normally much better at reading people, a major reason why he was good at his job. He'd let some preconceptions get in his way with Claire. Well, that and this feeling she stirred up in him.

Claire rubbed the arm she held loosely on the wheel.

"Tired?" he asked.

She smiled. "Surprisingly, no."

"Cold, then?"

"A bit."

Dion went below, returning quickly with a sweat jacket for her and coffee for both of them. He set the cups down and helped her into the windbreaker. He was close enough to touch her hair. And couldn't help himself. He leaned in, just enough to catch her scent, aware that his shampoo had never smelled this good. She shifted slightly. Had she moved closer to him or had he imagined it? Then she moved closer to the wheel, putting some distance between them.

He sat down and let her take lead, unwilling to break the moment with idle chatter. Eventually though, the wind increased, and he knew they'd need to reef the main a bit.

"Lash the wheel, Claire, and come help me lower the mainsail a bit now that the wind's increasing."

Without comment, she tied the wheel into place and led the way to the mainsheet, helping him to trim the sail back. She took direction well and worked without talking, except for the occasional question. Once again, she surprised him. She had done her homework well.

Dion leaned against the boom, thinking how much he'd enjoy a leisurely voyage with her. They would share duties, working in concert with each other like his grandparents had done. His mind took it further, to a tropical night much like this one, the sails down, wheel lashed, and a blanket on deck. With only the gentle slap of water against the hull and the stars as witnesses, they would come together.

He straightened then. The waking-dream caused a very physical reaction in him, so he quickly turned away, leaving her to finish securing the halyard.

Claire watched him hurry aft, confused. He trusted her to do this right? And he was actually being nice to her. Something was wrong. This wasn't the Dion she'd come to know and...well, this just wasn't the Dion she'd come to know.

Rejoining him at the wheel, she stood across from him. He didn't look at her. He watched the water and had left the wheel for her. Unlashing it, she settled in to a comfortable position, keeping one hand propped on the wheel so it wouldn't move without her knowledge. The silence continued between them. Before, it had felt like a silent bond, as though they had found some common ground. Now, though, Dion appeared tense. And as usually happened between them, he had to go and put a dagger in the harmony.

"Mind if I give you some advice, Claire?"

Wary now, she nodded her head.

"I would suggest you stay away from Aidan. He's a prankster and not serious about much of anything."

For a moment, Claire forgot to breathe as she stared at him. He just couldn't leave things on an even keel between them, could he? She took an agonizingly slow breath to cool the heat that suffused her body and reached for his hand, placing it on the wheel, steeling herself against the stab of desire that flooded her.

She leaned in so as not to wake the others, her voice low and melodious like a siren singing her song.

"You are sadly mistaken," she said, enunciating each word, "if you think I would have anything to do with *any* of you!"

Bam! Claire ran right into the wheel as she turned to leave. She slapped it with both hands, cleared it in one step and hurried below to her cabin. The chair was soon firmly in place under the door handle. She tried to pace, but the unfinished table got in her way. This seemed to be her life now, angry and pacing in this small cabin. Damn him. Damn him for taking something good and tainting it.

Claire realized she'd just left him alone on watch. *Serves him right. He can do everything himself. That's what he seems to want anyway.*

The tears started to spill over, and she willed them to stay. She would not cry over this man. He was bent on controlling her and willing to manipulate her for his own use and she would *not* let that happen again.

Claire lay down on the bunk, eventually drifting off to a restless sleep, where she dreamed of a two-headed monster, one hideous and the other handsome. Both beckoned her to do their will. Both treated her as if she were a pet, a treat for their amusement. In the end, the only one left in pieces was her.

CHAPTER TEN

An uneasy awareness crept into Claire's dreams, and she woke holding tightly to the bunk's edge. Something had changed.

Whoosh.

She jumped at the sound. Air rushed through the vent, and she shivered. Ear to the vent, she heard footfalls on deck.

Claire's chest squeezed like a vise as she strained to hear the voices, both frantic and muffled at the same time.

Her eyes widened. The pirates! They had been boarded. Heart pounding, Claire listened hard, searching for a familiar voice in the melee above but she couldn't tell.

The schooner lurched and the unfinished table crashed to the other side of the cabin. She lost her grip, fell out of the bunk and landed up against the table. Standing was an effort. The boat heeled over so far that she practically lay on the wall. Claire used the wall to balance herself and tried to get dressed.

The boat chose that moment to heel over in the other direction and Claire went flying back to the bunk. She clung to it and managed to finish dressing.

She secured the table so it wouldn't be damaged, then tore the chair away from under the door handle. Stopping to listen, the only sound she heard now was the almost continuous whooshing of the wind. Plus her own heartbeat, which felt like the frantic knocking of someone trying to get out of her chest.

Placing both hands against the door, Claire leaned into it, tried to draw strength from it, to find the courage to walk through. They'd been boarded. This is what Roger and Dion had told her would happen. With reality about to whip her in the face, the desire to find a cabinet big enough to crawl into and hide was intense.

But there wasn't one.

Trapped in the danger of the situation, she took a deep breath and opened the door.

She needed to use both walls to maintain some forward momentum. The schooner pitched again, almost dislodging her.

The main cabin was empty. That surprised her. All the commotion seemed to be happening topside. Slowly, carefully, she clawed her way up the companionway, astounded it was still night when she breached the top. Dion stood at the helm, both hands tightly braced on the wheel. His eyes didn't seem to be fixed on a person, though. They were turned skyward, toward the sails, not forward. What was going on?

As she cleared the companionway, Claire's hair immediately flew outward, covering her face and blinding her more effectively than the pre-dawn darkness could. Damn. She tried to gather it in one hand so she could see what was happening.

The wind had strengthened.

A lot!

The *Treasure* bucked, riding the turbulent waves crest to trough, then back to crest again.

Reaching for the wheelhouse, she stumbled, but a strong arm captured her before she fell and she found herself tightly entrenched at Dion's side. With the wind in her face now, she let her hair go, and it flew out behind her like a flag. Mike and Roger were tying off a rope that ran from one end of the boat to the other.

Claire turned to Dion's ear so she could be heard above the wind. "What is happening?

"Look!" he yelled, nodding forward.

She did then and finally saw beyond the schooner to the enormous black hole ahead of them. Even in the darkness, she could see the malevolent shades of gray and coal churning their way toward the schooner, weaving in and out, occasionally lit by a bold flash of lightening. She could hear the portentous thunder now, and her hair crackled with static electricity as she tried once again to confine it.

A storm!

There were no pirates. There was a storm coming. And it was almost upon them!

Dion hadn't loosened his grip, and she heard him now, insistent, urgent, in her ear. "Grab rain gear…life jackets. Wake Aidan. Tell him to stow everything below."

She saw the worry in his eyes, in the grim set to his mouth. "Will it be bad?"

Staring again at the angry force bearing down on them, he muttered, "Maybe." Surprising her, he kissed her temple then freed her.

"Hurry!"

That was all the impetus she needed. Claire flew down the ladder and into the forward cabin to wake Aidan, amazed he was able to sleep through the commotion.

"Aidan," she said insistently, shaking him. "Storm's coming. Wake up. Dion wants you to make sure everything's stowed."

Waiting only long enough to be sure he was up and reaching for his shirt, Claire dashed to the storage locker in the main cabin. Freeing the gear packs, she tossed one at Aidan.

"I'll be back with your life vest," she shouted and raced up the ladder. She was immediately hit by the spatters of rain the storm had begun throwing at them. The locker behind the wheel held the life jackets. As she passed Dion, she held out a rain-gear pouch and his free hand covered hers for just a moment.

She grabbed five vests and headed back to the wheel. The wind had increased another notch. Dion struggled to get his rain gear on, only able to use one hand at a time. So Claire reached for the wheel and was shocked at the strength it took to maintain their heading.

How long would they have to fight this?

Once Dion took back the helm, she went to deliver gear to the others. Dion's hand on her shoulder stopped her. Pointing at her, he mouthed the words "you first," so she sat and quickly got the pants, jacket and vest on. Standing up at the same moment the boat chose to roll violently, she once again lost her footing. And, once again, Dion caught her.

"Will she tear apart?" Claire asked, fear evident in her voice.

In the midst of the building fury, Claire melted as Dion smiled with no hint of doubt in his eyes. "She'll hold."

Claire leaned against him, and he tightened his grip, pulling her closer into his solid chest. She felt so safe here in his arms.

Too soon, he released her. "Go below...forward cabin," he said fiercely into her ear.

She shivered, thoughts of safety quickly replaced by a renewed dread.

"Forward hatch. Gear...Mike and Roger. Hook up when topside," he said, tugging a hook on her life jacket and pointing to the line stretched the length of the ship. "Save your life."

"Aye, aye, Captain," she said unconsciously then stumbled off. Walking anywhere was treacherous right now, even in the main cabin. The bucking grew steadily worse as the *Treasure* responded to the storm front. Claire had to move side-to-side, using walls, furniture, anything that maintained her upright position. A loose plastic bowl in the galley went flying past her, hitting the floor with a crash.

She found Aidan double-latching cabinets and cupboards and throwing loose items into the bench locker. She tossed him a vest without breaking stride and quickly reached the forward hatch. It wouldn't open. Bracing herself, she pushed with all her might, and it finally gave way. Poking her head through, she saw that Mike was right there.

"Rain gear," she shouted, handing the gear bags up.

"Vest," she added handing them up next.

"Thanks." She saw the words and knew he said them but the wind whistled the sound away.

Claire tried to pull the hatch cover down with her, but didn't have the strength. The wind held it captive. In the next instant, Mike grabbed it and lowered it over her head, tossing a quick, grim smile her way.

Racing back into the cabin, she tossed the now empty gear bags into the bench locker and sat down on top of it, clutching the back cushion.

"Did you lock the forward hatch, Claire?"

"No!" Her eyes widened.

"Don't worry. I'll get it. Standard procedure," Aidan supplied in explanation.

"What about Mike and Roger?"

"They know it'll be locked. They'll finish what they're doing and make their way to the aft hatch."

Queasiness welled up from Claire's stomach and lodged just below her throat. She couldn't stay down here. The motion was too strong, and she needed a horizon to right her equilibrium. She climbed unsteadily back up the companionway one more time, hooked onto the line, and made her way to Dion, who appeared focused on about three things at once. Her gaze moved to the sky in surprise.

The storm was rapidly swallowing them up.

Dion watched the sails, held the wheel steady, and continued an urgent discussion with Roger. She only caught the tail end of it as she reached the wheelhouse.

"Hold the wheel. I'll do it," she heard Dion order.

"I still need to stow the head sails. They'll blow away."

"Fine." Looking around, he saw her.

"Claire!" he yelled, motioning her over.

"Roger, show her, then go! I'll fix the slide."

Dion settled Claire's hands firmly in place on the wheel then, with a quick squeeze, left her and hurried forward to the mainmast.

"Claire," Roger yelled, trying to be heard over the deafening wind. "Keep the wheel locked. Don't let it shift. If he wants you to throw the wheel over, he'll signal."

Wide eyed, she nodded assent. "I can do this," she shouted.

"I know you can." With a quick squeeze of her shoulder, he started off.

Claire saw Dion already halfway up the rope ladder that led to the top of the mainsheet. Mike stood at the base, beaming a strong flashlight to help Dion find his way.

"Roger, what—?" The wind ripped her words away, so she pointed at Dion.

"The slide's stuck. He has to kick it loose."

"But, Roger. His injury!"

"He's the only one who can do it. It's his boat, Claire. He knows it best."

"His?" she asked.

Roger didn't hear. He was already on his way forward.

Looking back up the mainmast, her bewilderment turned to dread as she watched Dion. Almost to the top, he seemed to rest on his good leg.

The wheel started to pull, and she yanked her gaze away to increase pressure and maintain position. Searching him out again, she could see him on the spar. He seemed to test his weight on his bad leg by raising his good leg in the air. Then he started kicking. The sail? No. He kicked at the attachment to the mast, the slide, she guessed, trying to free it.

Whoosh!

A particularly strong gust of wind hit the schooner, almost wrenching the wheel from Claire's grip. Throwing her weight into it, she finally righted it. Then she screamed.

"Dion!"

He was hanging by his hands, his legs thrashing freely in the air, pulled by the wind and momentum of the swaying mast. She could hear something faintly. He was shouting.

"Up...wind!"

She threw herself into the wheel, turning it.

"No! No! ...other way! Into...wind! Into...!"

Muscling the wheel the other way, the schooner came out of the brace of wind, and the sails slackened. Just enough. She watched, wide eyed, as Dion found his footing. The slide had given way. Mike and Roger down below were able to reef the sail.

Dion stayed aloft until the main and foresail were both shortened.

Once the top and head sails were lashed, there was nothing left to do but ride out the storm. Dion didn't need to see it to know that the storm's full fury had hit.

He saw Claire doggedly shake her head as Roger tried to take the wheel from her. He smiled. It appeared that she wasn't going to relinquish command to anyone.

Dion held tightly as he shifted his weight, feeling a sharp jab of pain in his knee. The smile quickly changed to a grimace. It was time to get off the mast.

He climbed down slowly, using the underside of the rope ladder and pretty much letting his arms bring him down, giving his leg a rest. By the time he reached the deck, he felt weak with exhaustion. The storm was just beginning. Watching the fury surround them, he prayed he had enough strength to ride it out. Staggering back to the wheel, he went to take it from Claire, who still wouldn't let go. She was, however, giving orders.

"Roger," she hollered. "Go below. Get coffee. Dion needs it."

"You," she said to Dion, pointing with her head at the locker behind her. "Sit."

"Aye, aye." He threw up his hand in a haphazard salute and sank down to the bench.

After he'd finished a cup of coffee, he felt almost human again. She must have noticed a difference, because she motioned him to the wheel. As he stood, he gingerly tested the leg. It bore his weight, but it hurt like hell.

Suddenly, her low, sultry voice reverberated close to his ear.

"Where are your pain pills?"

"I don't need them."

She poked him in the arm. "Where?"

"I need to stay alert," he tried again.

"You'll stay alert. Where are they?" she insisted.

"In my…in your cabin. Middle drawer."

"Right."

She returned moments later with a pill and bottled water, which he gratefully accepted. During the short period of time spent standing, wrestling with the wheel and abrupt wind changes, the ache in his knee had created a whole new pain level.

"Will you give over command to one of your men now and get off your leg?"

"No."

It struck him then, and he looked hard at her.

All he saw was a granite posture. And recognition. She knew who's boat this really was. He didn't know how, but she knew. And there was going to be hell to pay because of it.

Claire found some satisfaction in the fact that she had proven herself an able seaman this day. The tempest raged, taking several hours to spend itself out. Dion wouldn't leave the wheel, but Mike and Roger were fully able to deal with any emergencies that occurred. Aidan, as it turned out, had a pretty violent reaction to the increase in motion, so she spent a good part of her time holding a wet rag on his head as he hung over the bowl. She noticed the small, round Dramamine patch just behind his ear.

"Aidan! You get seasick?"

"Mm-hmm."

"Why on earth did you take a maritime job?"

"It's my calling, babe." He gulped and continued weakly. "Can I help it if my body just doesn't agree with it?"

Claire uttered a sympathetic chuckle, then all conversation was halted by the next set of paroxysms racking his body.

Sneaking a break from Aidan, she refilled the covered travel-coffee mugs and started a new pot, not an easy thing to do when the sink and counter kept changing direction. Heading topside, she attached herself to the life-line then gave a cup to Dion at the wheel and secured the other two for Mike and Roger.

Far off, she could see a small break in the storm wall. She knew they had more time under this canopy of angry clouds that constantly formed and reformed, as if by the devil's own wind.

Still, it surprised her that she no longer felt frightened by the weather. Dion was right. Mother Nature put on one hell of a show, but the *Treasure* had so far proven to be a sturdy boat. She knew they were in tropical waters. Still, the storm seemed to have sapped the heat right out of the air. Everything was alive. She could almost smell the sizzle as the lightning flashed. The thunder cracked almost on top of them now, warning them.

No one would sleep tonight.

CHAPTER ELEVEN

By late morning the storm had spent itself out. It hit them with a fury, then left with a slow, gentle easing. The rain slackened, the wind slowly died down, the air grew warmer, and the darkness gave way to a temperate sun.

Exhaustion was etched in the men's faces. Dion's most of all. Once all danger passed, he slumped onto the deck. That was her cue, and she stepped in, barking orders.

"Roger, take over the wheel." Turning, assuming he would do as told, she directed her next order to Dion. "You, get below to your cabin."

"Let the others get some sleep."

"Get below."

She knew he didn't have enough energy to fight her and felt some satisfaction in seeing him rise and hobble over to the ladder.

While watching Dion's progress, she addressed Roger again. "Can you set up short watches so that everyone can get some rest?"

"Aye, aye, captain," he said, grinning. "And Claire?"

She looked at him.

"Thank you."

Grim-faced, she headed below, digging around in the first aid kit. She came up with an ace wrap and grabbed a plastic bag, a towel, and all the ice on board. She entered the forward cabin and halted. Dion wasn't in the bunk. Then she remembered.

He was the captain.

This was his boat.

The flush of humiliation at having been played filled her cheeks. She turned and headed aft to the captain's cabin and found him leaning against the bunk.

She'd been duped. The cabin she'd slept in this whole time had been his. He couldn't have told her that? He hadn't even trusted her enough to tell her this little truth.

Claire stopped in the doorway and watched as Dion peeled his damp shirt off and tossed it onto the heap of rain gear on the floor. Even that small movement tightened his muscles and accentuated his compact, well-defined lines in a way that caught Claire off guard.

She wanted to be angry. She needed to be angry. It was her only defense. It was hard when constantly bombarded with sights and sensations that made her want to reach out. That made her want to touch him, get closer to him. Their kisses permeated her mind, and she experienced again the pleasurable vibrations, all the way to the tips of her toes.

He saw her then. She caught a glimpse of misery in his face before he shielded it and returned to his steely outer visage. The look told her everything. She had no privileges and wasn't to be allowed inside. Most likely, no one was.

The fear she'd faced, when he was atop the mast, cut a quick, deep swathe through her heart. She cared about him. She cared a lot, damn it. About a man who would be whatever he needed to be to get the job done. No matter who got hurt.

"Don't."

"Don't what," she said.

"Fall for me."

Not expecting that, she was nonplussed and said the first thing that came to her mind, "Why not?"

"Because I'm not what you think."

"That's pretty apparent," she ground out. "I bet you say that to all the girls."

"It doesn't matter. We," he said, pointing to her and then back at himself, "are not going to happen."

He made it easy to be angry. He'd betrayed her by lying. Her past was too littered with similarities for her to be at all tolerant. Claire dredged up that past anger now, fed it, and used it as a cocoon, a temporary guard until she could get her walls firmly back in place. Still, it felt different this time, more like a tomb than a place of safety.

"You're absolutely right about that, *Captain*," she finished, stressing the name, allowing the frost to drip like an icicle from her words.

Dion watched her in silence, wary. He saw the hint of moisture in her eyes appear then evaporate. The sparkles diminished and grew cold. He'd extinguished that light. He knew it, but there was nothing he could do about it.

An ache started deep inside, one he would never let show. Moving to put his leg up on the bunk, the full force of pain in his knee hit him, and his face contorted in anguish.

"I think you'd better get me another pill."

She was already by his side, pill bottle in hand. While he took one out, she went for a glass of water.

"Thanks."

"You're welcome. Now lay down."

"Why?"

"Your knee needs ice."

Claire spent the next few minutes applying a compression wrap to his knee, winding the ace bandage around the ice pack she'd applied. It surprised him how gentle she was, considering her mood.

"Where did you learn to do that?"

"I had an accident-prone father," she replied coldly, settling his leg on a couple of pillows to elevate it.

"Ah, so you come by it naturally."

The levity fell like a stone in an earthquake.

"Look, Claire," he said, propping himself up on an elbow.

"I'll be back in fifteen minutes to remove it." Without waiting for a reply, she left the cabin. Dion stared at the door and realized how close he'd just come to an apology. He'd lied to her and didn't much like it. That was the job, though, and he'd better heed his own warning. He couldn't afford to give in to how she made him feel.

Drowsy now, he did exactly what he shouldn't do. He sank back down on the bed and let his thoughts drift. He pictured her again, at the helm when he'd been up the mast, panic in her face. Yet she'd wrestled the wheel of a violently bucking schooner like it was the only thing between her and that damn promotion. She had become an accomplished seaman. He only wished he could tell her. It was better this way, for both of them.

Shifting a little, he realized the ache in his knee had diminished. The ice and pills were helping, and he gave in to his exhaustion, drifting off to sleep with thoughts of her, held tight to his side, hair flying behind her, staring down the storm.

Claire checked on Aidan, blissfully slumbering, bucket held close as if his life depended on it.

She threw together some sandwiches, stowed two in the cooler then headed topside with the tray of food, a thermos of coffee, and mugs. The sun was overhead, just past its zenith. Only barely past noon? She felt as though they'd been struggling for days. She found Mike and Roger taking turns at the wheel.

"Thanks. We're famished," Mike said, taking the tray from her.

"Maybe I should have brought you iced tea instead," she said, holding the thermos up. "It's gotten hot and humid again."

"It was hot and humid all night. We just didn't recognize it," Mike said, biting gratefully into a sandwich.

Claire realized that things had settled back to normal. There was no storm anywhere to be found, no land around and no ships.

"How are our patients?" Roger asked.

"Both sound asleep."

Mike squirmed, having finished his food, and tried to settle himself in the short bench.

"Why don't you go below and take a nap?" Claire asked him.

"I wish I could. But there needs to be two people on watch."

"I'm here."

Roger took over the conversation at this point.

"And well able to take watch, Claire," he said, holding up his hand to forestall her ire. "You've proven that." He inclined his head in a gesture of respect.

"Thank you," she said, warming at the compliment.

Roger's next quiet words, though, had the effect of a blast of cold air. "They could show up at anytime. This afternoon is their best shot."

The pirates. For a short time, she'd managed to forget. Scanning the horizon again, she saw no boats in view. Lost in thought, she sat with them for some time in silence. Finally, she made a decision.

"I know you two can't sleep, but I think I'm going to try."

Going below, she went to Dion's cabin first. Carefully removing the ice wrap from his knee, she watched him shift slightly. A small moan escaped, yet his eyes never opened. Claire paused. In sleep his face had such a peace in it. She knew he had nightmares. She'd heard him. A quick scream, then a quieter, sadder sound, like someone in pain. Was he reliving the time he was injured?

If it were up to him, she'd never know.

Reaching out, she moved a stray lock of his dark hair back into place, feeling the softness, wishing... Claire straightened and forced the thought out of her mind. She left to check on Aidan, who still slept.

Her turn. Claire laid down in one of the open bunks in the main cabin. She hadn't expected to sleep with the takeover imminent, but drained, she dropped off into a deep slumber. The storm, it appears had taken its toll on everyone.

Claire woke to the noise of someone thrashing about. Groggy and disoriented, she wiped her eyes and forced herself to focus. There was the noise again, only this time, she heard a moan, also. She put her hand over her mouth. The pirates? Claire slid off the bunk and tried to pinpoint the direction of the noise.

"No-o-o-o...!"

Her cabin. His cabin, she corrected herself. Easing the door open, she saw Dion. His body moved restlessly in response to what must be a nightmare. Another noise, this time a cry, forced its way through this clenched teeth.

Claire turned at a sound behind her and waved Roger away, closing the cabin door behind her. She moved to Dion's side, again wondering what had happened to haunt him this way. More than likely, she would never know. She reached down to soothe him with slow, gentle strokes through his hair, her voice low and gentle. "Shh. Shh. It will pass. It's only a dream."

At first there was no reaction. He continued to toss and turn, firmly entrenched in the nightmare. Eventually, though, her soothing voice seemed to get through his tortured slumber, and he calmed.

Keeping up the ministrations, she watched him as he slept. Lines etched his face, stories that could never be told. She touched a small scar at the edge of his scalp near his ear. There was so much about Dion she didn't know and very little that she did know. He was the captain of the schooner. That made him the grandson of the gentleman who had been so involved in the festival.

Claire frowned. The festival. It seemed like another life far removed from the present. What was happening back in San Diego? Did anyone search for her? Or even miss her? Had they given her job to someone else?

This adventure would end everything she'd worked so hard for. And now, here she was falling for some guy who either couldn't or wouldn't open up to her. She thought he cared. Just not enough or in the right way. Even if he did, he led a lifestyle that wouldn't allow him to acknowledge it.

The shadows under his eyes were even more pronounced in sleep. Unable to resist, she leaned over and placed a soft kiss on his forehead. As she pulled away, a hand on her arm stopped her, and she looked down into deep, dark eyes. Normally unreadable, this time they flared with...regret? And the beginnings of something else. Passion?

I can't give you what you want. I also can't manage to stay away.

Dion knew he shouldn't do this, but reason fled in the wake of her gentle touch. Keeping eye contact, he stroked the back of her arm and smiled. Her skin felt like velvet, even covered with goose bumps.

He needed more. He needed to touch her, to see her, to satisfy this craving that sat deep in his gut like a fuse. This thing between them wasn't going away and, in fact, he felt drawn to her more now than ever.

His eyes lowered to her breasts, molded by her bra and covered by the tank top she wore. Small but well-shaped, his groin hardened as he imagined how perfectly they would fit in his hand. He watched as her nipples tightened underneath the cloth to perfect, kissable points.

He was lost.

He returned his gaze to her face, then reached behind her head, wrapped a strong hand around her neck, and pulled her to him.

Please don't hurt me. I don't think I can bear it.

The thought flickered through her mind and Claire chased it away. She didn't care. Anger fled. Reason left. She was tired of wanting...and waiting. As his gaze lowered, fire began to flow through her veins.

He pulled her to him, but she resisted, just for a moment. Placing her hands on his chest to gain some distance, she held his gaze, letting him see.

You can hurt me.

She was both afraid and starved at the same time.

Hunger was about to win. She lowered her lips to his and they met in a feathery kiss, a tentative acceptance of the inevitable. He deepened the kiss, but Claire pulled back, arching her neck, begging for a moment's reprieve. Every place he touched branded her with a sweet fire that she could not control.

You are exquisite.

Dion reveled in the feel of her as his hand followed the taut lines of her smooth neck. Any lingering thought of resisting fled as the need to taste her consumed him. He peppered light kisses along her skin in a slow, languid move to the cleft at the base of her neck. She shuddered and returned her lips to his with more urgency. He caressed her cheek with his free hand, so she leaned deeper into his touch, breaking the kiss. His hand moved over her lips, tracing the lines, feeling the softness. Then he tasted her again, moving his tongue gently over her bottom lip.

A quick sigh escaped her mouth, and Dion's answering throb almost undid him, sending him from hard to granite.

He pulled her bottom lip into his mouth, sucking lightly. She opened to him and he invited her in, let her taste him.

Another sigh escaped her lips. Dion shuddered as the small sound infused his body with a molten, crushing, need.

Is this what it's supposed to feel like?

The sensations overwhelmed Claire. She felt like he was making love to her lips. Never...

"Oh!"

As he pulled her lower lip into his mouth, she felt spikes of pleasure course through her. A shiver followed the length of her spine, her stomach, lower, and settled as a restive need in her very core. She hadn't felt this before. Oh-h-h-h! He was...savoring her, using his tongue to guide him. Tentatively, she reached out, learning, tasting, drawn into the sheer sensuality of the kiss.

He moved his hand again, up and down her arm, brushing the underside, touching the swell of her breast. She gasped and was rewarded by a tightening of his body.

When Dion pulled back, Claire moaned in dismay, but he only shifted in the bunk, inviting her to lie down beside him.

Yes.

She wanted more.

She joined him and Dion immediately captured her in another kiss, his hands beginning to roam more freely now that he had better access. She couldn't believe a simple touch to her neck could cause her whole body to ache with this need.

He scorched a trail with his hand to the sensitive center of her clavicle and down. She arched, begging for his touch. He only brushed through the dip between her breasts and circled, never over. His touch remained light, increasing her desire, her need, her ache. Never had she imagined...

"Oh!"

So responsive.

Another one of those quick gasps escaped Claire's lips as he brushed her nipple through the shirt. The sound seared him, went straight to his rock hard manhood.

Then he paused. She responded as if this were all new to her. He pulled back.

A frown supplanted the frenzied need on her face as she opened her eyes. "What?" she asked, huskiness filling her voice.

"You've made love before, haven't you?"

"Of course," she answered as she arched her back, begging for more.

He held her off. "Claire?"

Claire slumped back onto the bunk and looked away for a long moment before answering. "Once."

"Only once?"

"Just that one time. Now, please—" she said, moving against him as she spoke, her hands sliding along his back with sensual need.

But Dion's brain had taken charge. Only once? She was damn near a virgin. And she acted as if it was *all* new to her. He needed to know more, to understand, and clamped a vise-like control on his desire.

"Was it enjoyable for you?" he asked.

"It *is* more than enjoyable."

"That's not an answer."

She blew out a breath filled with frustration. "It doesn't matter, Dion." She reached for him, but he captured her hand, pulling it to his chest, holding it captive there.

"It matters to me," he said earnestly.

She grew silent for a moment, and he held his breath, praying she wouldn't leave.

"Do we have to discuss this *now*?"

"Yes."

"Why?"

"Because I asked. Because I can't move forward until I know."

"What do you want? Every detail?"

"No. Just one." He released her hand then and traced her mouth with his finger.

"Fine, then." Claire pushed his hand away. "It was not very enjoyable for me. Is that what you wanted to hear?"

Dion bit back a curse. Reality had just chucked him smack in the groin.

His hand moved to touch her face, to stroke her forehead, down the side of her cheek, to trace her lips. She didn't stop him, but she wouldn't look at him, either. He touched her chin and turned her toward him, profoundly sorry that he had snuffed the desire from her eyes. "I'm sorry."

"You should be."

His felt humbled by the gift she had given him. "I want to show you how it *should* feel."

Claire buried her face in his chest. "I'd like that," she mumbled.

Dion nudged her upwards, kissing her forehead. His fingers traced the bridge of her nose and he followed it with a kiss. The heat began to return. It wasn't smart, what they were about to do. He could no longer deny the need, though. He'd just have to take this very slowly.

"Are you sure you want to do this," he asked.

"Yes," she answered, her voice a rush of breath.

That one word was all he needed.

"You say stop, I'll stop. Do you believe me?"

"Yes."

Using his hand, he stroked her parted bottom lip.

"Do you like this?"

"Mmm. Yes."

He lowered his head and kissed her, a deep, slow, searching, erotic kiss.

"And this?"

"Oh, yes," she answered breathlessly.

He traced the outline of her tank top.

"And does this feel good?"

"Mmm-mmm." Quieter now.

He found the cleft between her breasts, lightly caressing it through her shirt.

"This, too?"

"Uh-huh." He almost couldn't hear her answer.

He ran his hand lightly over her nipple.

She shivered.

And he was ready. Slow had become painful. He caressed her nipple again, then around the swell of her other breast and over the tip, ever so gently.

"I never knew—" She arched into his touch.

"It could feel like this?" He continued to use one finger, designing trails, learning the curves of her body.

"Dion," she pleaded.

His hand softly surrounded her breast, but it wasn't enough. He wanted more. Reaching in through the side of the oversized tank top of his she still wore, he unclasped her bra.

Pulling the impeding clothing aside, he lowered his head, taking her taut nipple between his lips, playing, sucking, swirling around the tip with his tongue.

Oh! How much more can I take before shattering?

He sucked on her breast, and she felt it all the way to her core. What was happening to her? Claire was on fire. She raked fingernails along his arm, then gasped as he moved to the other breast, paying equal attention. Lost in the sensation, she didn't realize at first when his hand began to move, wandering erotically down her stomach, stopping at her shorts. His head came up. She missed the sensation, wanted him to go back to what he was doing. Wanted to feel...

"You can touch me if you want," he said.

She hesitated.

"It's okay, Claire. There are no rules. You can touch or not. Trust me. I'm hot enough without any help."

Then he lowered his head and renewed his interest in her breasts, sending new bolts of electricity thrumming through her. His hand moved lower until it rested between her legs. Instinctively, her thighs tightened around his hand. It all felt so wonderful, so right, so overwhelming. *Please*, she silently pleaded. *Don't stop.*

He removed his hand, and she protested.

"I want more," he said.

"What more?"

"All of you." He helped her shed the tank top, then the bra. Reaching out, he touched one breast, cupping it almost reverently.

He seemed shy now that she was bare to the waist. Claire took that as her chance to try being in the lead. Stepping off the bunk, she reached down and tugged the belt free. She pulled shorts and underwear down and stepped out of them.

Climbing back onto the bed, she faced Dion. She helped him out of his t-shirt, then began her education, first satisfying her recurring daydream by running her fingers through his soft, wavy, hair.

God, I love the feel of her hands on me.

Her breasts brushed his chest, and it was his turn to gasp. Round and small, they were as perfect as he'd imagined, with rosy areolas tipped with glorious nipples. It took all his willpower to remain quiet, letting her do what she wanted.

Mimicking his earlier actions, she traced lines down his cheek, his neck, his chest, spending the most time circling his nipples. When she leaned in to taste them, white-hot pokers drove straight through to his ramrod stiff penis.

Dion pulled her down next to him and yanked his shorts off in one fluid movement, drawing her attention downward. She reached out, but he didn't give her a chance.

He returned to his play, claiming her mouth, her neck, and finally returned to her breasts. Pulling a tip into his mouth, he razed it lightly with his teeth, and her chest rose in answer. His hand gently kneaded her other breast, then wandered over her stomach and lower, resting again between her legs. He kept still, giving her time. Time to know she had choices. Time to adjust to new sensations and catch up with what she was feeling. Hell, what he felt was exceptional, but he wanted so much more.

This time, she didn't flinch or close up. He teased her, moving his hand up and down, never quite touching her.

"Please," she whispered.

A little pressure on her thigh and she opened wider for him. He delved deeper, finding her center. She moaned as he removed his hand. Then he bent down to taste her.

"No," she cried, clenching her legs.

"Let me taste you, Claire. Let me show you what it should be like."

Can this really be happening? Is he truly treasuring me?

He continued his gentle attention and any protest died in her throat as the waves of ecstasy peaked. He sent her over the edge. Still he kept on, bringing her once more to the brink of climax.

"Wait for me," he whispered as he reached for a condom and sheathed himself.

He shifted between her legs. She felt his full arousal pulsate against her, yet he stopped, watching her, waiting.

For a long moment, she stared at him. Then she smiled seductively, spread further and reached to pull him inside her, first with one gentle thrust, then a building momentum. She tried to lightly caress him, the way he had done for her, but she quickly lost herself in the intensity of the fire that consumed both of them. Her fingers dug into his back as they both climaxed in a glorious explosion.

For long moments, Claire was awash in more emotion than she'd ever felt in her life. Gradually, she became aware that he had moved to lay beside her. He stroked her, talked to her. She didn't know what he said, only heard the sound of his voice, low and soothing.

Claire reached up and touched his cheek so he would look at her.

"Is that really what it's supposed to be like?"

A small, precious smile lit his face just for a moment. "Yes." He kissed her, and she pulled him close, lengthening the kiss, enjoying the attention he paid to her mouth and lips.

"What happened to you before, Claire?"

Claire tensed. "I try not to think about it."

He didn't say anything.

"Dion, this isn't some quick and easy story to tell."

"We've got time," he said, waiting.

Softly, she sighed, then continued. "I grew up in Martha's Vineyard, but not as part of the elite. My father did odd jobs for the residents there. We didn't have much money. My education was paramount to him, so he got me into St. Mary's prep school. There was definitely a class distinction there, and I was...alone most of the time."

She averted her eyes, caught up in the memory. "Jay began to date me halfway through my junior year of high school. I don't know why I was important to him as a conquest, but I was. He was a senior and school president. I was starved for attention. Hell, I was more than that. I thought myself to be in love."

She took a deep, shaky breath and Dion's arms tightened around her.

"On prom night he worked very hard to talk me into sex. Making love, he called it. I didn't want to. I knew I wasn't ready."

Claire's eyes squeezed shut as the memories flooded in. "He...convinced me. And it was...rougher than I ever imagined. When he finished, he rolled off the bed without a word and left."

"Hell."

"That's one way of describing it. It gets worse. I brought charges. But they had too much money. And word got through the school. Things weren't too fun for me my senior year. I couldn't wait to graduate and get the hell out of there."

Bastard.

Dion wasn't sure what to do. Anger raged through him. He wanted to kill the boy who'd done that to Claire. He also wanted Claire to know the feelings, the pleasures, making love brought. He forced his fury to the back of his mind and stroked her hair. She wouldn't look at him and, in fact, turned her head away. He reached for her chin and pulled her gently around. "You are not what this man tried to do to you."

"I know that in my mind. Sometimes my heart has trouble remembering."

"He's a bastard, Claire."

"I know."

"He never paid for his sins?"

"No. He was a prominent son and his family was very wealthy. My father and I lived in a small apartment and struggled financially every single day of our lives. Who do you think they believed?"

He nodded his head. He'd seen the injustice before.

He was a bastard, she reminded herself. She'd never told anyone what happened, not since she'd graduated and gotten the hell out of there. Claire lay beside Dion, awash in bad memories.

She felt Dion move, felt him kiss her cheek, then move to the corner of her mouth. Passion flared anew as she turned to him, wiping out all thought of that past.

His kisses moved across her body, feather light in one spot, eager in another. Her already hypersensitive breasts ached for more, and he didn't disappoint her.

They came together again in a way that convinced her she had never known love before now. Afterward, sated and content, Claire lay still as Dion casually ran his fingers over her breasts.

"Thank you," she said.

"You are so very welcome. Trust me, it was my pleasure."

She lay there, staring at the ceiling, then frowned. "What's that shiny thing up there?

Dion never got the chance to answer. With no warning, the door to their cabin burst open. His quick reaction barely got them covered in time and he glared at the intruder as Claire gasped.

"Uh...whoa. Gee, guys, sorry to interrupt," Aidan said, quickly turning away. Claire caught a glimpse of his profusely red face. "Roger sent me down here to let you know there's a powerboat closing on our position."

CHAPTER TWELVE

The pirates! Claire's heart thudded in her throat.

"Damn!" Dion was dressed before Claire could even get up. She jumped from the bunk, hit her head, and lost her balance. Dion grabbed for her, steadied her, and held her close for just a moment longer than necessary.

"It's okay. I'll keep you safe," he stressed. As he left, she could see that his limp was still more pronounced. It must hurt like the dickens.

"Grab two coffees," he said over his shoulder, "and join me at the wheel."

Her hands shook as she poured the coffee. Music wafted down from above. She'd never once heard music on board. Why now?

She managed to fill two cups and cap them, then head cautiously up the ladder. No one had boarded yet. Aidan and Roger casually sunned themselves forward. A boom box played country music beside them.

Dion stood at the wheel. She handed him a coffee.

"Try to relax."

Easier said than done. She started to turn, then jumped as Dion's hand brought her attention around to him. Gently stroking her cheek, he leaned close as if to kiss her neck.

"Don't look to starboard. That's the direction they are approaching from, and we want them to think they have the element of surprise."

She leaned into him, comforted by his solid body.

"Where's Mike?"

"Might as well let him sleep while he can."

Dion settled his arm around her like that of a long-time lover.

She started to pull away, but he stopped her.

"The best way I can protect you is to keep you with me. Stay put."

Her eyes flashed, and he continued before she could speak. "Claire, please. Do as I say."

The command in his voice was enough to still her. She sipped her coffee, yet didn't taste it. Her mouth felt parched by a mounting dread. "Why the music?"

"To make it plausible that we didn't hear the boat."

Before long, that was all she could hear, a steady droning that grew louder with each passing moment. Almost involuntarily she started to turn and look, but pressure from Dion once again stopped her.

"How could the victims have not heard that roar?" The sound filled her ears.

"You know it's coming. The others didn't."

She tried to be still, listening, knowing there was nothing to do except wait. Feeling a lump of fear anchor in her throat, she swallowed. What had she gotten tossed in the middle of? This was crazy. They were about to be boarded by pirates, for crying out loud.

She stood stiffly, drumming her fingers against the wheel housing behind her.

"Relax."

It was barely more than a quiet whisper in her ear. "You'll do fine. You'll be fine."

Nothing reassured her. Standing, waiting, was unbearable. Soon her legs started tapping in time to the music. She felt like she would burst into flight, she was so keyed up.

Suddenly, there was a shadow over her, then Dion's voice. "Don't hate me for this."

His lips captured hers. Hard. Struggling against him, she soon felt fear give way to another wave of desire. Claire stopped the struggle and gave in to the sensation. He bit her lip, backing up slightly, finding her eyes with his. She didn't wait for him to claim her lips again, but leaned toward him, provoking, begging. Everything else blurred. There was nothing except Dion, his kisses, and the sensations coursing through her body.

He captured her mouth, had just about caged her soul when they were rudely pulled apart.

Dion's plan to distract Claire worked well. So well, in fact that he forgot the present situation himself. He reacted instinctively when separated, whirling, veins throbbing in his forehead, ready to attack whoever had yanked them apart. Turning into the barrel of a rifle, he stopped mid-thrust, slowly raised both arms up into the air, and carefully shifted until he was between the Russian-made AK-47 and Claire.

He could see only the man in front of him, tanned and hard-looking. With a rifle. No one else.

"Down. Knees."

"What—"

"Down. Now." For emphasis, he pointed with the AK-47. Dion could have taken him at that moment. The man was vulnerable, but he didn't know how many were on board. He couldn't keep Claire safe that way, nor could he fulfill their objective. He knelt down slowly, head slightly lowered, praying he appeared submissive and without courage. Claire reached out a hand to his back. *Don't move*, he prayed, trying to convey the thought with a slight shrug. Staying in between the pirate and Claire, he remained alert for any interest in her.

He could not let her be harmed. He buried the slight shudder that raced through him. He would not let it happen again.

It wasn't long before Roger and Aidan were forced, also at gunpoint, to join them near the wheel. Dion now saw that there were four men topside with another two heading below. They all appeared to be of Mexican descent.

All except one.

One man gave quiet commands. The only thing he had in common with the other men was his darkly tanned skin. Everything else contrasted. The other pirates had short dark hair while his white blond hair was pulled back in a tail. The leader's light blue eyes boldly contrasted with the darker ones of his men. They were stockier, shorter. He seemed a giant in comparison, probably topping six foot five.

It wasn't long before a groggy, half-awake Mike came up the ladder. A shove tossed him into their midst.

As the captain, Dion remembered that he had a role to play. Standing up slowly, he fired his first salvo.

"Who are you, and what the hell are you doing boarding my vessel?"

Three rifles turned on him, and he once again raised his arms, but he didn't back down.

"I asked you what you think you are doing," he said, trying to mimic a demanding yet slightly fearful tone.

"No talk," one of the men said, raising the butt of his rifle as if to hit Dion.

"Jorge, no." One of the older Hispanic men said to the man, who glared back at him."

Dion flinched appropriately and knelt back down. He'd managed his objective, though. He'd shifted closer to Claire. Acting more fearful now, Dion tried again, keeping his head down.

"Please. Tell us what you want. You want money? We don't have much, but you can have it. Just leave us alone."

"Cut the act, agent."

Dion's head snapped up.

The tall, blond leader walked up to the group as he spoke. "I thought that would get your attention. Yes, Agent Gaetani. We know who you are. And you, agents Stone, Walker and Borland," he continued, eyeing them individually as he said their names.

"We know exactly who you are. Even you," he said, eyeing Claire with an appreciation in his glance that made Dion's blood boil.

"Clara? No. Claire. A yacht club secretary. Pretty one at that. There might be a little bonus in this raid, boys," he said, directing the last part to his men, a couple of which smiled in response.

"If you know who we are, then what the hell do you want?" Dion said with venom in his voice. He fought the urge to wrap an arm tightly around Claire, to declare she would not be touched by this man, or any man.

"I expect you already know that, agent. Do I really need to spell it out?"

Dion remained still.

"Yes," the pirate leader continued. "I guess I must for clarity's sake." Moving until he was directly in front of Dion, he continued.

"We want your boat, Agent Gaetani."

Looking around him, he laughed. "Actually, we already have it."

"You'll never take the *Treasure*."

"Ah, but we already have," he laughed again. "As to your earlier question? Well, you'll just have to figure out who we are for yourselves. You can call me Hawk for now."

Furious, Dion found himself torn between staying near Claire and the reality that he might actually lose the *Treasure*.

"Enough of this," Hawk grew serious, speaking to his men. "Take them below."

Prodding Dion and the others with their guns, the men pushed them to go below. As they descended the stairs, though, Dion heard one last order.

"Isolate them as much as the boat will allow. Put her in the captain's cabin. Oh, and make sure the forward hatch is secured from the outside."

A panic filled Dion. He couldn't protect her if they were separated.

Turning, he tried to fight his way back up the ladder. The butt end of a rifle stopped his momentum, and he fell the length of the ladder, his consciousness slipping away as he hit the floor of the main cabin below.

Dion woke up hours later in the forward bunkroom with a monster ache pounding through his head. He got up too fast, making matters worse, swaying and almost blacking out again. He squatted and grabbed his head in both hands. Several long moments later, he took a slow, deep breath, and finally, the world stopped spinning.

"Where's Claire?" he grunted.

"I don't know for sure," Aidan answered. "I think she's in your cabin."

"Damn." He looked around. He and Aidan were alone.

"Roger and Mike?"

"They've separated us all. Mike and Roger are in the two private bunk rooms."

"That's a new tactic for them," Dion murmured thoughtfully. "Hatch?"

"Blocked from above. They found a way to bar the door, too."

Dion tried the door and found it immovable. He searched the top of the door jam and pulled out a nail file embedded in the wood.

"What the heck is that there for?"

"Spying. Useful when Grandfather sent me to bed early."

"I don't get it."

By then, Dion had already pried the knot of wood out of a small notch about halfway down the door. The hole appeared barely the size of his little finger, but big enough to see through into the main cabin. Turning a grim face to Aidan, he pointed to it.

"Spy hole."

"Aha."

He saw no one in the main cabin, but there were blind spots beyond his vision. The radio room, the bench behind the table, and the open bunks on the other side were all out of sight, He could, however, see the rope tying the two single bunkroom doors closed.

Damn. He could pick a lock faster than most people. But how do you untie a rope you can't reach? The only positive was his clear view to the captain's cabin door. He'd know if they went in there. Not that the knowledge would help. Dion turned and ran both hands through his hair, wincing when he touched the lump from the rifle hit.

"They know who we are," Aidan said.

"Yes."

"How?"

"I wish to hell I knew."

"Someone on the inside?"

Dion was quiet for a moment, staring at empty space. Finally he answered. "Seems likely."

"But who?"

"That's a good question."

Now it was Aidan's turn to be quiet. Dion started to move, alternately pacing and plastering his eye to the knothole.

"So do we stick to our original plan?"

"I don't see that we have much choice."

"Okay. We wait."

"And watch. And pray they don't deviate any further from their normal pattern." Apprehension filled his veins with ice. He was back at the door now, crouched down, peering through the small hole.

"I'll take first watch."

CHAPTER THIRTEEN

Claire had seen the blow Dion took. He'd dropped like a lead weight, falling in a heap to the floor of the main cabin. Instinct took over, and she struck out at the younger man who had rifle-butted Dion. He was faster, though, and the stalk of his gun connected with her stomach before she could inflict any damage.

"No!"

She barely heard the blond man's missive. Doubling over, she gasped in short spurts, panting. Slowly, agonizingly, her breath returned to a more normal state. The thief who'd hit her waited until then to prod her with the barrel of the gun.

"Move."

Looking down, she saw that Dion and the others were not in sight. As she stood, her stomach reacted and she retched.

"Madre de Dios!" The pirate jumped back too late.

Her nausea worsened at the rancid smell of her own vomit. Still, she couldn't resist a smile.

The rifle came up as if to hit her again, and she flinched, but the strike never came. The leader barked an order in Spanish, and the man backed up a step. They spoke heatedly, waving in her direction once or twice. Claire didn't release her breath until the rifle was lowered.

The leader had won.

Thank God.

"It would be better for you," the blond giant spoke to Claire, "if you did not rile Jorge so."

"Take her below," he said quietly to one of the other men.

Shoved into the captain's cabin, Claire searched for Dion and was immediately disappointed. He wasn't there. None of the men were. She was alone.

Her legs finally reacted to events. They began to tremble, and she sat down on the bunk, curling her knees up and holding her stomach, wondering if Dion was okay and what she should do now. Things were horribly different from what Dion had predicted.

She began to replay what happened. Then it hit her. The leader had known all their names. Even hers, and she was a last-minute unplanned participant in this fiasco.

How could the pirates have known she'd be on board?

Claire sat up straight. They couldn't. Unless they had put her here. The noise on board the *Treasure* that last night in the harbor must have been them. She was sure of it! One of the pirates had hit her over the head and concealed her in the raft. It was the only explanation.

She paced now, as well as she could in the small cabin. The pirates must have planned to steal the schooner before it ever left San Diego harbor. It still didn't explain how they'd known her name as well as Dion and the rest of the team. How could that be?

What had Dion said? They always overtook yachts during satellite blackout periods. If they had planned this in advance, they must have had foreknowledge of the route Dion would take. How would they get that information?

She felt the shiver of goose bumps work their way down her arms.

They have someone on the inside! They must have. Who? Someone back at headquarters? Or someone on this boat?

Shocked, she sat down. How could it be one of the men she'd spent the last few days with? She discounted Dion immediately. This was his boat. It had been his Grandfather's before that. He wouldn't plan to have it captured and sold.

That left Mike, Aidan and Roger. She didn't like Roger, but she had to admit that was mostly because he had been so unbending when she'd first been found aboard.

Claire gasped, feeling sucker punched. Except it hadn't been Roger, had it? Roger wasn't the captain. He'd only taken the role to give Dion more maneuverability. Dion had made the decisions. It had been Dion's choice to keep her with them—to keep her from going back. He'd lied to her about more than just his position on the boat, she thought bitterly.

She paced again, frustrated at the lack of room. So she hit the door. Dion had kept her here, even let her beg and still refused her, all the while using Roger as a shield. She hit the table. He'd probably kept her from her promotion, too.

She stood looking at the bunk.

He'd made love to her knowing all of this.

Damn him!

Her shoulders slumped as she glanced at the door. There was only one other cabin on board. They must have put him in the foc'sle with the other agents. He was imprisoned only feet from her yet she couldn't talk to him.

She couldn't touch him.

She couldn't cold-cock him.

Damn it to hell. She'd been used again, thoroughly and completely, and then tossed to the wolves. Furious now, she whirled to stare at the door. Leaning against it, she listened, but was unable to hear anything. The door was tightly jammed. There was no lock, and it opened inward, so they must have tied it shut.

Claire examined the hinges, deciding they were probably beyond her abilities. Wait a minute. She had tools in here from her work on the table. A glance at the bench told her they'd been removed.

She was stuck here for who knows how long. And with a lot of un-resolvable anger. A vision of Dion crumpled on the cabin floor flooded her thoughts and Claire frowned. She hadn't seen any movement from him, but she'd only had a glimpse before going berserk. He'd been hit on the head, though, not shot. People survived head wounds, didn't they? She grimaced at the remembered pain. She had survived. He must be alive.

All she could do is hope. Her eyes narrowed. He'd better be. If anyone had the right to be personally responsible for his demise, it was her.

Claire kicked the door, then returned to the bunk and lay down, fanning her hand out along the sheet and allowing the memories to torment her. Had it been only a couple of hours since they'd been here? Dion had been so caring, so worried about how she felt. She stretched her arms out, feeling the fire build again at the memory of his touch, the kisses, how he had melted her.

She clutched a pillow tightly, rocking slightly back and forth. Had seduction been part of his job?

Her hand struck the cabin wall. God, she hated being stuck here with nothing to do but think.

Muffled discussion filtered through to her brain. She could not isolate it enough to hear clearly, though. At the door to her cabin, all seemed quiet. Not even a whisper. Back at her bunk, the sounds were easier to hear.

Muted voices.

Claire remembered the air vent. The other end was near the wheel housing. She smiled grimly. A nice way for the captain to make sure all is well topside, eh?

As she crouched on the bunk to get as close as she could to the vent, the voices became more coherent.

"It went pretty well, don't you think?"

She didn't recognize the voice and assumed it was pirate leader.

"Smooth, yes."

This voice sounded a bit more familiar, but she hadn't heard enough to place it. The first man spoke again. "You are in agreement that this will be our last venture together?"

"Yes."

Claire still couldn't tell who was talking. Something else began to invade her senses. A woodsy aroma–pipe smoke!

"So what are you planning to do with the money?"

"It's time for a change of locale, mate. I'll be heading for parts unknown just as soon as we're rescued."

Roger! It was Roger. Claire sat back on the bunk, her hands covering her open mouth as the mystery tried to resolve itself in her head. Roger was the informant. Dion said they'd been friends for, what, ten years? What could have caused a rift like this between the two?

"Leaving friends and family behind?" Hawk said.

"I've no family to speak of. Not anymore. And friends? Well, let's just say there's no one I owe any allegiance to."

"What about Gaetani. I thought you two were pals."

Claire leaned closer to the vent.

Roger's next words came through, dripping with hostility. "We were. Right up until he got my girl killed."

This is the incident that Dion wouldn't tell her about. She would bet her life on it. And the reason Roger had turned into a traitor.

"Ah, so you are motivated by vengeance, then?"

"It's as good a reason as any."

"Not in my book, it's not."

"You're no better, leading this rag-tag group, stealing sailboats, and selling them for your own profit."

"That's where you are wrong, my friend. The profits are not my own. I work for a cause."

"And what cause would that be?"

"My own and none of your concern."

"Fine. It's of no matter, anyhow. I've gotten what I need out of the venture. That's all I care about now."

"Yes. I can imagine. Now, we'd better take you back below so no one gets suspicious. I'd imagine you want to get out of the country before that happens."

Roger's chuckle faded away. Claire heard what sounded like two men climb down the ladder outside her cabin. Soon, one returned. Had Roger been returned to the other men? She had no way of knowing.

After propping up pillows and anything else she could find, Claire fell asleep sitting up, listening to the silence at the vent.

She woke with a start as the door to her cabin opened. She'd seen no one for the past two days except for the two times they had passed a tray of food and water through to her. The one called Jorge motioned her to come out of the cabin. Standing well back from her, he pointed his rifle at her, then at the stairs. A brief, tight smile came to her face as she realized he was keeping his distance. Good.

The bright sunlight blinded her, and she froze on the stairs while her eyes adjusted. A prod from behind sent her the rest of the way up. She rounded the hatch and stood holding on to the cover until she regained some sight. The sun looked to be a short way past its zenith. It was just after midday.

"Ah, there you are, Miss Saunders."

She recognized the voice this time. Turning, she found herself scrutinized by the pirate leader. "Hawk."

"I'm flattered. You remembered my name."

"I've had two days to think about nothing else."

"Yes. That's so, I guess. Come," he said, indicating the deck chairs set up amidships. "Have a seat."

Claire stood immobile.

"Don't worry, Claire. I have no intention of hurting you. I'd simply like the pleasure of your company for a little while."

Claire sat on the edge of the chair provided for her. She glanced around but could only see Hawk and the one called Jorge topside.

Hawk left the wheel and sat in the chair across from her. That left no one at the wheel. Claire noticed the boat was on an even keel. They had stopped. The sails were all down, although not stowed.

"We've stopped."

"Yes. It's time for us to part company."

She saw the island in the distance, looking very small and very inhospitable.

"Which island are you leaving us on?"

"San Benedicto in the Revillagigedo chain."

"All of us?"

"Now that's a strange question, Claire. What would make you think I wouldn't send all of you on your way? After all, it's the schooner I want, not you."

Damn. She needed to be more careful. She didn't want to tip her hat and let him know she was aware of the spy in their ranks. He could warn Roger before she got to Dion. She had to say something.

"You couldn't have done this without help. Someone on board must have aided you." True enough.

"And you think you know who that is?"

"I wish. Care to give me a clue?" Good, she'd managed just the right amount of scorn. She hoped.

He cocked his head, considering her. "It doesn't matter to me if you know or not. Once you're away, you can do whatever you want, say whatever you want. I think, señorita, that you will find it harder to convince your lover than you think."

"He's not my lover," she said stiffly.

Hawk smiled. "If he's not now, he will be." The smile disappeared quickly as he gazed out over the water. It almost seemed as if regrets shadowed him.

"Not if I have anything to say about it."

"Well, time will tell. I regret I cannot stay to see how it turns out."

He was silent, and Claire wondered what he was up to. Did he want something from her, bringing her up before the others?

"What do you want from me?"

"Why, nothing. Only a small bit of your time. You see, it will be hard for you to convince the captain of anything if he thinks you are colluding with me."

"Dion wouldn't think that," Claire said.

"Wouldn't he?"

They sat there in silence for a while. But Claire had too many questions to keep quiet. The more she could learn, the easier it would be to capture them. She looked around again. "Where are the rest of your men?"

"Curious? Well, they are around. This is all you need to know for the moment."

"What will you do after you strand us?"

"I don't know. Maybe I will sail around the world. This is by far the best of the lot we have captured. A sleek, well-built vessel." He ran his hand over the wood, almost caressing it, much the same way Dion had.

He appreciated the *Treasure*.

"Do you sell the boats you steal? What do you do with the money?"

"So many questions. And no answers to be had. I'm sorry. You won't find out what I've done or will do from this conversation." He frowned. "There is too much to protect here."

Frustrated, she couldn't think of any way to get some details out of him. She sat back in her chair, silent, racking her brain. Nothing came to mind.

Soon, two more men came up, carrying two small bags and a couple of jugs of water. They passed Hawk and Claire and threw the bags overboard. Claire saw then the life raft had been lowered into the water.

"It's time, Claire."

Just then, Dion and the rest of his men were brought topside. Grateful to be seated, Claire felt alternately weak with relief that he seemed okay and wobbly with anger at his betrayal. And Dion's own face showed a myriad of emotions. Had she seen surprise and relief? If so, it was short-lived, soon replaced by the scowl she'd come to know so well. *Will he trust you?* Hawk's words came back to haunt her.

Dion endured two nights of captivity. Barely. He rarely left the door and kept an almost constant watch on Claire's door. He knew someone kept watch in the main cabin since he could occasionally see feet stretched out into the cabin aisle. By the quiet, muffled voices when they changed guards, he could tell they were working in two-hour shifts. He saw no sign of Roger or Mike. He'd seen someone twice go to Claire's door, untie the ropes and pass a tray in. At least they were feeding her. That was more than he could say for the rest of them.

It was late morning. Something had to happen soon. By his reckoning, it should have taken no more than two days to reach the nearest island, San Benedicto.

As if in answer to his thoughts, the pirate called Jorge came down the ladder and opened the door to the master cabin. Moments later, Claire emerged, appearing sleepy and disheveled and thankfully unharmed.

Claire was safe.

Drawing his first deep breath in days, Dion felt his shoulders loosen from the constant state of readiness he'd been in. It looked like the time had come for them to be set adrift. He replaced the knot in the door and waited.

Except no one came for them. Ten minutes passed, then fifteen. A half hour later, still no one had arrived to release them. Finally, after a full hour, he heard movement. Soon his door opened, and Jorge motioned topside with his rifle.

With his hands raised in a non-confrontational pose, Dion led the way. Claire wasn't by the wheel. Neither was the leader, Hawk. He saw them both amidships, seated as if having a casual conversation.

What was that all about?

He approached slowly, masking his relief that she was okay. Something was up and, until he knew what, he'd better keep his thoughts to himself.

Aidan followed closely behind Dion. It wasn't long before Mike and Roger joined them.

Hawk wasted little time on pleasantries.

"I'm afraid it's time for you to leave. Since you've been trying, unsuccessfully I might add, to capture me, I'll assume you know the drill," he said with a quick nod of his head to starboard, eyes on Dion.

Dion stared him down for a moment then glanced to the right. He recognized the island immediately, even from this distance. Half of it was flat and covered with sparse, low-lying, vegetation. The other half had a very distinctive prominence, as if a volcano had erupted out of the water and attached itself to the island. There was nothing there except a small mountain of coarse, dark rock, leftover lava cooled and formed by nature into a conical shape.

"San Benedicto," he murmured. They had guessed right, but it was an empty victory at the moment.

"Yes, Agent Gaetani. You do your homework well."

Dion watched as Hawk made a subtle motion with his hand. In answer, the gunmen raised their rifles, prodding them all to transfer to the life raft.

Dion didn't budge.

Hawk didn't move, didn't talk. He just returned Dion's stare.

"You know it's a three-man Zodiac," Dion finally reminded him.

"Yes." Hawk smiled. "I do."

"How do you expect us to fit?"

"I *expect* you to get in the raft, Agent. How you make it to land is entirely up to you. Though I have supreme confidence in your ability to survive."

Disgusted, Dion barely had time to think before a jab in his back reminded him how little time he had. He turned to the others.

"Aidan, you first. Then Claire and Roger. Mike, you and I get the first shift in the water.

Without a word, Aidan climbed down to the raft, helping Claire, then Roger. Mike waited until Dion was ready before he jumped into the water.

Dion hesitated, taking one last look around. The *Treasure* was a priceless legacy from a well-loved Grandfather, and he was more than reluctant to give her over to these thieves.

"You have no choice, agent," Hawk read his mind. "Get off *my* boat."

"I'll find you, you bastard," Dion said. "You'll pay for this. I swear it."

"You are welcome to try, Agent Gaetani," Hawk said, his grin widening. "First, though, you've got to make it to land."

This time, the prod wasn't gentle, and Dion went tumbling over the side, landing in the water a few feet away from the raft. He swam over, grabbed one of the ropes, and glared up at the pirates.

"Oh, and Agent Gaetani? Catch!"

A small object came flying at Dion, only caught through instinctive reaction. As he lurched, the raft rocked violently, and water gushed over the sides. Claire screamed.

"I won't be needing that," Hawk raised his voice to be heard over the noise.

Dion saw he'd caught one of the tracking devices planted on board the schooner. Closing his eyes in frustration, he missed the next bit of metal that went flying by and quickly sunk beneath the water. It didn't matter. He knew it was the second tracking device.

"This one, either."

The thieves had found two tracking devices, Dion thought bleakly. His head slumped briefly onto the side of the raft. He felt Claire's hand touch his arm and shrugged it off.

Without another word, the pirates cut the raft loose and the *Treasure* slowly slipped out of his grasp. He could only watch as the currents pulled them farther and farther apart.

Damn it to hell! Everything about this op had been botched. The pirates seemed to always be one step ahead of them. The IMB had known the thieves were getting satellite data from someone. Now he suspected that person was close, maybe even with him on this raft.

Crap.

He knew his men well and didn't think and of them capable of turning. And Claire…well, he hadn't known her as long, but he couldn't believe that she would be involved in this.

Claire applied a light pressure to his arm. He didn't want her sympathy. This time, though, he didn't brush it off. He simply didn't react to it.

The first of the sails went up on the fading schooner. Soon, it was nothing but a spec heading in a southeasterly direction. A wave, larger than most, topped the raft and soaked everyone. Claire's gasp reminded him there were more important issues looming.

Time to prioritize. They needed to get to safety. Then he could take time to sort recent events out. Tightening his grip on the raft, he turned toward the island.

Claire's relief at seeing Dion and the men was short lived. She hadn't truly believed they had a chance to survive until that moment.

Now, here they were, barely afloat in the dinky Zodiac, and relief quickly gave way to thoughts of survival. She needed to talk to Dion, yet knew this wasn't the time.

She watched him, eyes locked on the diminishing view of his schooner. They needed to make it to land before they got swamped. The four to five inches of water inside their small lifeboat didn't bode well for the attempt.

"Roger, Aidan, you two start rowing," Dion said, spitting salt water out of his mouth. "We'll push for now."

Well, at least they finally had his attention, Claire thought, sitting still while Roger and Aidan repositioned themselves.

Dion pulled himself halfway up onto the raft to talk.

"I estimate about a mile to the island, then we'll have to drift around to the beach side before we can land. We've got a good three hours of work ahead of us."

Claire looked at the island, then down at the raft. The water was getting deeper.

"Uh, guys?"

"What?" Dion answered distractedly.

"We may sink before we make it to land, at this rate." Claire pointed at the water inside the raft.

Leaning in further, Dion watched as Aidan started feeling around gently with his hands, then froze.

"Damn," Aidan swore.

"What?" Claire questioned.

"There's a small hole in the seam."

"How bad?" Dion asked.

"Bad enough. The air chambers in the Zodiac will keep us afloat long enough, I think. Claire, bail. Come on guys. We've got to get to land."

Her eyes widened and she started bailing with her hands as fast as she could. Aidan took off his windbreaker and handed it to Claire.

"Try using this to cup the water and bail," he said as he started rowing.

Claire watched Dion, already swimming, one arm holding on to the rope that threaded along the outside of the raft, the other working in unison with his legs to powerfully propel them toward the island.

"Will we make it to shore?" she asked Aidan.

"We should." He shrugged. "It'll be close."

"Didn't we check the raft before we left San Diego?" Roger piped up quietly.

"Yes. It was fine. The tear seems man-made."

Roger's face turned ashen.

That was the clue Claire needed. She knew then the tear was deliberate. If they weren't in such dire straits, she'd have enjoyed the shock on Roger's face. Could he be wondering if this deliberate attempt was for his benefit? After all, he knew who the pirates were. He was going to get them all killed.

"How?" Roger managed to ask in a fairly normal voice.

Aidan answered. "The cut is straight, not jagged, and in a place that doesn't have a whole lot of stress on it."

"Enough talk. Row!" Dion said between strokes.

"You look a little green around the gills, Rog," Aidan said.

Smart man. He knows something's wrong.

"I'm fine," Roger said, leaning against the side of the raft for a moment. "Just fighting a little sea sickness of my own, I think."

"Well, buck up. We need you on an oar."

Roger rowed, but it was apparent he was having difficulty keeping up with Aidan. Eventually, Mike climbed in and took over for him. Roger went over the side and clung to the back of the raft, more dead weight than assistance.

Claire kept on bailing. She didn't gain much ground, but she didn't lose any, either.

They worked this way, as a team, for over two hours. Dion refused to let anyone spell him and kept swimming, only occasionally letting the raft pull him as he floated on his back.

Roger appeared to get sicker and sicker and they eventually tied a rope to him so they wouldn't lose him. Claire knew what was making him ill. She opted to keep her silence until she could speak to Dion in private.

Focused on getting to land, the harshness of the island surprised Claire as they closed in.

"Is the volcano active?" she asked, in between throwing jackets of water overboard."

"No," Mike puffed, rowing hard. "Well, not since, uh, about 1952." He pulled on the oars again. "The island was half the size it is now. The volcano attached itself with lava."

Another pull.

"All's quiet now. But all these islands are visible peaks of an underwater mountain chain." He pulled again. "They're called the Eastern Pacific Rise. It stretches all the way to the Arctic."

Finally, the water lightened to an aqua blue, and they were in sight of the beach. Roger thrashed at the ropes until Dion untied him, then staggered through the water, crawling onto the beach and collapsing.

Good, she thought, watching him. He should feel lousy. She'd have a chance to talk to Dion soon. Before then, they all needed to feel dry land underneath their feet. Dion helped Claire out then handed a small bag of supplies over. Mike and Aidan both clambered over the side and waded in to shore.

Dion left the raft last, pulling it further onto the beach. The captain is always last, Claire thought bitterly, remembering the lie.

CHAPTER FOURTEEN

Several gasping minutes passed before Claire could move. Her exhaustion was total. She knew that food and a good night's sleep were the only remedy for the strenuous passage they'd just completed, but those weren't luxuries they could afford right now. Survival was the priority.

Sitting up, she could see there wasn't much to work with. The sandy beach quickly changed to scrubby grass, rising gently to the peak of a small hill. There weren't many trees to break up the monotony of the landscape. The few that did were scraggy and offered little or no shade.

The other direction didn't offer any better options. The volcano appeared much more ominous from land. It loomed above them, large, dark, and formidable.

She looked up, seeing the sun still high in the sky. There were still several hours of heat left and, based on her observations, no respite in sight.

A hand settled on her shoulder, and she jumped, clutching her chest.

"You all right?"

It was Aidan. She expelled the breath she'd been holding. "You startled me."

"Sorry, angel. Just checking in."

Claire raised her arm, testing a shoulder that would soon be complaining. "I'm okay. Tired mostly. And I think I'll be sore from bailing."

"Yeah. We're all going to pay for this little adventure. Hang on. I'm going to see what the plan is."

He strode over to Dion and placed a hand on his shoulder just as he had done to her. Only Dion didn't flinch. In fact, he barely moved. Aidan spoke quietly at first, but as she watched, his conversation with Dion became more intense...and very one-sided. Finally, he stood, threw his hands in the air, turned, and walked back to Claire.

"What's the matter?" she asked.

"Beats me. He's in his own little world."

Mike walked up then. "We need to find some cover, Aidan. This sun is going to bake us."

"It already is. All right. Mike, you and I'll go scout. Claire, can you keep an eye on these two and check the provisions? We haven't eaten in two days."

Claire's eyes widened as she heard that.

"So let's hope they gave us some food." With a pat on her arm, he and Mike set off for the other side of the hill.

Claire threw withering glances at both remaining agents then headed for the two small bags that the pirates had tossed into the raft. The supplies were meager. One gallon of fresh water for five of them wasn't going to go very far.

The other bag held a full loaf of bread and...peanut butter? That was it, except for a buck knife and a book of matches. *They call this survival food? What a joke! Energy food that makes you thirsty and very little water to wash it down with.* Still, food was food. She wasn't hungry yet. But Dion and the other agents had to be starving by now. *Beggars can't be choosers*, she thought as she went to work.

Cleaning the knife as best she could, she slapped two sandwiches together and tossed one on Roger's stomach without a word. Resolutely, she walked over to Dion with the second sandwich. He stood staring off into the distance.

"We need to talk."

"Go away, Claire."

Go away, Claire? He sounded pissed at her. What the hell did he have to be angry about? She was the one with the righteous beef. Frustrated, she tried again, but Dion beat her to it.

"Why is it so important," he asked, pinning her with a stare, "for you to get that promotion at the yacht club?"

"Huh?" She shook her head in confusion.

"I said why is that promotion so important to you?"

"I *heard* what you said. Why do you want to know? And why now, of all times? We have more important things to talk about."

"Answer the question."

Dion's face seemed to be carved in granite, like a man who'd been tortured and knew there was more in his future. He wouldn't give in. And he wouldn't let the topic go, either. Claire knew that like she knew he was ticked off about something.

"Because I need the money, okay? Is that what you want to hear?"

He didn't answer her instead turning to look out over the water.

Claire tried again. "There's something you need to know, Dion."

"Not now," he said, walking away.

Great. The one time I need him to actually play agent and he's too busy. Doing what, for crying out loud? We're stranded on a frigging island!

"Fine," she said through gritted teeth. "Do whatever you want." She followed him, holding out the sandwich. He didn't take it, wouldn't even acknowledge the offering. "Eat."

"Eat it yourself."

At which point Claire hit boiling and shoved the sandwich in his face.

"I was fed on board. *You* apparently were not. Now you can eat this sandwich voluntarily or I can shove it down your throat. It's your choice."

His eyes bore into her. After several long seconds, he took the sandwich from her and kept walking.

She kept up with him. "Take a bite," she ordered.

"If I do, will you leave?"

"Gladly."

He took a bite, chewed, and swallowed. "Satisfied?"

"Yes. Now finish it. We don't have enough to waste." With that she stomped away, leaving him to his miserable self.

Damn it! Dion paced along the beach. Could things be any worse? He checked the empty expanse of ocean for what seemed like the umpteenth time. The *Treasure* moved farther and farther away with each passing minute.

Damn.

He picked up a rock and threw it at the horizon.

It didn't help.

His other problem was just as frustrating. The *Treasure* was gone, in the hands of a thief. And somehow, someone he knew had helped that happen. There was a traitor among them. One of these people, these friends, these... It could only be one of them who told the pirates about the second GPS transmitter. He hadn't decided to place it until after setting sail.

Another rock sailed out over the water, landing with a plop and disappearing. He should be doing something. He should be doing his job. The idea of pounding whoever betrayed him to within an inch of their life wasn't leaving much room for anything else at the moment. The problem was, he didn't know who the informant was.

Mike? He couldn't believe it was Mike. He was a good agent and a workhorse when it came to getting a job done. Happy-go-lucky Aidan? His mind moved back to three months prior, on board that tanker. Aidan had saved the day then stayed at his side, staunching the flow of blood, until the helicopter flew Dion out to the hospital. To date, Aidan had done very little undercover work. He just didn't have the poker face for it. Dion had a hard time believing Aidan could pull off this type of subterfuge.

Roger had been his partner for ten years and was the closest friend Dion claimed. Roger had never blamed Dion for Mary's death. He could have. Hell, he should have. He and Mary had only been dating a short time, but it had been serious from the start.

Roger's friendship meant a lot to Dion. Even with Mary's death, he'd stayed with Dion at the hospital until he'd been airlifted back home.

That only left one person. Claire. He glanced at her. Could he be that wrong in his judgment? She just didn't seem to fit the profile. She was trying to fit into the yacht club, yet not carrying it off too well. She obviously cared for people. He'd seen that on multiple occasions.

His mind kept going back to that hour on board ship. Why had she been taken topside so much sooner than the rest of them. Had she looked relieved or guilty when he'd joined them? And she'd admitted to having been fed while they were confined.

All the stolen yachts had been owned outright. She certainly had access to information about who owned and who still owed on their boats. She didn't have access to the satellite data. Still, she was pretty enough and savvy enough to con someone in one of the agencies to check on it for her, or worse, give her access. It would certainly explain how she'd ended up on board. The knot on her head had been real enough, but some people would do a lot for the right kind of money. She'd said it herself. She needed the money.

He seriously doubted she could pull it off, though. She didn't seem to have a good enough handle on her emotions. And the...intimacy they'd shared...Dion hardened at the quick flash of memory...it had felt real. Although, he'd managed to woo women where necessary so that possibility had to be considered.

No. Claire as a mastermind was ridiculous. She just wasn't that heartless.

Seeing Mike and Aidan returning, he walked back, deciding that he had better start acting like a captain again, until he had a reason not to.

Claire watched Dion walk the beach, deep in thought. He glanced at her once then turned away. What was going on in his mind? She'd give him until Mike and Aidan returned. If he hadn't snapped out of it by then, she would tell Aidan what she had learned. Sitting far away from Roger, she kept an eye on both of them. Roger hadn't moved, except to sit up. The sandwich she'd thrown to him was gone. Beyond that, if the faraway look in his eyes was any indication, he appeared to be in some other world. He had the appearance of a haunted man, and she couldn't think of a better penance.

Before long, the scouts returned, grim shadows forecasting the lack of resources found. Dion walked up just as they reached Claire.

"Welcome back, boss," Aidan commented dryly.

"What did you find?" Dion asked, ignoring the comment.

"Not much," Mike said. "There's not much except scrub and sand on this Godforsaken island. Oh, and a couple of patches of these trees inland a ways. I don't think it will afford us any more protection than right here," Mike answered.

Claire covered her eyes, noting that the sun was well into its descent. "Are we going to have to sleep on the beach?"

"Not exactly. We started pulling loose scrub and tree branches to make a shelter, but we need help. We should be able to build a lean-to to sleep under."

"All right, let's get going on it," Dion said.

"What about food and water?" Claire asked, handing Aidan and Mike one of her gourmet peanut butter sandwiches, both of which were just about devoured before she got her next sentence out.

"We don't have enough to last more than a day."

"We'll worry about that later," Dion answered, not looking at her.

"But—" Claire tried to continue.

"First things first."

Since when is shelter more important than food and water? They'd never make it more than a day or two without water. Claire decided to pick her battles and remained silent.

Roger was close to catatonic, so they left him on the beach and headed inland to move the materials closer and build a shelter. Dion strode at such a fast pace that Claire had to run to catch up to him.

"Dion?"

He didn't answer.

"Dion!" she said more insistently, grabbing his arm to slow him down. Feeling the prickle of electricity shoot through her, she immediately let go.

He glanced sideways at her yet he kept going.

"What is wrong with you? You can't just ignore me."

"I can try," he muttered under his breath.

"What?"

"Nothing."

"Dion, I need to tell you. I overheard something on board the boat while we were being held captive."

That got his attention. He stopped, waiting for her to go on, but she let Mike and Aidan pass them and move out of hearing range before she continued.

"You suspect someone's feeding information to the pirates, right?" she asked.

"Maybe."

"Well, you're right. Dion, I don't know any good way to tell you this, but—Roger is the inside man."

Instead of the eye-opening epiphany she expected to see, the only perceptible response she got was a slight narrowing of his eyes. He stared at her, and still wouldn't say a word.

Why didn't he acknowledge what she'd just told him? She hurried on. "I overheard him talking to the leader of the gang.

They were right above me, must have been right beside the wheel house."

"What makes you think it was Roger?"

Finally. A response. "First, I smelled pipe smoke through the vent in my cabin." She blushed. "I mean, your cabin."

"That's not conclusive."

"I know. I listened through the vent. It was easy to distinguish his accent. And then, well—"

"Spit it out, Claire."

"Well, he said he didn't owe his allegiance to anyone, least of all the one who got his girl killed."

Dion blanched. Good. At least she got a reaction, but it didn't last long. The stone wall fell firmly back in place.

"Nice try, Claire," he said, his cold eyes matching the ice in his voice. "I'm not buying it."

He walked off, leaving her standing there, gaping. "Then who else knew about the tracking devices?" She had to yell to make sure she he heard her. "That's what that thing on your ceiling was, right?"

Dion didn't answer and, in fact, didn't even bother to acknowledge her statement.

Claire lagged far behind the men, trying to make sense of the conversation. It hadn't been a conversation, really. More like the death of a relationship in two sentences or less. He hadn't believed her. Not only that. He'd outright denied the possibility and called her a liar as if she was the one in the wrong here.

Seeing Aidan, Mike, and Dion all starting back her way with scrub and branches, she hurried past them, grabbed an equal amount and turned to follow them back to the beach, all the while reeling from Dion's unspoken accusation. If he didn't believe Roger was the traitor, then who did he think it could be?

Her forward momentum stopped. Could he possibly think she was the informant? She was breathing hard, whether from the exertion of pulling the brush or the realization that Dion might actually consider her a suspect, she didn't know. Slower now, she started out again, eventually joining the rest of them on the beach.

"We were about to come back for you, hon," Aidan said, taking the branches from her. "What took you so long?"

Looking askance at Dion, she couldn't think of a single thing to say. Her life had been turned upside down by this team, by Dion Gaetani most of all. Right now, talking to any of them was more than she could tolerate. So she simply stomped off to sit on the beach, away from all of them. Hugging her knees, it was her turn to sit and stare out at the water.

It took a while, but they finally got a makeshift shelter built. Dion searched the sky and found no clouds anywhere in sight. The sun, now almost set, wouldn't bother them any more tonight, so it seemed a moot point. Tomorrow they might need the shade, though. Rubbing at the small, healed incision in the underside of his arm, Dion wondered how long they would be on the island.

Roger joined them then. He still looked out of it, but it was good to see him up and about.

"You okay, buddy?" Dion asked.

"Right as rain."

The shadows under his eyes and the pallor of his skin said he was anything but.

"I know it was a long way in here, but you should have recovered by now." Dion put a hand on his friend's shoulder. Roger stiffened and moved away.

Dion frowned. Roger had never reacted this way to any part of an operation before. What the hell was going on?

Mike and Aidan grabbed bunches of scrub and started a fire. Once the sun went down, the air would chill quickly. Early evening was a quiet one, with all of them slowly moving closer to the fire as the night weather moved in. Claire made them each a sandwich, with only a half for her. The meager supplies were now officially depleted.

Dion watched as Aidan sat next to Claire and tried to give her part of his sandwich, but she shook her head and moved away.

Roger moved to the shelter without a word to anyone. Before long, exhaustion showed in all of their faces. Mike was next, followed by Claire. Aidan was quick to join her. Just like a puppy dog, it seemed. Dion remained by the fire, keeping watch with only his thoughts for company.

Sometime after midnight, the rain started, and he joined them under the shelter. Roger slept on the end, then Mike and Aidan, with Claire sandwiched between them, snuggled against Aidan to ward off the chill of the night. A burst of green lightning surged through him. Reminding himself of their earlier conversation, he clamped the lid on his jealousy. Tight. He had no relationship with Claire. Never could and never would have. He might as well get used to that right now.

Claire slipped away from the shelter quietly, careful not to disturb the sleeping men. Stretching, she tried to work out the kinks from her night on the hard sand. She brushed her wet khakis off. Sand seemed to have gotten everywhere. The rain had ended with the morning sun, but the night had been miserable. The shelter had dripped in a myriad of places. She hadn't been able to find a dry place to sleep. Aidan and Mike had tried to be as accommodating as possible. Still, they were all soaked by the time first light had broached the horizon.

Her arms reached upward to the sun god, praising its return, vowing her eternal gratitude.

Then a shadow loomed over her. Before she could scream, a hand clamped over her mouth.

"Shhhh."

Her heart hit the wall of her chest, and she used both hands to push it back inside her rib cage. Dion. It was only Dion.

"You'll wake the others."

"You scared me," she whispered through his hand.

"Sorry," he said off-handedly, releasing her.

He didn't sound too sorry to her. She scowled at him in answer, giving him a dose of his own medicine. Moving to the fire he had re-started, she reached out to ward off what little morning chill remained. Any coolness to the morning was quickly dissipating. The day already forecast excessive warmth.

Dion walked off, who knew where or why. Who cared, she thought sourly as she watched him go.

"Good morning, Claire."

Once again having to still her wild heart, she noticed Roger had taken the seat next to her and was warming himself by the fire.

"Right bad night that was, eh?" he continued.

Claire moved to the opposite side of the fire and glared at him. She didn't care that it gave her away. She refused to be anywhere near him.

His face took on a mask of pure malice, and fingers of apprehension trickled down her spine.

He took a moment to look around, then he quietly confirmed her suspicions. "He won't believe you if you tell him, you know."

She remained silent.

"Ah, so you already tried. And I'm right." He frowned. "But you've probably planted a seed that will complicate my life to no end. Buggers. First the pirates try to off me, then you make matters worse."

She picked up a stick and started to draw circles in the sand.

"Well, no matter. I'll be long gone before the possibility gets through his thick skull and becomes reality. There's nothing you can do to stop me, Claire, so don't even try."

She spoke then. "Why?"

"You wouldn't understand."

"It was an accident, Roger."

"He was in charge. He could have stopped it. He *should* have stopped it. Now, when it comes out that I'm the informant, he'll be ruined."

"How could that possibly ruin Dion?"

"Oh, not in the agency's eyes," he interrupted her. "In his own. It will haunt him the way Mary's death haunts me!"

"Her death preoccupies him, too. You see that."

"Not enough," he said, standing as he saw Dion approaching. He glanced at Claire. "Not nearly enough." Then he walked off toward the hill.

Before long, everyone was up and circled around the fire.

"What will we do for food?" Claire asked. "We don't know how long we'll be here."

"Not long," Dion supplied by way of an answer.

"You can't know that for sure," Claire said, frustrated over his reticence to search for food and water.

"Yes, Claire," Aidan supplied. "He can. Look." He pointed out across the water. A vessel sped toward the island. It was close enough, in fact, for her to see the red slash of the Coast Guard logo emblazoned on the side.

"How did you know?" she asked, turning to Dion.

In answer, he held up his arm to show the small scar.

"Transponder," he said, keeping his gaze on the cutter.

They watched as the cruiser slowed and came to a stop, then a zodiac hit the water to rescue them.

"A small GPS locating device inserted under his skin," Aidan filled in when Dion didn't elaborate. "It's a proximity device as well as a GPS. Dion didn't just plant two transmitters on the schooner. He planted three. He didn't tell any of us about the third one until last night. Anyhow, when Dion was physically separated from the third unit on the *Treasure*, a signal went out that sent the other half of this operation into action, zeroing in on our location. We got lucky. The pirates deposited us on the island we thought they would. Otherwise, we could have been here for a day or two more."

Scowling now, she looked back at Dion. "And you couldn't tell me? You must have enjoyed listening to me bellyache about the need for food and water."

Claire got up and walked to the water's edge as fast as the sand would allow her to. Her shoulders slumped. He really must hate her.

Aidan came up and put an arm around her shoulders. "Don't worry, hon. He'll get his head out of his ass sooner or later," he said loudly enough for Dion to hear.

"I don't think I'll bother to wait," she answered just as loudly, slightly mollified to see Dion's scowl deepen.

Before long, they were making good speed across the Pacific Ocean, following a faint signal from the *Treasure*. Dion was grateful for whatever instinct caused him to put a third locator on board. He could only pray now that they would get to the schooner before the pirates started hacking away at her, changing her, prepping her for resale on the black market. Their speed was greater than the *Treasure's*. Dion estimated it would take a day to catch them. All he could do now was wait and see. And hope.

Turning from the scope tracking his boat, he saw Claire sitting out in the wind and sun, a mug of coffee in her hands. Funny. After the time on the island, he figured she'd be ensconced in a bunk, huddled under blankets trying to catch up on sleep and keep warm.

He had to admire her for the choice to be outdoors. It would be his, too. Scowling, he remembered she was a suspect. One that he didn't seem to be able to stay away from. Dion grabbed a cup of coffee from the nearby pot and went outside.

She watched as he approached, her face as blank as someone who'd been trained to keep emotion hidden. Maybe she was better than he thought at masking.

"We need to talk about what's going to happen," he said.

"So talk."

"We won't be able to plan the capture until we see what we're up against. One thing I do know, though. When we reach shore, you stay with me until we've got the pirates in custody."

"Keeping your enemy near, are you?" Claire shook her head. "I'd prefer to go back to San Diego as soon as we dock."

"That's not going to happen until we get this all straightened out, Claire."

"Because I'm a suspect."

His lips tightened. "Just stay by Roger or I until the capture is over, okay?"

"Stay with Roger—the spy. Sure. Whatever you say, Dion. It's your op."

"So I can keep you *safe*," he countered.

"I can keep myself safe. Answer me!" she said angrily. "Am I a suspect?"

He paused then confirmed it for her. "Yes."

She turned away, giving him only the quickest glimpse of the sheen of tears.

Damn. He hated tears.

"Claire—" Dion stopped himself. There was nothing he could say.

"Go away."

He stood there a moment, pangs of regret slicing through the wall around his heart.

"Please, just go away." She jumped up before he could move, pushed past him, and headed below.

CHAPTER FIFTEEN

The little bay was easy to miss, hidden by an outcropping of rocks that seemed to have no break. As the cruiser passed by from a distance, a narrow opening gave them a glimpse into a tiny natural cove and a village beyond. There were two boats in the harbor. One showed visible signs of activity onboard. The *Treasure* sat calmly in the bay, peaceful and apparently unchanged. A light fog had rolled in, offering Dion and the crew cover, with opportunities here and there to see what they were up against.

Claire sat tensely at the back of the salon while the team of agents planned the attack. Three teams were needed, so everyone but a skeleton crew would be involved. Team Alpha, led by Mike, would go first, moving up the coast, circling around to block any chance of exits via land. Once they were in place, teams Bravo and Delta would move in. Delta, under Aidan's leadership, would go in underwater to incapacitate anyone on the *Treasure* or the other boat. Bravo, led by Dion and Roger would move in to take the leader, Hawk.

Hawk. Aidan had finally come to her last night and asked her about what she knew. He'd been visibly shaken at her accusations but had taken the information about the leader to Dion. Claire had heard them in furious, low-voiced discussion. As it ended, Aidan stomped out red-faced, leaving Dion deeply scowling when he headed to the wheelhouse a while later.

Now here she was. It wasn't too hot this morning, yet the smell of adrenalin permeated the air like heat waves in a desert. She watched in fascination as the men prepared. Very little conversation went on, just a lot of activity. Guns were broken down, checked, re-assembled and ammunition loaded. Microphones and ear buds were tested, vests fitted.

"Try this on."

She jumped as Dion came up behind her. Turning, she saw him holding a sleeveless jacket that looked like a thin, black life vest.

"It should fit you."

Taking hold, she almost dropped it. It was heavier than she'd imagined.

"Bullet-proof?"

"Bullet-resistant. Don't take any chances."

Wide-eyed, she tried it on. The fact that it was too big was immediately apparent. Shaking his head, Dion left, returning shortly with another one. This one fit much more snugly.

She stood there, arms out to each side, while he adjusted the straps to fit her. Anger, sorrow, and yearning mixed together to make a pain cocktail that was almost too much for her heart to bear. He was so close, bending over now, concentrating on the task. His hair smelled different. He must have used someone else's shampoo. Still, the scent of him blended with the shampoo, all sea salt and sun…it was too heady to resist.

"Turn, please."

As she did, his fingers brushed her neck, and a shiver trailed down to the tip of her spine. She could feel the instant throb. Her nipples became tight with desire, and she was grateful the vest covered her.

Dion paused. He'd apparently felt her shudder. Stoically, Claire held her arms rigid and her face forward, willing her body to obey. She failed miserably as her body started to shake. She didn't want to react to his nearness, didn't want to hurt, didn't want to love…

She closed her eyes as the word popped into her head, recognizing the truth in it. She loved him. She shouldn't. He had hurt her. Hell, he was hurting her now and would continue to do so if she let him. Apparently, falling for the wrong type of guys was her destiny. Only this one would end up hurting far worse than that other one had. This one felt like it might kill her.

Just then, Dion pulled tightly on a strap, causing her to jump.

"Hurt?"

"No," she gulped, afraid to say anything more than that, afraid to even look at him. She had to get out of here. Quick.

"We done?"

"Yes. I think the fit is good."

"Fine. I'll be on deck."

"No. Stay below until we're ready to board the Zodiac. We're too close to shore. And keep quiet."

"Certainly, *Captain*," she sputtered, moving swiftly and quietly away. Once in the hallway, she wiped and errant tear from her cheek.

Aidan was in the galley when she entered. "What's wrong, love?"

"Nothing." She turned to go, but his arm stopped her.

"Come on, hon. I've come to know you better than that. What did the bastard do to hurt you now?"

"Nothing. He didn't do a damn thing, okay?" Hitting the table with her fist, she slumped into the seat next to him.

"Ah, finally figured out you've fallen in love with him, have you?"

Placing her head in her hands, she leaned over until her elbows met knees, letting the misery wash over her. Aidan's arms gently pull her into an embrace, and he spoke words meant to soothe. She couldn't hear them through the roar pounding through her chest like waves on a beach. She instinctively clutched him as her silent tears fell.

She didn't see Dion pause in the doorway, observing them.

Aidan did, though, and set his jaw in a firm line. He'd have this out with the man sooner or later. He knew Claire loved Dion, and he suspected Dion had strong feelings for Claire. He wasn't about to let him push her away like this. These two needed each other.

First things first, though. They had a job to do.

"Time to go," a scowling Dion said, then left.

"I'm so sorry, Aidan." She pulled her head away, wiping the tears as best she could.

"No worries, angel. I've got strong shoulders," he smiled. "We'd better get going. We'll finish this later, okay?"

Claire hedged. "We'd better go," was all she said.

They left the zodiac in a hidden cove of the rocks. Dion led the way quickly, but minutes of scrambling over the rocky beach felt like hours to Claire. Eventually, they reached a small cleft in the breakfront that allowed them an uninterrupted view of the village and bay. They waited there for a signal that teams Alpha and Delta were in place. Claire settled onto a rock for a much-needed rest, doing shoulder rolls and neck circles, anything to dislodge the knots of apprehension that dug painfully into her back.

It was midday according to the sun. Climbing carefully up to the edge, she peeked ashore. There was activity all over the place. The village itself seemed to be in a process of rebirth. In one section, new cottages were under construction, small houses made of thatch and stucco. Another area seemed more like a war zone, with a graveyard of weather-beaten materials haphazardly strewn around. Yet, here and there, a wall stood testament to the fact that this had been a part of the village at some point.

The *Treasure* was anchored and looked untouched. Good. No matter what its master was like, it would be a shame to see the schooner modified.

Glancing at Dion, she could see his eyes were riveted on the bay. The schooner wasn't the only boat, and Claire could see that most of the activity seemed centered on the blue yacht, slowly being turned to white except for a small line of the original color right at the waterline. This must be the yacht that had been stolen just before the festival, she thought. Thankfully, it appeared to have distracted them from disguising their newest acquisition.

Abruptly, she was yanked down. Her heart in her throat, she glared at Dion.

"What the—?"

Dion clamped a hand over her mouth. "Keep out of sight!" he whispered urgently in her ear.

"I was!" she said through clenched teeth.

"Shhh!" Dion held his hand up to his ear, listened, then passed a "ready" signal to the team. "Stay close to me," he said to Claire.

Still near her ear, his breath sent ripples of need through her body, overshadowing the waves of irritation that preceded them. He moved away and Claire took a deep breath to clear her head.

Dion climbed over the last set of outcropped rocks, crossed the short spit of sand and slipped into the water by the dock that butted up against the promontory on which they stood. Claire followed, grateful for the tropical temperature when her body shook with the realization that danger crept toward her again. As part of this stealth mission to capture thieves, she was an untrained liability to the team. Hell, she didn't even have a weapon to protect herself with. Not that she could shoot if she needed to.

They moved slowly, silently, underneath the dock, stopping frequently to reconnoiter. Suddenly, Dion's hand came up in a motion to be silent, and Claire froze, along with everyone else. As he pointed upward, she heard the footsteps. People on the dock! And they were speaking English.

"How much longer do you think it will take?" The man's heavy accent made him difficult to understand.

"Another day, two at the most." This voice was very distinct. She knew it. Hawk, the leader of the pirates! So close. Claire concentrated hard to hear over the pounding in her ears.

"Is the buyer lined up?"

"*Si*," the other man replied. "We are to meet him in four days time."

"You'll need at least two days sailing time to get to the transfer point."

"*Si*."

"Then we'll be done tomorrow. We have no choice."

"*Si*."

"How goes the reconstruction?"

"Well, *mi hijo*. Very well. The West end will be completed in another two weeks, and we can begin to clear the mud and rubble away on the south end."

"Good, Manuel. You've done well. But there's still much to do, eh?"

"*Si, si*."

As the footsteps echoed through the pilings and their voices faded away, Dion used his arms to rise up briefly, peering over the dock edge. The man with the accent, Manuel, headed toward the village, but Hawk entered the small building at the edge of the pier.

Good. It was accessible without being seen.

"You four," Dion said as he pointed, "go for the one called Manuel. He seems to be second in command. The rest of you, follow me. We'll take the leader."

Checking again, seeing no reason to hold back, Dion led his group out of the water and to the shelter of the building that Hawk had entered. Dion gestured to two of his men, then to the main door of the building. He, Roger and Claire worked their way around to the back door. Quickly glancing over a windowsill, he could see Hawk bent over what appeared to be a rug on the floor. Turning back, he pointed at Roger, then down at the ground, mouthing the words.

"Keep her safe."

Rounding the corner of the building, Dion crept onto the porch. He turned the doorknob as silently as possible, but the building was old and everything squeaked, including the door. He knew the noise would alert Hawk.

"Go. Go. Go," he said urgently into his mike. Throwing the door open, he rushed in. The room that Hawk had been in just thirty seconds before was now empty.

"What the hell?"

Where was the pirate? Reaching for a crumpled corner of the rug on the floor, he yanked it back and saw the trap door.

"Shit!" Not waiting for a reply, he threw the trap door open then moved quickly aside so he wouldn't end up a target to anyone hidden in the darkness below.

Jumping through the hole, he found himself in some sort of cage that led from the trap door to the edge of the building. He crawled to the end and cursed again at the locked wire door barring him from going any further.

"Hell!" He backed up with as much speed as his throbbing knee would allow him to crawl in the small quarters. When he jumped up through the trap door into the room, his men were there, including Roger.

"Where's Claire?"

Roger rubbed his head. "Sorry, partner. He came up on me before I had a chance to react. Knocked me silly for a few seconds. By then it was too late.

Dion froze. Hawk had Claire.

He stopped breathing. Stopped thinking about the op. Hawk had Claire.

The words ran through his mind over and over. Time slowed as his focus shifted to this new threat. It was more than a threat. It was his past colliding with his present. A flash of oozing red blood—no! It wouldn't happen that way. Not again. Not to Claire.

Dion rushed outside. "Which way did he go?"

"I'm not sure. I think that way." Roger pointed to the trees.

"Stay here. Wrap things up."

Dion raced to the tree line, favoring his bad leg, and crashed through the underbrush. He could hear Hawk ahead. The man didn't bother to hide his retreat. Claire must have slowed him down considerably, because Dion soon caught up to him.

"Stop!"

In the midst of pushing aside another banana palm, Hawk froze and turned slowly back around. Claire stood in front of him. Dion saw the glint of metal in the pirate's hand.

"Don't think I won't shoot her, agent."

It was Malaysia all over again. Only this time, it wasn't just his friend and co-worker.

This time it was Claire.

He moved out into the open and slowly turned the gun up and away from his target. With both hands in the air, he spoke. "You can't get away, Hawk."

"Maybe, maybe not. Put the gun down, agent."

Dion bent to set the gun down in front of him.

"No. Toss it far into the brush."

"Hawk—"

"Just do it, agent, or I *will* hurt your girlfriend."

"All right." He started to toss his weapon, but a shot rang out first. As if in slow motion, he watched Claire crumple to the ground.

"No!" he shouted, firing at Hawk, hitting his shoulder. The force threw him back, and away from Claire.

Dion ran over, kicked the gun away, and leveled his own at the face of the pirate. His hands shook with the effort to control himself.

Hawk raised his hands in surrender.

"You win, agent," he said quietly. "I give up."

At that moment, Roger clambered out of the bushes into view.

"Watch Hawk," Dion yelled, then bent to check on Claire. She was out cold. Blood oozed from a wound near her shoulder. A lot of blood.

"Medic. Get the medic here," Dion yelled into his mike. At the same time, he reached into a pouch on his vest and tore open a steri-pack. As he applied compression to the wound, Claire moaned and began to thrash about.

"Be still, Claire," he urged, knowing she probably couldn't hear him. He forced his voice to calm and lowered his body so she could hear. "Be still, sweetheart. You're going to be okay. Just lie quiet. I'm here. I'll take care of you."

Her eyes opened, and Dion almost cried out in relief. He began to stroke her hair with his free hand. "Hell of a way to get me to talk to you."

Claire didn't answer, and her eyes quickly closed again.

"What the *hell* were you doing?" Dion stared daggers at Roger. "You could have killed her!"

"I thought you needed some help."

"So you shot Claire?" Anger coursed through Dion.

"I wasn't aiming for her. I missed."

"You've never missed a shot in your life. You pick now? You pick Claire to take that chance with? I thought I told you to stay back at the village."

"It seems to me it was a good thing I didn't, wasn't it, partner? You'd be in a world of hurt right now if I hadn't distracted Hawk."

"Roger, if Claire doesn't survive—"

The medic showed up then, and Dion's attention reverted back to Claire. "We'll settle this later," he said over his shoulder.

Once the medics had Claire and Hawk stabilized, they marched back to the center of town. As badly as he needed to go with Claire, Dion knew he had to mop up what remained of this operation. So he sent Aidan with her instead. He watched as the helicopter took off then turned to his first good look at the villagers. Hawk's wound turned out to be minor, so they handcuffed him like any prisoner. The people of the village didn't appear scared. In fact, it was just the opposite. They seemed upset. Some actually cried. For Hawk? What kind of hold did he have over this village anyhow?

As they waited for the other teams to bring in the rest of the thieves, Dion spoke to Hawk. "You don't fit the profile for a criminal. In fact, you seem to command some respect among these people."

"Yes."

"Why steal boats then?"

"Check it out," Hawk said, gesturing with his head.

Dion did, seeing the village as more than an op site to be analyzed. Situated on a hill sloping down to the bay, it had been terraced to allow for huts and small houses to be built. A few of them appeared brand new. Some were still in the process of being constructed. Others, though, showed signs of devastation, some with only one or two ragged walls remaining. Closer to the bay, a communal washbasin and drying lines had been constructed, recently by their appearance.

"What happened?" Dion asked.

"This village was all but destroyed by a mudslide." It seemed, for a moment, as if a shadow passed over his eyes, but it quickly disappeared.

"What's your tie to this village?" Dion asked. "You are not from here."

"No," Hawk agreed. "My wife was." He was silent for a moment before continuing. "No one would help to rebuild, not the government or the philanthropists. Trust me. I tried. I thought I had some connections and made all the political and social rounds. Felt like I was prostituting myself, begging for help. I spent two months circulating in Washington and elsewhere and I couldn't secure one dime of funding. No one is interested in a Mexican village so small it's not even on the map. So I took matters into my own hands."

Reaching to resettle his injured arm, Hawk continued, quiet yet resolute, "You haven't caught a thief, agent. You've set in motion the death of a village."

Dion remained quiet.

"Do you know what they call this village, Agent Gaetani?" Hawk asked.

"No."

"*Tierra Bonita del Dios*. Beautiful Land of God." Squinting against the sun, Hawk continued. "Now it will never again get the chance to live up to its name."

Dion looked around. Where was Roger?

"If you're searching for your loyal partner, he's gone."

"Gone?" Dion repeated.

"Yep. Ran as soon as your back was turned."

Why would Roger run? It made no sense.

"Where?"

"Who knows? Probably the quickest route out of here."

"Just out of curiosity, why'd you sabotage the Zodiac. You've never done that before."

Hawk shrugged. "I knew you'd make it to land. And I wanted to send a message to our spy, remind him there are ramifications to what he does."

Frustrated now, Dion tried to analyze the situation. Suddenly, the proof he needed hit him like a sledgehammer. Claire had known about the third GPS unit. She'd asked what that was on the ceiling of his cabin. Yet Hawk and his men had not known. Claire hadn't told them. He clutched the gun in his hand tighter. She had tried to tell him and he'd refused to listen.

Roger had betrayed him.

Not Claire.

And now she was on her way to the hospital because of it.

Dion looked at Hawk. "Is he—"

Hawk sighed and stared out at the water a bit before he answered.

"You know, what I did may not have been right, but at least I had the right reasons. Your partner, now, there's a true criminal if I ever saw one. I asked him once how he felt about stabbing you in the back."

Dion ground his teeth. "And?"

"Tell me, agent. Did you really murder his girl?"

Dion's blood ran ice cold and white hot at the same moment as everything crashed into place. He saw the opportunity, the motive, all the little comments that should have sent up a red flag.

He started to pace. "I can't believe I fell for it."

"Yes. Hits you where it hurts, doesn't it?" Hawk asked. "Don't be too hard on yourself." He frowned. "It's easy to be deceived by someone you care for. Trust me. I know."

But Dion wasn't listening. He had to get to Claire. To convince her he believed her. He knew she wasn't the traitor.

First, he had a criminal to catch. Roger would pay for this betrayal. Dion would make sure of that.

He searched the beach and called Mike over.

"Watch him," Dion called over his shoulder. "I'll be back."

Dion took off at a run for the promontory where the zodiac waited. There were very few men on the cruiser, but he knew

Roger wasn't stupid enough to try that. There was, though, enough gas in the zodiac to get him well down the coast, someplace he could get lost in. If he didn't catch the man now, he might never find him.

He raced across the dock and onto the shoal, rounding the rocks just in time to see Roger push the zodiac out and jump aboard. Dion launched himself over the rough ground then stumbled, his knee screaming.

He righted himself, then stumbled again.

Reaching a point where he felt he had the best advantage, he stopped and sighted in on the zodiac.

One bullet. Two. Three.

It took five bullets, but he finally got enough holes in the raft to see it deflating. Moving carefully, he reached the water's edge before Roger made it back to shore as the raft sank beneath him. Dion stood, gun ready, as his partner crawled out of the water and sat on a nearby rock.

"Why'd you do it?" Dion asked.

"You know why."

"Because of Mary?"

"Yes, you bastard."

"She made a rookie mistake, acted on her own. I couldn't have stopped her, Roger. I was too far away."

"You should have known better than to even take her."

"You talked me into it," Dion countered.

"And you were always better at sizing up agent abilities. You were the boss. You should have overridden me."

Dion paused. "Maybe."

"No maybe about it. And now she's gone. I want you to pay." Roger shifted his position.

"And Claire?"

"She was a bonus."

"A what?"

"A bonus. I could see you were attracted to her right from the start."

Dion straightened as the realization hit him. "*You* hit her over the head!"

"Yes," Roger answered, his voice puffed up with pride. "She provided a very nice distraction for you in case I made some stupid blunder. And, in the end, I knew I could cause you the same pain as you caused me."

"You intended to kill her?"

"I intended to find a way for you to do that. You're so good at it."

Dion's face went red. He'd bought into it, damn it, and Claire had almost paid the ultimate price.

"So, partner," Roger said, standing up. "This is where it all ends, eh?"

"Not for you. You'll rot in hell ten times over first."

"No, I won't. Jail's not for me."

With that Roger thrust upward, knocking Dion's gun hand off the mark. An uppercut to the chin came next. Dion went flying, dazed. By the time he found his senses...and his gun, Roger was well ahead of him, heading for the bay where the boats were moored.

Dion caught him just as he reached the water's edge. He grabbed his shirt and hauled Roger around until fist met chin. Roger reeled but didn't fall. Coming back at Dion, he feinted to the left, then tried for a right upper cut. Dion had sparred too many times with the man to fall for that. He ducked at the right moment then sucker punched his ex-partner in the stomach.

"That's for lying to me," he ground out as Roger fell to the sand. Panting, Dion still stood, ready for any move. As Roger stood, Dion didn't wait, throwing all his strength into another blow to the chin. Blood spattered in an arc as Roger went down like a heap of Jello.

"And that," he said, "is for Claire."

CHAPTER SIXTEEN

Claire floated in and out of consciousness. She was in a helicopter, en route to the hospital. She turned, searching for Dion, but found Aidan instead.

He smiled broadly and winked at her even as he continued to talk on the phone.

"Yes, we bagged the leader. We got the whole gang." There was a pause before he continued. "Yes, sir. The authorities here have agreed to hold him pending the outcome of extradition hearings."

He patted her hand as he listened.

"We should be back tomorrow night, the next day after at the latest," he said to the person on the other end of the line. "We'll be in the office for debriefing as soon as possible, Chief."

Another pause.

"Yes, sir. I'll pass that along." Finally, he hung up.

"You've got cell coverage?" she croaked. "Here?"

"Spy phone," he said with a crooked smile. "How are you feeling?"

"Like I've been shot."

"Yeah," he said. "Hurts like hell, doesn't it?"

"Yes. Um, Aidan?"

"Yeah, darlin'?"

"Dion—"

"He had to stay back in the village, to finish everything up." I'm sure he'll catch up to us at the hospital."

She didn't know how else to say it, except straight out. "I don't want to see him, Aidan. I just want to go home."

"Well, let's get you fixed up first, Claire. We'll sort the rest out later."

"No, Aidan. Promise me you'll keep him away."

"Claire, I really think you need to give him a chance. Once this op's over and things calm down, he'll see how badly he screwed up."

One of the medics spoke up then. "She needs to rest. We're going to give her something to dull the pain, and it will make her drowsy."

She watched as he injected something into her IV.

"Promise me," she said again to Aidan, gripping his hand.

"All right. I promise. But I don't have to like it."

She heard him in a fog as she succumbed to the drugs.

Dion showed up at the hospital a few hours after Claire had been taken into surgery. He'd kept up an almost running dialogue with Aidan and knew that she was out of danger. The bullet had been removed with no permanent damage. Claire would be fine.

Aidan met him at the nurse's station and pulled him into the empty waiting room.

"How is she?" Dion asked.

"In recovery, sleeping it off."

"Which way?" Dion started down the hall, but Aidan held him back.

"She doesn't want to see you, bud."

"What?" he almost shouted.

"Shhh. Keep your voice down."

"What do you mean, she doesn't want to see me?"

"Can you blame her? You kidnapped her and kept her against her will."

"Yes." He hung his head. "I didn't have much of a choice."

"Then you screwed her."

His head came up. "Now wait a minute."

"And you followed that up by accusing her of being a spy."

Dion winced and stopped trying to interrupt Aidan.

"How the hell did you expect her to react?"

Dion sat down. "I don't know. You're right. I really screwed it up. And almost got her killed in the process."

"Yep," Aidan said. "So what are you going to do about it?"

Standing, he walked to the window and stared out at the darkness. Finally, Dion turned back to Aidan. "Nothing. She's got a right to make her own decisions. A right to be in control." Dion walked away then. There really was nothing else he could say. Everything Aidan said was true. And there wasn't a damn thing Dion could do to fix it.

The door made no sound as it opened. He walked in carefully, silently, and moved to the bedside. He saw the IV tubes, the oxygen, her bandaged arm and shoulder. Even with all that, she looked beautiful. He reached out to touch her hair but stopped himself, his own words echoing in his mind. She had a right to be in control. She'd earned that.

Grimly, Dion turned around and walked out.

"Take care of her, Aidan."

"I will."

Dion left the hospital, then, and walked out of Claire's life.

Two days later with her arm in a sling, an aide wheeled Claire out of the hospital and into a smiling Aidan's waiting SUV.

She drew in a breath of fresh air. It felt so good to be outside. She'd missed it.

"I've had the authorities call ahead to the embassy, so they know we're coming," Aidan told Claire. "You'll have to wait while they clear your passport, and that could take some time. The jerks won't start the process until you arrive."

"Thank you, Aidan. I appreciate everything you've done," she said quietly.

"I'll be able to stay until I know you're going to be okay. Then I have to catch my flight back to London. I'm overdue, and the chief is starting to chafe." He chuckled.

Claire smiled at the play on words. "I understand. I'm grateful you can take me this far."

"Claire?"

"Just let it go."

"You two are good for each other."

"We never had a chance. C'mon, Aidan. Think it through. We're from two different worlds, and it's better off left that way."

They traveled in silence, and before long, Claire was settled in at the embassy to wait for clearance to fly home to San Diego, where she hoped to pick up what was left of her life. She needed to focus there. Nothing else mattered, at least, not anymore.

"Is there anything else I can do to help, Claire?"

"No. You've done more than you should have already. I'll be fine."

Taking her hand, he drew her into his embrace.

"You sure, hon? I can go to bat for you with your boss, make him see the error of his ways."

"No." She pushed away from him with her good arm. "I'll take care of myself."

"Well, at least let me talk to Dion."

"Absolutely not." Claire sighed. "It would never have worked anyhow. I refuse to be part of the world you all live in. You can't trust anyone. If I've learned anything, it's that I no longer want to live like that."

Giving her a hard look, he finally relented. "All right, Claire." He slipped a card into her hand. "Here's my work, home, and cell number in England. You need anything, *ever*, you give me a call, okay? Collect or otherwise."

Damn. The tears were going to start again. She gulped them back as she handed him a folded piece of paper.

"Could you give this to Dion for me?"

"Sure."

She saw the sympathy and concern apparent in his face.

"I guess I fell in love with the wrong guy, didn't I?"

"I guess you did. Hmmmm. Maybe there's hope for me yet," he said, smiling. And then, with a quick peck on her cheek, he was gone. Claire laughed in spite of the tears.

CHAPTER SEVENTEEN

On board the *Treasure*, Dion threw himself into getting the schooner back in order. Mike stayed to help, since their flight out didn't leave until morning. Thankfully, they'd gotten to the vessel before any major alterations happened.

Hawk and his crew had been turned over to the Mexican authorities. The village men would be dealt with locally, but extradition proceedings had been started for Hawk. The thefts had occurred in international waters. However, since the stolen boats were registered in U.S. ports, they would try their best to get him to San Diego for trial.

Sitting on deck, he and Mike ate dinner and kept watch over the quiet village. Beyond the devastation, it really was a picturesque little town. A bit rustic, but that was a small trade off for the view of the bay.

"Claire's okay?" Mike asked.

Dion hesitated before answering. "Yes."

"When's she going home?"

"Day after tomorrow, I hear. They want to make sure her anemia improves before they send her home. Turns out she lost more blood than we thought."

"No long term effects?"

"No."

Mike took another swig of his beer. "You going after her?"

"Nope."

"Boss?"

"Leave it alone."

With a disgusted look, Mike got up and grabbed Dion's plate, muttering to himself.

"What did you say?" Dion asked.

"Nothing except that you are one stubborn son of a bitch, boss." With that, he went below and didn't return.

Dion tossed a rope onto a hook. It held for a moment, then dropped to the deck. This boat is as out of sorts as I am, he thought. He checked the cove for any activity, but all was quiet. The anchor was in place, and he could give in to his exhaustion. Lifting his bad leg to the railing, he grabbed the rigging for balance. He was more tired than he could ever remember, even more than after that storm they'd come through.

He thought of Claire. She had amazed him with her ability to deal with Mother Nature's fury. She'd turned out to be quite an able seaman. Sea-woman. All woman.

Just not his.

Not now.

Not ever.

His life didn't leave room for relationships. Hell, he spent so much time undercover, he wasn't even sure anymore who he really was. It had never felt old, though, until now.

Dion finally gave in and headed below. Reaching his cabin, he almost didn't want to go in. The last time he'd slept here, he hadn't been alone. He opened the door and saw the refinished desk. He ran his hands over it, admiring the beauty. She'd turned his grandfather's inscription into a focal point on the desk. His hands traced the carved words. *My Treasure, My Love.* He stared for a long time at the bunk bed they had shared. Finally, he walked away and grabbed a bunk in the main cabin, trying unsuccessfully to get some sleep. They would be flying to England tomorrow for debriefing, and he needed to have his wits about him.

Waiting for the wheels of bureaucracy to turn gave Claire altogether too much time to think. She'd been here for hours, stuck in this little room. It was amazing how long it took the American Consulate to verify a passport that she didn't have in her possession. Short-handed, the undersecretary had told her. Budget issues. Apparently, that theme carried through to the décor also.

When Aidan had brought her to the embassy, she'd been interviewed, then placed in this sparse little waiting room and told not to leave. More like a holding cell or interrogation room, she thought, tracing the letters carved into the metal table. *La vida loca*, the crazy life. Appropriate. Her life had certainly felt like that the past couple of weeks.

She squirmed for what must be the hundredth time in the uncomfortable plastic seat, wishing her heart could be as hard and unyielding as the chair.

She missed Dion. And wanted to hate him, all at the same time. But she couldn't. The man was only doing his job. She'd been the one who screwed up, letting her heart get involved.

The door to her little cell opened, and she jumped. It was the undersecretary.

"You've been cleared to return to the states, Miss Saunders," he said. "Thank you for your patience."

"I'm real pleased, son. Real pleased," the voice boomed.

"Thank you, Director."

"You did good, catching that pirate and his gang."

"Yes, sir."

"Did a lot for the agency, too. Yes, there are a lot of people real happy with us right now. A lot of people. That'll mean some good funding for future ops."

A lot of people were happy. Just not Dion. Things weren't the same. He'd filed his reports, attended debriefings, all the normal stuff that went hand in hand with closing out a covert operation, but he was on automatic.

"How are you feeling about Roger's duplicity?" the director asked.

Dion tensed. "He can rot in that Mexican jail for life as far as I'm concerned."

"They don't want him and have agreed to extradite him to England. I believe the paperwork is already on its way. He should be home within the month and will stand trial here. They'll put him away for a very long time, I'm sure."

"Good." Dion slumped back in his chair. Even the satisfaction of Roger's long incarceration couldn't flip his mood.

"You okay, son?" Director Ecker asked, getting Dion's attention. "You seemed a million miles away."

No. Only a few thousand. "I'm fine. Just tired, I guess." *Tired is as good a way of putting it as any.*

"Well, catch up on your sleep, man. We've got a back load of cases to get to and, for right now, a blank check to fund them."

For the first time that he could remember, the thought of another op didn't thrill Dion. He logged out and went home to his apartment, jet lagged and in dire need of a shower. Turning the key in the lock he knew that, even as tired as he felt, he still he didn't want to go in. It would be exactly as he left it, maybe a little cleaner since he had a lady come in twice a month. Black leather furniture, wood floors and uncluttered surfaces would all gleam. It always took him a while to get used to it after living aboard the schooner. Somehow, he knew, this time it would take a lot longer.

He opened the door to no surprises. A stack of mail sat on the raised kitchen counter, the sink was free of dirty dishes. It was pretty much as he left it.

Dark, sterile, and lonely.

Disgusted with himself, he headed for the bedroom and threw his duffle onto the bed. After peeling off his clothes, he stepped into a hot shower.

It didn't help.

So he went downstairs to the gym and spent the next hour and a half driving his body almost beyond endurance, at least as far as his knee would allow. He was back in a brace after getting a stern lecture from the orthopedist about how close he'd come to permanent injury.

Exercise didn't help any more than the shower had, and now he needed another.

Back in his apartment, he mixed himself a drink—a strong one. Nothing worked. He felt too keyed up. Finally, he picked up the phone. A sleepy voice answered.

"Can I come over?"

"Uh, sure. Come on."

"Thanks. Be there in ten."

True to his word, Dion knocked on the apartment door eleven minutes after he'd hung up the phone. A still sleepy Aidan opened it, a full mug of coffee in his hand.

"Hey, boss. Come on in."

Dion followed him inside, closed the door, and stood there.

"Uh, want some coffee?" Aidan held up his cup.

"Sure." He handed a bottle of whiskey over. "Put some of this in it. On the rocks."

"Okay. So no coffee." Aidan left and came back momentarily with a glass filled with ice. He poured a healthy dose for Dion then handed it over.

"Want to sit down?"

"I don't know what I want. I'm not sure why I'm here." He sat down anyhow, staring at the gas fireplace Aidan had lit to ward off the chilly London night. Funny, it hadn't seemed so cold here when he'd left for San Diego.

"I am."

"What?"

"I'm sure why you're here."

"Really," Dion said. "You know something I don't?"

"Apparently," Aidan answered with a smile plastered across his face, finally showing signs of waking up.

"Okay, smart ass. Why don't you tell me why I'm here then?"

"We'll get to that. First, the agency seems pretty happy with us. How'd debriefing go for you?"

"Fine. No problem."

Aidan dug deeper. "How'd it feel?"

"What do you mean, how did it feel? It felt like every other debriefing."

A stillness filled the room as Dion thought the last statement through. It hadn't felt the same. He'd distanced himself from it more than ever before. There hadn't been any pleasure in completing this operation. In fact, what he'd done to the village felt pretty damn rotten.

"No, it didn't feel like the other briefings," he finally admitted. "It felt...hollow."

"Do you know why?"

"Because this criminal was doing the wrong thing for the right reason."

But was that all? This was the second operation in a row that hadn't gone according to plan. He didn't like it. Something gnawed at him.

"I was blinded to the fact that Roger was a traitor." Dion said.

"Hell, we all were. That's not your fault. No one could have figured that one out. He was a master at deception."

"Still, there were clues."

"Yes, there were. Remember, he wasn't always a traitor. Recent events turned him. That's why you trusted him so much. Because, right up until this mission, you could."

"I feel like I've lost my edge."

Aidan paused as if considering. "Does Mary's death still haunt you?"

"Not the way it did. I haven't had a nightmare since before we were captured onboard the *Treasure*. That's unusual in itself. They'd been occurring almost every night."

He remembered then the last thing he'd done before the takeover. He'd made love to Claire.

"You had some waking nightmares too, didn't you?"

"Yes, though none lately. I think..." he was quiet for a moment. "I think that making it through this operation without getting anyone killed may have helped that. Kind of a getting back on the horse type of thing, you know?"

"Yeah, maybe. I think Claire might have had something to do with how you feel, too."

"Claire?"

"You finally care about something, or someone, more than the past."

Dion had no answer for that. Gut churning, he stared into the fire.

Aidan changed tactics. "What are you going to do about work?"

"This business ages you, you know?"

"Yeah, I think I do."

"I'm starting to feel old. I'm tired of living in a world where I can't trust anyone."

"I think there's more to it than that," Aidan said.

"Okay, swami. Out with it. You're not going to let me off the hook until you've had your say."

"You're in love with Claire."

The sip of whiskey Dion had just taken went flying.

Aidan hooted with laughter. "Problem?"

"Shut up!" Dion said, ineffectively trying to wipe the droplets off the coffee table with a napkin. It took a few moments before he was under control again, having managed to wipe the booze off his leather jacket and test another sip.

He'd always been one to face the challenges put to him, but this one...was it true? His heart lurched. Was he in love with Claire? As soon as he asked himself the question, he knew the answer.

Yes.

And he'd pushed her away by not having faith in her.

Leaning forward, he set the glass down and put his face in his hands. "What the hell am I going to do? She'll never have me after the way I treated her."

Aidan got up and went to his desk, returning with a slip of paper.

"She gave this to me when I dropped her off. You didn't deserve to see it until now."

Unfolding the slightly crumpled paper, Dion saw a short note in a neat script. Funny, he'd never seen her handwriting before. There wasn't much to it, but it drove a stake into his heart.

Dion,

I love you. More than I thought it was possible to love. And that's the price I'll be paying for this little adventure for a long time to come. Still, I hope you find what brings you peace.

Claire

CHAPTER EIGHTEEN

San Diego International Airport, as busy as always, still managed to appear more like an upscale shopping mall than a travel destination. Claire's gate, of course, was at the very end of the concourse. By the time she'd walked its length to the main terminal, her shoulder ached like the devil and weariness had won the battle. She wanted to go home.

A good soak in the tub and about ten hours of sleep ought to help. She had no luggage, just a bag with a toothbrush and her pain medicine in it. TSA had confiscated her toothpaste, and she had just enough money for a taxi home.

As she walked out of the terminal intent on finding a cab, the bright sunlight caused her to miss the limousine that pulled up, at least until Mr. and Mrs. Seton stepped out.

Oh, great, This is all I need. Maybe they wouldn't notice her. Claire tried to step back out of the way, but it was too late.

"Claire!" Mr. Seton called, scurrying to her side, his wife right behind him.

"Mr. Seton? Mrs. Seton?" she said, turning from one to the other in confusion.

"Claire," Patricia Seton said with a smile. "Welcome home! You look—" She paused as she took in Claire's disheveled appearance, biting her lip as she appeared to search for the right phrase before continuing, "Well."

Claire ran her hands through her hair, which she knew needed a good wash, and scrutinized the khakis that hadn't seen an iron in days. Dion's t-shirt, and a well-used brown sweater one of the nurses had given her completed the ensemble.

I look well?

There was no need to respond, since the Setons wouldn't have heard her anyhow. They never spoke to her without an agenda on their minds. She prayed it didn't require anything from her for at least a couple of days since she desperately wanted to feel human again before she dealt with work.

Before she could think of a way to extricate herself, they each grabbed one of her arms and propelled her toward the limousine.

"Ouch!"

"Oh, dear," Mrs. Seton said, releasing Claire's arm. "I'm sorry about your injury. Does it hurt much?"

"Yes," Claire said through gritted teeth. She needed a pain pill.

"Well, time will make it all better. Now come, dear. We must hurry. We're almost late already."

"Late? Late for what?"

"Why, for the party, my dear."

"What party?" Claire demanded, confusion wiping all remnants of deference out of her voice.

"Why, the party for you. You're a hero, Claire, for stopping the pirates. Don't you know?"

Claire balked then, stopping right in the middle of the sidewalk, causing both Setons to whiplash as their momentum came to a sudden halt.

"I'm not going to *any* party!" she said vehemently.

"Of course you are, dear. It's all been arranged. And you don't have to lift a finger. We've even got a clean-up crew," Mrs. Seton said with a peacock's pride in her voice. Claire was certain the woman was most pleased with herself for having thought about that.

"How do you even know what happened?"

"Oh, a young man called and explained what happened. How horrible that you were knocked unconscious. You could have had a concussion. And you were shot? My, you have had an adventure."

"I guess you could call it that," she said. A flash of dark hair and unreadable eyes made the pain in her shoulder dim compared to the ache in her heart. She focused on Mrs. Seton. "What man called? Did you get his name? Who was he?"

"Oh, goodness. I can't remember his name at the moment."

"Aidan," Claire said, more of a statement than a question. It had to be Aidan that called.

"No, I don't think that was it. What was his name? Doug? Danny?"

Claire held her breath. "Dion?"

"Dion. That was it! A very...succinct young man. He wasn't much for conversation. He was, however, very clear about how helpful you were in the luring and capture of those nasty men."

Claire was stunned, which allowed the Setons to hustle her into the limo. Once settled, Mrs. Seton continued.

"Like I said, dear, he wasn't much for talking. He did say that you had a pivotal role in the capture of those thieves that have been preying on our poor friends. Do you know they only stole yachts from this harbor?"

George Seton patted his wife's hand. "We want to show our appreciation, Claire. So we decided to throw you a welcome home party."

If you want to show your appreciation, then give me a bonus or a pay raise, not some meaningless party that increases your visibility in the area but doesn't help me one whit.

"I don't want a party. I want a shower."

She saw the surprise register on their faces at her bluntness. She didn't care. She was tired. Couldn't they see that? Her shoulder hurt, and she needed sleep. Lots of sleep.

It was like they didn't even hear her.

"You look just fine. And there are so many people waiting to greet you."

Claire had had quite enough of their posing. She wanted to go home, so diplomacy went flying out the window.

"Mr. and Mrs. Seton," she began in a voice the school principal reserves for students who just can't stay out of his office. "You're not listening to me. I. Do. Not. Want. A. Party. Take me home."

Finally, they took notice.

"Oh, dear," Mrs. Seton said, wringing her hands together.

Mr. Seton "harrumphed," then tried again to convince her. "It's important that you go to the party, Claire. There are several very public personas there, including the mayor of San Diego."

"I don't really care—" she started, but he interrupted her.

"The other reason is that it will look good on your resume. There is still the matter of that promotion."

Claire's eyes narrowed. "Are you saying that the promotion is still available?"

"I'm saying the possibility is still there."

"And that I don't have a chance in hell at it if I don't go to this party you've arranged?"

"Crude, yet possibly accurate."

Claire gazed out the window, trying to calm her anger. After everything, she still had to jump through hoops. She couldn't believe it. Turning back, she answered him.

"Fine. I'll go."

The relief on both of their faces was so evident Claire would have laughed if she weren't still so angry.

"But—"

Their faces fell.

"You *will* first take me to my apartment. I need a shower and to change clothes, or I'm not going anywhere."

A bit ruffled, they looked like they were going to argue but acquiesced without saying a word.

The party was a disaster in Claire's mind. First, the guest of honor arrived almost an hour late. Second, while the open bar had been flowing since the start, no one was allowed near the food until she arrived with the Setons. So a good number of the upper crust were feeling no pain by the time she got there. When she realized this, she immediately served herself up a plate of hors d'oeuvres, which allowed the rest to get something to eat. They must not have used their regular caterer because the food wasn't that great. There was no one to take coats at the door, no valets outside, not even a band or quartet to provide a little music. Whoever set this up bungled it big time.

She smiled sadly. *They don't even realize just how much better off they would be if they gave me the promotion.*

"Claire, sweetie." The voice came from behind her and dripped sugar. Claire recognized Trish, Mr. Seton's daughter and her competition for the promotion.

Great. This was all she needed. Maybe if she just ignored her...

Trish sat down next to her, leaving her no way out. "It's good to have you back."

Yeah. I just bet it is. "Thank you," Claire said.

"You've been missed, Claire. In fact, I'd like to take this opportunity to offer you a position as my assistant. I know you're tired and probably don't want to deal with this right now, but there's a lot to be done, and I think together we can accomplish great things. I'd like you to think about it."

Claire swore she could hear a note of desperation in Trish's voice. That brought the ghost of a smile to her face. It disappeared when she realized what Trish was saying. "You want me...to work for you?"

"Yes, Claire. I think we'd make a good team."

"You were a receptionist when I left."

"Well—"

"They gave you my promotion," Claire stated bluntly, her lips tightening more with each word.

"It wasn't *your* promotion," Trish responded in a huff.

"It was based on how well the festival turned out."

Trish's voice returned to the conciliatory tone she'd used previously. "You weren't here. They didn't have any idea where you were and they had to fill the position. So, yes, I took the job." She held her head up higher in an obvious bluff.

Trish's nostrils flared. She was scared. Good. She ought to be. Then Claire's thoughts took another turn. "Tri-s-s-h-h," she began, her eyes narrowing. "Who reported me missing to the police?"

"What do you mean?"

"I mean, who called the police and filled out a missing persons report on me? You said you all had no idea where I'd gone."

"Why, I don't honestly know if anyone here did that."

"No one reported me missing when I didn't turn up to finish the festival?" Claire's eyes closed even farther.

"Not that I'm aware of," Trish hedged, looking a bit like a cornered animal.

"And no one reported me missing when I didn't show up at my job?"

"Hmmm." Trish tapped her chin. "I believe someone asked me if I'd seen you. You would have to ask my fa—Mr. Seton to be sure."

Claire's vision shriveled to a thin line of disbelief, tainted by the red veil of anger. No one had contacted the authorities?

Trish tried another tack. "Well, Claire, it's not the responsibility of the people you work for to report you missing. Your family should have done that." She got up, transparent in her desire to get away from this conversation. "Look, just think about the job offer. It would be a step up for you."

As Claire watched her walk away, she realized that no one here knew she had no family. They had never asked. Sitting alone in a room filled with people ostensibly there to honor her, she let the sadness wash over her. It was time for her to leave. She was tired, irritable, and her shoulder ached like the dickens. She headed for the coatroom to get her jacket, but was waylaid by Mr. Seton.

"Claire, may I have a moment of your time?"

"I've done what you asked, Mr. Seton. I'm going home now to get some sleep."

"I understand, Claire. I'd like to thank you for agreeing to the party, and I have something I'd like you to think about."

She was silent, waiting. George Seton, once again, had something on his mind. By the way he fidgeted, he was having trouble coming out with it.

"I love my daughter."

That's a strange opening.

He began again. "I love my daughter. However, it's obvious she's not cut out for the position she's in right now."

"You mean the position that should have been mine?"

"Well, yes, I guess so. Anyhow, we'd like to make amends and offer you the position now."

"Why?"

"Because it's obvious you are the better candidate."

"Meaning I get the job done?"

"Yes, Claire. You get the job done."

"And do I do it well, Mr. Seton?"

"Of course you do it well. We wouldn't offer it to you if you didn't."

No, but you'd offer it to someone who doesn't have the brains to do it just because she's got the right bloodline, wouldn't you?

"Mr. Seton, I'll have to think about it. Can I let you know?"

"I'm afraid I'll need to know tomorrow. You see," he said, shuffling his feet, "there's an opportunity for Trish to go abroad for the next few months, but she has to commit the day after tomorrow. She won't go if she's still in this position."

"Fine. I'll let you know tomorrow, then. Goodnight, Mr. Seton."

"Goodnight, Claire. And...thank you, for everything."

The limousine dropped her off at her apartment. Unlocking the door, she went inside with a heavy heart. Her efforts to make her little piece of real estate a home had always lightened her mood, yet tonight it felt empty. Empty and...alone.

She missed him. Dion. More than she thought possible.

He had called to smooth things over with her boss, but she doubted he'd done it for reasons she'd prefer. Dion Gaetani was a conscientious man. She knew that much about him. He felt responsible for her predicament and so had called to discharge that duty. Goody for him.

Resentment welled up in her. Just once she'd like to win. Just once she'd like to come through something better, not worse. Just once she'd like to know she wasn't alone in the world.

"Arrrgggghhhh! This isn't getting me anywhere," she said aloud to no one. Turning off the lights, she headed into her bedroom and the first chance in a while for a nice, uninterrupted sleep.

She was still awake at eleven p.m. She saw midnight on the dial of her clock. Then one o'clock.

Two o'clock passed by. And three o'clock.

Finally, somewhere around four she drifted into a dreamless sleep, only to be shrilly awakened by her doorbell at eight.

"I'm coming, I'm coming," she hollered as she grabbed for her robe. *And I'm going to kill whoever you are when I get there.*

When she opened the door, a tall man flashing a detective's badge was standing there. Blinking at the brightness outside, Claire didn't respond, and he took the initiative.

"Detective Lansing with San Diego P.D., ma'am. Can I talk to you for a moment? It's about the piracy case."

Still not entirely awake, Claire moved away from the door and motioned him in.

"I'll only take a few minutes of your time, Miss Saunders."

"First," she said, finding her voice, "you'll have to wait while I put some coffee on and get dressed."

"Certainly."

"Fine. Make yourself comfortable," she waved at the living room. "I'll be with you in a few minutes."

She emerged from her bedroom ten minutes later with a freshly washed face and clean but comfortable clothes on. The detective looked like a blond Tarzan sitting uncomfortably on her prim, padded straight chair. Heading for the kitchen, she spoke over her shoulder to the detective. "Would you like a cup of coffee, detective?"

"Please, call me Tom. And yes, I'd love a cup."

"Okay, Tom." He came and sat at the kitchen table while she poured two cups. "Cream or sugar?"

"No, ma'am. Black and leaded is perfect for me."

"And you can call me Claire."

"Okay." He indicated her sling. "How is the shoulder?"

"Hurts like hell."

"I bet."

Setting two mugs down on the table, she sat across from him and picked hers up. Even though September remained warm in San Diego, nothing beat the smell of that first cup of coffee in the morning. Smiling, she gave in to one of the pleasures of being home—coffee made exactly the way she liked it.

"What can I do for you?" she asked.

"It's about the boat thefts."

"Yes."

"The decision has been made to only pursue extradition hearings for the leader of the band."

"Hawk."

"Yes. That's what he's known by. His real name is Hakon Thoralssen."

"I didn't know that."

"We've been informed that you were on board when the vessel *Treasure* was overtaken and stolen."

"Yes, I was."

"We'll need an official statement from you. I'd like to bring you downtown."

Claire sat up a little straighter at that. "I just got home, Detective," she said in a slightly colder voice.

"Tom, please," he smiled as he spoke. "I know it's sudden. And I'm sorry to have to do this so quickly, but we'll need your report for the extradition hearings."

"I've only had about four hours of sleep since I got home, *Tom*," she tried again, steel working its way into her tone.

Thinking a moment, he offered a compromise. "How about late this afternoon. Would that work? We could transcribe it overnight and still have it ready for the attorneys first thing in the morning."

Sighing, she realized that was the best she would probably get. "Fine. What time?"

"Four o'clock? I'll have a car pick you up."

"If it's all the same to you, I'd rather drive." She pointed to her injured left shoulder. "Thankfully, I'm right-handed. I know where the precinct house is and, well, I'm just a little tired of not having much control over my destiny, okay?"

He smiled. "That will be fine." He got up to leave then. "I'll see you at four."

As he reached the door, he turned to say one more thing. "Oh, and we'll give you the reward paperwork then, too."

"Reward? What reward?" she asked.

"The one for information that leads to the capture of this band of pirates. Don't you know about it?"

"Haven't heard a thing."

"The yacht club—you work for them, right? Yes, you do," he went on, answering his own question. "The yacht club put up a one hundred-thousand-dollar reward. They didn't tell you?"

"No. They didn't." She compressed her lips.

"Then, if I were you, I'd mention it to them. Until this afternoon, ma'am." He tipped an imaginary hat in her direction and let himself out.

"I certainly *will* mention it to them," she said under her breath.

All thought of sleep went by the wayside as Claire contemplated the reward she knew nothing about. There'd been no talk of it before her disappearance, but someone should have mentioned it last night at the party.

Not quite ready to go into the yacht club, Claire took a long walk down to the Embarcadero, passing all the little shops she'd always enjoyed so much and the restaurants she'd eaten so many wonderful meals in.

No one called her by name.

No one knew who she was.

She stopped at the bench where Dion had helped her with little lost Billy. Sitting, she closed her eyes and could almost feel him standing beside her, helping her, strengthening her own abilities. Claire imagined the *Treasure* still there, right behind her. She could turn around and see him, focused on his work, just like she had so many times during the festival without his knowledge.

She pictured the schooner as she'd last seen it, swaying at anchor in the little bay. Then bucking wildly, challenging the storm to do its worst. And finally, her mind's eye went below deck and into the captain's cabin, to kisses that had awakened her first true feeling of sensuality. Dion had given her a taste, and now she wanted more.

More than he could apparently give, Claire thought as she opened her eyes. The problem was, she couldn't imagine life with anyone else.

An older couple walked by, nodding a greeting to her as they passed. Hand in hand, they continued on. Claire stood up, watching them. She wanted what they had.

She had learned a lot during her captivity. She'd proven some things to herself. She had more strength than she thought. Not even storms and pirates could stop her.

Claire smiled.

And she was good at a lot of things. Her smile broadened, then disappeared. She'd run away from Dion rather that have it out, unwilling to face him and listen to his accusations. And unable to say, "I love you," and chance rejection.

She still had a lot to learn and only herself to satisfy. San Diego no longer held any of those answers for her. One hundred thousand dollars would certainly help her afford the time to find some of them.

Claire turned her face to the sun, feeling its warmth, letting it wash away the final dregs of negativity. She started walking again, but toward home this time, not away.

It was two in the afternoon when she let herself into her apartment. She still had time. She grabbed her purse, got in her car, and drove to the yacht club. Some new cute, fresh face greeted her arrival. Claire introduced herself then entered her office. To her surprise, nothing had been moved or changed. This superficial societal cult hadn't even cared enough to erase her existence.

She'd busted her butt putting that festival together and she felt proud of it on a very personal level. Yet, not a single one of them had displayed pride in her abilities. All they cared about was the fact that the festival had been a success, and that someone from their club, even if it was a mere employee, had been instrumental in capturing the pirates.

She picked up her nameplate, intent on chucking it, but stopped to run her hands over the smooth metal and the indentations that spelled her name.

Claire Saunders.

She had done a great job here. And she had also wasted way too much time on this place.

The nameplate hit the trash can with a metallic bang as Claire squared her shoulders and walked to the end of the hall. She didn't wait to be announced by Mr. Seton's new assistant. She simply walked right in. He was alone, sitting behind his massive dark cherry desk, surrounded by walls covered with sea-going paraphernalia.

"Claire," he said, getting up and pasting a smile on his face. "How good of you to come in so quickly. Have you made a decision?"

"Yes, Mr. Seton, I have. I quit."

The smile disappeared for a moment then returned. "Claire, come sit down. Let's talk about this."

"There's nothing to talk about. I am turning in my resignation, effective immediately."

"But we need you, Claire." He slumped back into his chair.

"Really? That's nice to know. In fact, that's about the nicest parting present you can give me, because I no longer need you."

He must have realized her resolve because he dropped the smile. "I'm sorry you feel that way. I won't try to stop you. If you need any assistance with your things, just ask Tammy at the front desk, and she'll help you." He began to read the file folder in front of him, effectively dismissing her. The new Claire would have none of it.

"Oh, and Mr. Seton?"

He looked up, appearing distracted. "Yes?"

"Whom do I talk to about getting my one hundred thousand dollars?"

At the mention of the reward, the very tanned George Seton, of the Mayflower Setons, of course, blanched a perfect shade of white, which then fused into pink, and then the loveliest shade of red.

"How did you find out about that?"

"A nice police officer mentioned it to me."

"Good. That's very good," he blustered. "Actually, it had slipped my mind, so I'm glad you brought it up."

Claire stood silently as her ex-boss fiddled with the folder on his desk, looking everywhere but at her.

"Claire, um, there's a little problem with that."

"Oh, and what problem is that?"

"We don't exactly have that kind of cash available at the present time."

"Well, you'll have to figure something out. I'm on my way over to the precinct to file my report, and they said they'd have the appropriate reward verification forms ready for me. I'll be returning with them first thing tomorrow."

Not waiting for a reply, she walked out of his office. As she reached the edge of the reception area, she heard him barking through his intercom.

"Trish, get in here this minute. And bring your rolodex with you. We've got some calls to make."

Smiling, Claire graciously said goodbye to the receptionist on her way out the door.

CHAPTER NINETEEN

Freedom.

It smelled like the warm breeze flowing in through her car window and the faint cinnamon scent coming from the wild orchids that seemed to be everywhere.

It looked like the miles of pavement she had put behind her.

With a wide smile, Claire leaned her head out the window and shouted.

"I'm free! Woohoo!"

Settling back in behind the wheel, Claire still couldn't believe the changes the past two weeks had wrought.

As she'd promised Mr. Seton, she showed up the very next morning at the yacht club to file for her reward. They were ready for her, attorneys and all. She'd sat calmly while they postured and subtly threatened her. In the end, she held firm and told them to come up with the money. She agreed to take a third up front and the rest in monthly installments. They had exactly one week to draw up the paperwork to her satisfaction or she'd go to the news media.

She had worked closely with the police and the district attorney's office, giving statements and depositions to help bring Hawk stateside for trial. She'd finally gotten the almost finished table project done and returned to its owner. Then she gave up the lease on her apartment, gifted some special things away to the few people she thought of as nice acquaintances and moved most of the rest into a rented storage locker.

But the most satisfying thing of all had been writing out the check to pay down her father's gambling debt. His vice had waylaid her for too many years. The money she would be getting every month for the next two years would more than pay off the debt and even allow her enough to live on if she was careful.

That was what freedom felt like. For the first time in her life, Claire could do whatever she wanted to. It didn't take her long to figure out what that was, either. She planned to put her furniture making skills to good use.

Now, here she was, in Mexico, driving with her car packed full, along with a little trailer she'd purchased. Her clothes, her tools and a few other necessities, like good coffee, shared space with lumber, paint and stains. She was going somewhere she could make a difference.

There was no road into *Tierra Bonita* that a car could travel. So Claire got as close as she could, then hired a boat to take her by water. She saw the rock promontory she had scrambled over with Dion's team and was surprised at the stab of pain that shot through her.

As they rounded the corner into the little bay, Claire's breath caught in her throat, and she grabbed the boat rail for balance.

The *Treasure*! The schooner was still moored in the harbor.

Dion? Was Dion here? No. He was in England. Aidan had confirmed that when they'd spoken last week.

There seemed to be no one on board. It swayed peacefully in the slight swell as they passed by. Everything flooded her consciousness. The fights, the storm, the love-making.

Especially the love-making.

Claire hung her head and turned away, turned toward the village she hoped to help rebuild.

Even though her arrival in *Tierra Bonita* was unannounced, Claire was warmly welcomed. The town patriarch, Manuel, was overjoyed at the unexpected help, and she was soon ensconced in one of the new huts. A quick tour by Manuel verified the deplorable conditions she'd remembered. Ending in the town square, where she was introduced to the team of locals supervising the rebuilding and given her own workspace. They had a long list of furniture needs, and she'd be able to start work immediately.

Claire smiled as they graciously agreed that tomorrow would be soon enough. She returned to her little one-room hut to unpack and settle in. It didn't take long. She blew up her air mattress and set it in place.

Laughing, she realized she was still sleeping on the floor. Funny, this already felt more like home than her apartment ever had. She muscled one of the wood crates she'd packed supplies in over beside the bed. It would do just fine until she could build a night stand.

Lastly, she placed her father's picture on the makeshift table, lingering to run her hand along the frame. It seemed like his smile had widened.

"You're proud of me, aren't you, Dad. Well, I'm pretty proud of myself, too."

She squatted down in front of the picture.

"Oh, and Dad? I forgive you for the debts. I know it was your way of spending time with me. Gambling seemed the quick way to earn money, at least at the beginning. And I love you for putting me first. I am so, so grateful to share your love of wood. Thank you for that. You have helped to set me free."

Claire joined the village for a festive communal meal, meeting pretty much everyone at once. After some food and a lot of hugging and back-slapping, she eased her way out of the tent and took a walk.

It had been a hectic and satisfying day, and Claire felt tired but restive. Without knowing where she was going, she wound her way down to the beach, taking a seat in the sand and hugging her knees. She stared at the schooner, giving in to a strong desire to remember. Remember loving. Remember leaving. Remember Dion.

She sat up. With the *Treasure* still here, would Dion come back for it himself or send someone?

She might see him again.

The thought both thrilled her and scared her to death. He'd gone back to his normal life, whereas she had completely changed hers. Some of that was because of him. Hanging her head, she let the ache of loving him spread through her again. How long would it take to get over him?

Forever.

She looked up again and watched as someone in nothing but khaki shorts came topside and walked along the deck of the schooner.

Who was that?

Her eyes widened. Standing, she shielded her eyes from the setting sun just as Dion glanced toward the beach.

Both froze as recognition hit.

Dion wasted no time, not even bothering to put the zodiac in the water. He flew off the deck, cleanly sluicing into the water, swimming with powerful strokes to the beach.

Claire!

Claire was here.

He didn't know why or how and didn't care. All that mattered was that she was here.

With each stroke he told himself he wasn't going to screw it up this time. It took very little time for him to reach the sandy beach. His bad leg gave out in the shallow water and he tripped, falling into a wave and swallowing sea water. Before he could stand again, she was at his side.

They spoke at the same time, standing knee deep in water.

"Are you all right?"

"Claire!"

Then neither spoke as Dion squeezed her to him. He touched her face, running his hands over her cheeks, her chin, her hair, anything to help him believe she was real.

They tried again to speak, but again, both started at once.

"You're really here," he said.

"I can't believe it," she said.

He kissed her then, taking all chance at talk out of the equation. She was here. And she felt wonderful. The kiss, at first tentative, deepened quickly into a fierce urge, as if only this tactile contact would reassure them both.

Claire returned his kiss, moved with him as it deepened. He could feel it as she gave herself over to him.

Then a wave toppled them both. Sputtering, they laughed. Dion stood and helped Claire up. Once on the beach, they saw several villagers who had no qualms about watching the spectacle.

"This isn't the place for this," he said.

"No, it isn't."

"Let's go," he said, drawing her toward the dock.

"Where?"

Dion looked out at the schooner. "Home."

"Uh, how?"

He stopped mid-stride.

"You swam in, remember? The lifeboat is still onboard."

"We'll find something," he answered, moving again.

A small dinghy that seemed badly in need of repairs sat on the beach near the dock. Dion pushed it into the water as Claire watched. As he turned to help Claire get in, he saw the unease in her eyes.

"What?"

"Um, am I going to have to bail again?"

Laughing, he pulled her to the seat next to him.

"Maybe. But," he said, giving her a kiss that left nothing to the imagination, "I promise it will be worth it."

She didn't have to bail, yet she would have gladly. Reality wrapped Claire in a cozy, warm towel. Dion was here. Except it was going to take forever to get to the *Treasure*. Every time she turned his way, he stopped rowing to kiss her.

Once on board, Claire knew she was meant to be here. She couldn't believe it had been only three short weeks since she'd last stood on this deck. It felt like it had been years. The creaking noises welcomed her. Dion was right. She'd come home.

Dion set the dinghy adrift to find its own way back to the beach. Claire knew they would have to talk. Now, though, a more primal need for fulfillment seemed to be controlling them. He walked over to her, a look in his eyes she'd never seen before. A feral hunger that matched her own need.

He reached up, cocooning her face in one strong hand. She welcomed it and kissed his palm, gratified at the shudder that ran through his body.

"Before anything else, I have to tell you something," he said.

"There's nothing that can't wait." She leaned in, raining kisses along his neck.

He set her at arm's length. "Yes, there is. I...can't go further with these things between us."

Weeks apart already felt like years, but Claire sighed and resigned herself to a few more minutes of torture. "All right."

"I need to tell you what happened."

Dion released her then, walked over to the railing, and gazed out over the village. Claire didn't think he saw it. He already seemed to be in another world, so she moved beside him, not touching, just settling in to listen.

"We were working the Malacca Straits, a hotbed for piracy. A large shipping company had contacted us, offering a covert chance to tag an elusive band that had been terrorizing the straights for months. We planned to go in undercover. Roger, Aidan, Mike and I. Roger demanded Mary come along. I didn't want her. She was too green, and this was an important op. Roger insisted. He said she was capable. I knew she was a crack shot and had a good head on her shoulders, so I relented. Biggest mistake I ever made."

He shook his head. "Anyhow, I decided to keep her by me, so she and I went in as cooks. It was a large crude oil carrier and easy for five people to be absorbed into the crew. Roger and Aidan were laborers and Mike was part of the bridge crew." He paused.

"What happened to the people you replaced?" Claire asked.

"We held them. Not exactly legal, but we had to be sure no one leaked that we were aboard. Only the Captain knew who we really were."

Pursing his lips, he leaned down to grab the railing. Claire's heart ached to tell him it was all right, but she didn't dare. He was still locked in the hell of the story.

"The first couple of days were uneventful, except that Mary had to teach me how to cook for thirty people."

Claire watched a smile touch his face, then disappear, wishing she could bring it back.

"On the third day, we entered the straights. That night, the crew put the usual anti-piracy measures into effect. Deck lights were turned on. Engine room and cabin doors were locked. Fire hoses were at the ready to spray any intruders down. The bridge watch kept a close eye out for any small craft, but the speedboat managed to come in under the radar. They threw a grappling hook up to board."

He sighed. Claire let the silence linger and watched Dion, hurting for him, waiting for the story to be over.

"Our job was not to capture the pirates, but to place a locator on as many of them as we could to track them to their hideout. We all carried little beacons in our pockets, always at the ready. Mary forgot that, got caught up in the moment, I guess."

He started to pace now, a few feet one direction, then back. And again.

"We were all herded into the main salon, made to kneel in a group. Then the bridge crew was brought in. There were only five thieves in the group that boarded us, yet it was enough."

The shadows under his eyes seemed even more pronounced. Claire wanted to kiss them away, but knew he had to finish the story.

"Mary was edgy, nervous. These situations are tough on the uninitiated. Hell, *I* was scared. And I've been doing this for years. Anyhow, we were a group of about twenty kneeling there, and Mary and I got separated. She was at the other end. Roger tried to sidle towards her and got a rifle butt in the gut for it. While he was doubled over in pain, I saw a signal from Mary. She had a gun and reached for it.

"I knew it was too soon to make any moves. The pirates were too organized. She'd never pull it off. I shouted for her to stop, managed to divert their attention. It wasn't enough. One of the men saw her move and opened fire."

Claire gasped at the horror, but Dion didn't notice.

"I leapt toward her, tried to protect her." He gave a haunted little laugh. "It was too late. All it got me was a couple of my own wounds. I laid there, not able to move, and watched her die, just feet from me."

"Oh, Dion."

"I've had nightmares about it ever since. I keep seeing her blood spreading out, like it was trying to reach me, to devour me."

"How horrible," Claire said, trying to nudge him back to the present.

"It was a rookie mistake, pulling her gun so soon. I know that. But I agreed to take a rookie on a highly dangerous mission. I felt responsible. Still do."

Claire searched for some way to alleviate his sense of responsibility. "Roger holds some blame here, Dion."

He just looked at her.

"You said once he was as good an agent as you. He should have known she wasn't ready. In my mind, he's the culpable one, not you. You did everything you could, even took bullets to try to save her."

Dion reached out then. She wholeheartedly entered his embrace, clinging to him for dear life. He returned the strength of her hug tenfold.

"I know I did everything I could."

"Do you still have the nightmares?"

"No. I think you stopped them."

"Me?"

"Aidan helped me realize that they diminished when I met you," Dion answered.

She continued to rain kisses along his neck, his chin, his cheek.

"Claire?"

"Hmmm?" she mumbled, finding the warm, salty taste of his earlobe had a very erotic effect on her.

"There's one more thing."

"Dion!"

"I'm sorry."

"Fine. You're sorry. Now can we—"

"Claire, I'm sorry."

She stopped, digging deep for some shred of patience. She had waited so long. Another couple minutes longer wouldn't matter, would it?

She searched his face and gave him the time to say what he needed to say.

"I didn't trust you. Hell, I didn't even believe you."

"We've had this conversation, Dion."

"Yes, but we never finished it. I hurt you, deeply."

She tried to pull away from the embrace, but he held her tight.

"You did hurt me."

"I know. I've only been here a day, Claire. I came back to outfit the schooner. My intention was to sail her back to San Diego and find a way to make you forgive me."

"You were coming back for me?"

"Yes. I love you, Claire."

She looked into the eyes of the man she loved. No longer guarded and unreadable, she saw the emotion. The gratitude. The love. She smiled then, settling back in to his arms, feeling all the right things in her world click into place.

"Then I forgive you."

Feeling comfortable in their closeness, Claire wondered what would come next.

"So, that's it?" Dion asked. "I say I'm sorry, you forgive me, and it's over? A little anti-climactic, don't you think?"

"Oh, no. It's not over by a long shot." Meek, mild-mannered Claire did something she'd never done before. She stepped away from him, walked backward toward the companionway to below deck, slowly, agonizingly unbuttoning her shirt one button at a time. When she got through the last button, she stepped onto the first rung of the ladder.

"By the way," she shot over her shoulder, tossing the shirt at him. "I love you, too."

She quickly dropped down the steps, turned and beat feet for the master cabin. There she stopped short.

The master cabin. Dion's cabin. Here is where the possibilities had begun and where they would become reality.

Dion, having quickly closed the distance between them, came up behind her, shirt in hand.

"What?" he asked, raining kisses on the back of her neck, sending shivers of excitement threading through her entire body. H moved to her shoulder, sliding the strap of her bra aside so nothing stood between him and her skin.

She felt like she was on fire. "I was just—ummmm," she said, losing her train of thought under the onslaught of his kisses.

"Hmmm?" He began to trail his hands down her arms then reached in front to undo the clasp of her bra.

She tried again. "This is where, um, well, where it all started. And I can't help but wonder—"

"How you never knew making love could be so fulfilling," Dion finished.

"Well, yes."

Turning her, he reached under her chin, pulling her head up so she would look at him.

"You just never had the right teacher, sweetheart."

She closed her eyes, and he kissed them both.

"Do you trust me?" He kissed her lightly on the lips, returned to trailing fingers down her arms, around her wrists, up the inside.

"Umm-hmm," she answered distractedly.

"This is real, Claire," he mumbled as he kissed the edge of her mouth. "And this." Then her neck. "And this."

She leaned in to him, kissing his cheek. "And this?"

"Yes."

She moved to his neck. "This, too?"

"Mmm-hmm. That, too."

She used her tongue to trace sensuous trails in the hollow of his shoulder blade. "And this?"

"Oh, God, yes." He pulled away, then, reached down and picked her up, letting her bra fall away, moving over to the bed to set her gently down.

"I won't hurt you, Claire."

"I know." Her eyes were flooded with desire.

He lay beside her then, bracing himself on one arm, using his free hand to roam. First her face, with his hand soon joined by his lips. They kissed, tenderly now, knowing that they had all the time in the world. He ran his fingers through her hair, stared at her as if memorizing her face.

He kissed her again. Slowly, sensuously, using his tongue to learn the nuances of her mouth, giving her time to explore, too.

He moved from her face to her neck. All the while, his hands wandered trails across her shoulder blade, down her arm and up the inside, grazing the flare of her breast.

Claire gasped at the strength of her response. She reached for his shoulder, caressed his chest, tangled her hand in the hair there.

Dion pulled her hand away.

"I want—"

"Me, too."

And without another word, his mouth lowered to her nipple, sending shards of pleasure coursing to the tips of her toes and the ends of her hair. Gently, he played, first with one breast, then an agonizingly slow move to the other. All other thoughts fled, and Claire arched her back.

"Oh!" She gave herself over totally to the sensations that were making her groin pound with hot-blooded desire.

"Please, Dion." She didn't know what she begged for, more sweet torture or release. She reached out, searching with an untrained hand yet finding instinctively what made him gasp.

He responded by moving his hand downward, spiraling past her waist, following the zipper of her shorts, causing her to moan as he reached between her legs. Just a quick touch, then he returned to the band of her shorts, unbuttoning them, pulling the zipper down.

Claire reciprocated, reaching to free him from his shorts. But she had trouble unbuttoning them, so he pulled away just long enough for her to utter a moan of dislike. Standing, he shucked his pants. He stood there for a moment, letting her see how she affected him.

She helped him peel her shorts and panties off. Standing there, beside the bed, for just a moment longer, he reached over and ran his hands across her stomach, loving the feel of the smooth skin, making erotic trails all over. Up, around, and down. Until finally, he reached the triangle of hair, lightly touching, learning, watching her react.

Arching toward him, she reached out to pull him back to the bed.

"Soon, sweetheart. Soon. I want to see you first."

His fingers convinced her to open to him, to let him go deeper, to find her core. She moaned as he played. The sound of her sigh almost undid him. Lowering his face, he tasted her, took her in his mouth, used his tongue like he had his fingers, teaching her new sensations with each motion, each kiss. Her movements became more frantic, more pronounced. And finally...

"Dion!" she screamed as she arched her hips off the bed on a long, rolling climax. The waves kept washing over her, sensations too strong to resist. As they subsided, he returned to her side. He cupped her breasts, but she brushed his hand away, instead getting to her knees and straddling him. She knew by his sharp intake of breath exactly when she made contact. He reached up to caress her breasts, and she leaned forward, obliging his need to taste, all the while rubbing against his erection.

"I...can't wait much longer, Claire," he mumbled.

"Then don't," she said, repositioning and sliding onto him partway. He groaned as she stopped, but she only laughed.

"Patience, my love."

She continued to play, moving up and down. Lowering herself slowly until she knew they were a perfect fit.

His hand moved between them, found her again.

She moaned, and increased her tempo as desire began to peak again.

He took control, thrusting them both to a new plateau of pleasure.

At that moment, the *Treasure* rocked sharply, then settled back into a smooth, slight rolling motion. Dion and Claire looked at each other.

"I think she approves," he said, laughing.

"Ahoy, the boat." The voice droned on, saying the same thing over and over again. "Ahoy, the boat."

They tried to ignore it. Finally, quiet descended...momentarily. Suddenly, the cabin door burst open. Dion jumped up, ready to defend against the intruder. Claire gasped and grabbed the blanket to cover herself.

"Are you two ever going to get up," came the now familiar voice.

"Aidan," Dion bellowed. "What the *hell* are you doing here?

"Just making sure, that's all."

Claire grinned as Dion continued to glare at him.

"What are you talking about?"

"Hey, man, I was here when the sparks first flew between you two. It's only fair I get to see the end result." He blushed then. "Well, not actually *see*, mind you."

Laughing, Claire tossed a pillow at him. "Aidan, get the hell out of here."

Dion, still glowering over the intrusion, turned his back on Aidan.

"Okay, love," he said to Claire. "But it's morning, and I'm cooking breakfast. You've both got ten minutes to join me or I'm coming back in."

"Get. Out," Dion growled.

As soon as the door shut, Dion turned to Claire.

"How the hell did *he* get here?"

"Don't look at me," she answered, laughing. "Besides, does it really matter?"

"Yes. I want you all to myself," he said, pulling her into his arms.

"We'll have lots of time."

"I know. I love you, Claire Saunders."

"I love you, too, Dionisio Gaetani."

"How did you learn my full name…never mind," he said, glaring at the closed door. "I think I know."

"He's a good friend, Dion."

"Yeah, but whose?"

Laughing, she squirmed out of his embrace. "Ours. Come on. Get dressed. I'm in need of energy and someone else is cooking."

He tried to reach for her again, but she screamed, once again bringing Aidan to the door.

"Do I have to come in there and break you two up?"

Gleefully, Claire started to answer him. Dion clamped a hand over her mouth. "Don't you dare invite him in here." But he, too, laughed.

Shortly, they joined Aidan for breakfast on deck. Dion carried what looked to be a very old bottle of whiskey and three glasses, pouring a shot for each of them. Claire's eyes widened.

"No time like the present to toast to our futures," he said, handing each a glass.

They clinked glasses and cheered in unison. "To the future."

"You know, it's about time you two stopped being so pip-headed and realized you were in love with each other."

Dion reached for Claire's hand. "Yeah."

"So you quit the agency, eh, Dion? Without telling me or anyone else?"

Claire turned to Dion, her mouth open in shock.

Squirming, he tried at first to dodge the issue. "I told the director."

"Why, Dion?" Claire asked.

He gave her the only answer he could. "My heart just wasn't in it anymore."

"And you, Claire," Aidan continued, pulling more information out of his hat. "You quit the yacht club?"

It was Dion's turn to be surprised. "You did?"

"My heart wasn't in it, either," she answered.

"What will you two do now?"

"We haven't gotten around to discussing that yet. Someone," Dion said, directing a mock glower at his friend, "came to call before we had the welcome sign out."

"I can build furniture," Claire answered. "And I'm pretty good at it. I came to help the village rebuild."

"I had planned to try to help, too." He smiled at her then. "Right after I convinced you of how much I love you." Taking both of her hands. "Will you?"

Almost breathlessly, she asked. "Will I what?"

Dion took a deep breath and plunged ahead, kneeling in front of her, right there on the deck of the schooner, in front of Aidan. "Will you marry me and help me pick up where Hawk left off here, only the legal way this time? We'd have to live aboard the boat for a while, until enough is done that we can move into a house in the village."

For a split second, he thought she would turn him down. She wasn't looking at him but around the deck of the *Treasure*. After seconds that felt like minutes, she turned back to him, glowing as she answered.

"I can't think of anywhere else I'd rather live."

"Is that a yes?" Aidan broke in.

Dion made as if to hit him as Claire laughed and gave him his answer. "Yes." She turned to Dion. "Yes, Dion, I'll marry you."

Aidan let out a whoop and started dancing around on the deck. Dion watched him until he was close to the railing, then casually reached out with his leg and gave Aidan a shove, sending him flying into the water, complete surprise blanketing his face as it disappeared.

Turning to Claire, he paid no attention to the shouts coming from the water. Taking her in his arms, he kissed her, sealing their pact.

"You are what I've been looking for my entire life," Claire told him quietly.

"I love you, too," he responded, kissing her in a way that left no doubt in her mind.

EPILOGUE

Claire shuddered as the bars clanked shut behind them.

"That sound is horrible, Dion."

"It's a prison, Claire. It's not supposed to sound nice and happy."

"Yes, but it just seems so...sterile and harsh. So final. Hawk doesn't belong here."

"You're right. He's not a criminal. But he did break the law."

"I know," Claire said, sighing. "I just pray he gets a light sentence. It's already been too long."

"I've heard he's got some hotshot lawyer who's going to try to get his sentence reduced on exceptional grounds."

"That's good to hear."

Soon, they were ushered into a small, gray room. The guard gestured to a table and they sat in two of the chairs, waiting.

Before long, Hawk was brought in by another guard. Confusion registered on his face as he saw the two of them and he said so, sitting down opposite them. The guard took up a watchful position outside the door.

"To what do I owe the pleasure of this visit, Agent Gaetani?" he asked in his old arrogant demeanor.

"We came to see how you are faring," Dion supplied.

Hawk gestured around him. "As well as I can."

"You remember my wife, Claire, don't you?"

His eyebrows rose at the introduction. "Ah, good. I knew I sensed something between you two. I'm glad to hear you acted on it." A brief shadow crossed his face. "Life is too short to let love slide past without notice."

Claire beamed at her husband. "You're right. We came here for another reason, too. Have you been in contact with anyone in your village?"

"No," he answered, pounding his fists on the table. The guard started to enter, but Dion held up a hand to stop him.

Hawk glared at Dion. "Why? Have you come to gloat? To tell me the village is in ruins?"

"Not exactly."

"Well, it couldn't be much better than that. The money must have dried up. Maria's homeland is probably a hovel by now."

"I wouldn't call it a hovel," Dion supplied, trying to keep his smile hidden. "Although there is still a lot of work to be done."

Hawk sat up then. "Have you been there? Do you have news? Are my people surviving?"

Claire smiled. "Yes, we have news." Turning to Dion, she asked if he wanted to tell Hawk.

"No, you go ahead."

"Honey, I really think you—"

"Well, somebody tell me. Please!"

"Your village thrives, Hawk," Claire quickly answered him.

"How?" he asked in confusion.

"You can thank Dion. Turns out, he's a bit of a philanthropist."

Hawk glanced from one to the other, bewilderment written all over his face.

"Hawk, Claire and I have been living in the village since a few weeks after your capture. Turns out, she's a pretty good carpenter."

"And he," she said, hitching a thumb in her husband's direction, "is quite persuasive when it comes to getting people and businesses to donate funding. We're funded for a few months now, and the building is going at a much faster pace than before. We should be done by the middle of next year, complete with a brand new well, and even a town generator!" Claire's enthusiasm was showing as she started gesturing in the air with her hands.

Hawk sat back in his chair, silent, rubbing his eyes, an obvious attempt to control the mist filling them. Finally, he leaned forward and uttered one word.

"Why?"

He looked at Dion as he spoke.

Dion answered. "Your means were faulty, yet the cause was worthy. We both decided that we couldn't live with the village's demise, so we did something about it."

"I'm...humbled."

"Haven't been there before, have you?" Dion laughed.

"No. It is foreign to me. I'm not used to needing help, much less having to ask for it. I think that's why I failed when I tried to get donations. My arrogance showed through." He sighed then, a sigh of peace. "You are finishing a dream of mine. I am...more than grateful." Picking up Claire's hand, he leaned over and kissed it. And paused, looking at her intently. "There is more to your story than you are letting on."

Both Dion and Claire widened their eyes in shock. Then Claire smiled and put a hand on her stomach. "We only just found out."

"Congratulations. It seems you have as many blessings as you have given to me."

At that moment, the loudspeaker intoned in a dull voice.

"Hakon Thoralssen, attorney inbound."

Hawk resituated himself in his chair, assuming a much more arrogant pose, probably posturing for the legal eagle.

"Is it *your* attorney that's here?"

"I believe so. I haven't met her yet, though. I only know what the guards have told me."

"Her?" Claire asked.

Any answer was forestalled by the opening of the door, as a drop-dead gorgeous redhead walked in, dressed to kill in a sleek pinstripe suit with a skirt slit further up her thigh than propriety should allow.

Her eyes went directly to Hawk and she blushed, which amazed them.

"Sorry to intrude," she said. "I need to confer with my client."

Claire smiled. "That's okay. We were just leaving."

Hawk cleared his throat. "Dion and Claire Gaetani," Hawk said, "meet my attorney."

"Julia Branholt."

"It's nice to meet you," Claire said as Dion helped her with her jacket.

Dion extended his hand. "We won't crowd your time. This guy," he said, tossing a look over his shoulder, "needs all the help he can get."

"Gaetani?" the attorney asked. "The same Gaetani who arrested my client?"

"Yes. I'm afraid so."

"I don't think—"

"It's all right," Hakon intercepted. "They didn't come here to discuss the case. They brought me news...good news."

As Dion and Claire left the prison walls behind them, he encircled her waist. She was a perfect fit beside him.

"Did you see the looks that passed between those two, Dion?"

"Hmmm?" He was much more interested in gazing at his beautiful wife.

"Dion, did you see?"

"The sparks flying between Hawk and his attorney? Yes. I think, my dear, that our pirate is not quite done with adventures."

Placing her hand over her stomach, Claire agreed. "Neither are we, my love. Neither are we."

Thank you for reading **Stolen Treasures**. If you enjoyed this book, please consider leaving a review wherever you prefer, and know that it would be greatly appreciated.

And be sure to check Hawk's story in the sequel to Stolen Treasures.

For new release information and news about Laurie Ryan, please sign up for her newsletter .

BOOKS BY LAURIE RYAN

Contemporary Romance stories

<u>Billionaire Bachelor Pledge series</u>

Royal Flush

High Card

All In

Full House

Blind Bet

<u>Willow Bay series</u>

Last Resort

Finding Home

Chances Are

Tender Tide

Reluctant Christmas

Operation Ethan

<u>Tropical Persuasions series</u>

Stolen Treasures

Pirate's Promise

Dare to Love

<u>Standalone</u>

The Long Journey Home

Rudy's Heart

Lost and Found

Northern Lights

Healing Love

<u>Women's Fiction</u>

Show Me

<u>Fantasy</u>

Survival

Enlightenment

Birthright

Awakening

Wolf's Call

About the Author

Laurie Ryan writes about resilient, independent women who might stumble, but they dust themselves off and get the job done. Their men, whether commanding alpha or endearing cinnamon roll heroes, will do whatever it takes to ensure the happiness of the women they cherish.

Laurie lives in the Pacific Northwest with her "he can fix anything" hubby, but is always willing to travel to visit their children and grandchildren. Her creativity isn't limited to writing. She also scrap books and, when she really needs to disappear, she paints rocks and shells found on the beaches she walks at the ocean—her happy place.

Laurie has always had a deep connection to nature and the outdoors, which is reflected in her writing. She is a passionate writer who brings her love for nature, animals, and creativity into her work.

An avid cruiser, Laurie has visited many places. One of her favorites was a stop in Greenland, where the strength and endurance of the people living in those beautiful but harsh surroundings became an underlying thread in her stories. Her sensual romance novels are sure to warm the hearts of readers.

Connect with Laurie on Facebook, Instagram, or TikTok, or her website, and join Laurie's newsletter for up to date news and releases.

Laurie loves to hear from her readers and can be reached at laurie@laurieryanauthor.com

SNEAK PEEK

Pirate's Promise

(book 2 of the Tropical Persuasions series)

She promised her father. He promised his heart. Love will make them break every vow.

Everything attorney Julia Branholt has worked for is about to tank thanks to one stubborn, bull- Everything attorney Julia Branholt has fought for is circling the drain—and the culprit is one infuriating, bull-headed pirate, Hakon "Hawk" Thoralssen. It's bad enough she's been forced to take his case pro bono. But when someone mysteriously bails him out *in her name*, Julia's career—and the promise she made her dying father—teeters on the brink of ruin. Desperate to stop the spiral, she does the unthinkable: she follows Hawk.

Hawk swore he'd never let anyone close again. Not after the loss that gutted him. But when sabotage threatens to destroy the beloved village his late wife called home, he has no choice but to fight for it. What he didn't expect? A sharp-tongued attorney with fire in her eyes—and a pull he can't seem to shake.

To save Tierra Bonita, Hawk and Julia will have to work together, toeing the thin line between desire and disaster. But in a village built on second chances and open hearts, will they risk everything for a chance at a love that could finally set them free?

Prologue

Off the Baja coast

Three months ago

The small powerboat flew across the swells of the dark, gray-blue water at a breakneck pace, jolting the men with each surge and dip. The tall, golden-haired man stood despite the turbulence. One hand skimmed the wheel housing for balance, his only concession to their speed.

His other hand-held binoculars focused on the target directly ahead, a sailing vessel.

He smiled, much like a cat preparing to pounce. The yacht, single-masted, about forty feet in length and wood rather than fiberglass, appeared to be exactly what he wanted. Collectors loved sleek and expensive. Plus, he could discern no distinguishing characteristics that couldn't be easily disguised for quick resale. A nice bonus.

He saw the family then and watched them play, decked out in their designer clothing. Had they come from a yacht club event? More likely, they dressed this way for every outing.

The blond man shook his head. The sad part was that they'd done nothing but live the insipid lives of the rich. That alone made them the perfect mark for his plans. His free hand tightened into a fist as the shadow of still-raw memories gripped him, and his nostrils flared with a momentary regret.

With a quick jerk of his head, he banished the thoughts. That life was dead to him now. He followed the only option left open.

He plotted the takeover as they approached. They would board before the family noticed. These types made it easy, never considering an attack on the water a possibility. No one ever did. Before long, though, they would know their mistake.

It was perfect. Maybe.

Straightforward, certainly.

But never simple.

His team was well-honed and they were several boats beyond their first capture. God willing, this one wouldn't be their last. Even planned, though, anything could happen. The most dangerous part would be boarding, but his men knew their jobs.

The midday heat, magnified by humidity, blazed into his shoulders. Neither the wind nor the salty spray off the water banished the intensity. It baked the energy out of most people. Not him. He stood taller, basked in the heat, drew it in, and let it energize him. Dressed easy, in shorts, sleeveless T-shirt and sandals, he knew he looked more like a beach bum than a pirate. The smile returned. Even in lawlessness, he was a non-conformist.

He bound his hair back into a tail as they closed on their prey. The action wasn't enough to dispel the acid churning in his stomach. His hand gripped and re-gripped the windshield as the adrenaline began to scream through his body. His ears pounded in time with his heart, hammering away, matching the rhythm of the boat as they slowed to a crawl.

Indistinct voices filtered through. He heard their laughter.

Couldn't they hear the approach?

He could. The quiet whine of the engine dying down and the gurgle of water as it slapped the hulls of both boats. Even the seagull that screeched a warning from high above seemed magnified.

Almost alongside now, the oily, acrid fumes of the engine swept forward. His breathing went shallow and ragged as fear and exhilaration fought for control.

The boat maneuvered into place beside the yacht. He used the brief moment to inhale one long, calming breath. His muscles bunched like a lion ready for the kill, preparing for that launch into the unknown.

He didn't wait. He knew his men would follow him as one unit.

The blond man cleared the railing and landed on the yacht's deck. Within seconds, the vessel was secured.

It was over too quickly.

He needed an outlet for the wild adrenaline still coursing through him and let loose with a growl that would have made Tarzan proud.

What a rush!

Feeling very much like his conquering Viking ancestors, Hawk grinned broadly as he approached the captive family.

More information about Laurie Ryan and her books can be found at www.laurieryanauthor.com.